"I Never Looked Like This When I Was First a Succubus."

Yeah. You should see your hair.

"My—!" Melisan's hands flew up and woke a knot of very testy serpents. "Not my *hair!*" she moaned.

You wanted to be a succubus again. You didn't specify what kind. You still have a good figure, and your face is the same. A lot of men are willing to overlook unshaven legs, and they do say the tousled look is in.

"Maybe some styling gel . . ." Melisan considered. The snakes hissed their objections to being spiked, scrunched, or finger-waved. "Oh, shut up," she told them. "I've got my old powers back again, and if I want I can turn myself bald-headed. Being a succubus is like riding a bicycle: You never forget how."

▼HOORAY FOR▼
HELLYWOOD

ESTHER FRIESNER

ACE BOOKS, NEW YORK

Attributions

"Art imitates Nature."   —ARISTOTLE

"Nature imitates Art."   —OSCAR WILDE

"The most momentous thing in human life is the art of winning the soul to good or to evil."
                                         —PYTHAGORAS

Prologue

IN THE MIDST of the Egyptian desert, a demon moaned.

He had been born a demon, formed of primal evil, endowed with his present shape by the undeniable expectations of the youngest breed in all Creation: humans. Humans shaped him, but never made him. Humans: free, hated, his natural prey.

They were also imaginative, those mortal creatures, and over the centuries their potter's-wheel minds had thrown strange vessels for the essences of Hell to inhabit. The shell the demon presently occupied had sprung from the brain of a Burgundian sorcerer, more than five hundred years ago. A gaping Hellmouth lined with dagger teeth was the most flamboyant of the mage's notions of how a demon ought to look. There were also talons, and a subtle sprinkling of scales. Had this same fiend been summoned into a mortal's thrall in the age of Romanticism, he would have fared better, perhaps resembling Lord Byron with bat's wings.

Murakh never had been lucky.

He tilted his head back and howled his rage and frustration at the sun. The desert sands trembled with his wrath. The sunken ruins of an early Christian colony of monks shook with Murakh's fury, webs of hairline cracks shivering the baked clay domes. In the deep-sunk cemetery that the monks had left behind, their brothers' bones thrummed and split to the marrow. A demon's howl is enough to wake the dead, rouse the deepest sleeper.

Down below the sands, the monks' bones were not alone.

Abruptly, Murakh's bear trap jaws snapped shut. He cocked an ear to the north, his talons clamping the sand so hard that discs of glass twinkled up between his toes. Was it . . . ?

Yes, it was! He'd know that sound in his sleep, if he ever could sleep. It was a vehicle approaching the site of the demon's exile, and if he were lucky this time, then maybe—just maybe—

The demon's eyes widened as the vehicle in question mounted a final sand dune and balanced on the gritty ridge in full splendor. He had seen its like before, but never this close to the nether belly of Hades. The nether belly of New York, maybe. Out here, far from any paved road, anyone who had sense but lacked a camel drove a jeep. They did not drive white stretch limousines. White stretch limousines, like monks, died in the desert. By rights, that sleek piece of greed-fulfillment should have broken down three miles after it left civilization. Its occupants should be roasting like foil-wrapped crabs at a barbecue.

Murakh made himself invisible. Though he had lost his freedom and his principality, he still retained some power. The black-uniformed driver whose polished boots first crunched the sand did not see him. A gust of pleasantly chilled air struck Murakh's face as the car door swung closed.

Air conditioning? And after the sun-scorched miles from the nearest road, it still *worked?* Murakh might almost believe in miracles.

The driver stepped to the rear and opened his employer's door. With a smile as brightly white as his limo's hood, brown hair sleeked irrevocably in place, a tall and slender young man stepped out and surveyed the expanse of sand below. Apart from a spur of black rock protruding from the desert floor, there was nothing to mark this part of the wasteland as different from any other.

The traveler didn't seem to think so. His grin spread itself wide as a pair of welcoming arms. The infernal heat pulsed across the sand in frustration, unable to touch this strange visitor. His driver was already sweating profusely, leaning on the car door for support as the sun did what it must to those fool enough to dress for Boston and take a wrong turn at the Mediterranean. The passenger's brow wasn't even dewy. He remained crisp and natty in a three-piece navy suit that calmly stated, "Savile Row, of course; and you?" He carried a Mark Cross attaché case with golden fittings.

"Wait for me in the car, Neddy-boy. I'll whistle when I want you, and you jes' come a-runnin'."

Murakh almost tumbled tail over teacup with astonishment. At the very least he'd been expecting to hear the accents of Oxford and Eton when his visitor opened up a mouth. Instead he heard fluent Grits and Fatback.

"Yes, Mr. Lee, sir." Neddy-boy staggered gratefully into the air-cooled shelter of the limo, while his employer sashayed down the dune in a beeline for the black rock. Murakh crept after.

At the black rock, the young man knelt, opened the attaché case, and took out a trio of white mice. The rodents were more dead than alive, nearly suffocated by their confinement. They still wiggled feebly as Mr. Lee held them up by their tails.

"Awwww. Y'all had a rough trip, boys?" He clucked his tongue in sympathy and bashed their brains out against the stone. Blood trickled down the cracks and crevices. He popped one red-spattered white body into his mouth, smacked his lips, tilted back his head and hollered:

"*Come* and get it! Come and geeeeeeeet it! Yo! Big Fellah! Get your no-'count tailbone up here and—"

"You called?" Murakh's claws closed on the young man's shoulder, ripping a fortune in haberdashery to rags. The sulfurous fumes of a long-lost homeland still rose from the demon's flesh. A lock of hair fell into his captive's eye. The reek of Hell was enough to counteract the costliest of styling mousses.

The young man turned and stared Murakh full in the face. Grin for face-splitting grin, he matched him.

"*Dad!*" Mice flying, he threw his arms around the fiend.

"Raleel . . ." Murakh spoke his son's name in a strangely choked voice. It was not emotion. Raleel had gotten a hammerlock on the demon and was doing his damndest to throttle his sire blue. A jab of the talons and one good yank broke Raleel's hold and sent him caroming into the black rock head first. "Still the same little bastard."

Raleel rubbed the crown of his head. Still smiling, he said, "Aw, c'mon, Dad. You'd think less of me if I didn't try to off you. I owe you that much."

"You and your sister . . ." Murakh shook his head slowly and picked up the fallen mice, chewing them in a meditative manner. His children had always been a grave disappointment, but it was his own fault for coupling with a mortal woman. It had been three-hundred-odd years ago, yet time did not excuse mistakes, as witness his own exile. The mother of his twins had been a witch—there was that much consolation. Still, mortal blood would always out. Baal knew, the neighborhood Puritans had made quite sure that the witch's blood outed when they caught her.

"Still carrying a grudge because I didn't save your dam?" Raleel snorted. "Nah. Revenge for a reason, filial senti- ment, that'd be sister Lysi's line. Who gives a bat's fart what you did or didn't do for the old bitch?"

"So why try to kill me every time we meet?"

A shrug. "Why not? It's fun." The logic was demonic in its inescapability. "And if I can kill you—if it turns out you *can* be killed—I'm your only heir. Raleel, Prince of Parvahr . . . Kinda *sings*, don't it now?"

"You have an American's cheap fascination for royal ti- tles. Why I ever went to Massachusetts . . ." Murakh settled himself against the black rock. "Got any more of those mice?" As his demi-demon son rummaged through the attaché, Murakh studied him more closely. "You didn't just come here to pop rodents with your old dad, Raleel. You're after something. What?"

Raleel found another trio of the unfortunate varmints sand- wiched into his Week-at-a-Glance. They were already dead, but still tasty enough. He gave his sire one and gobbled two for himself before replying.

"I've come to give you some good news, Pops. What do you want more than anything in this or any other world?"

Murakh's eyes flared yellow. Overwhelming anger throt- tled the words from his lips, but the demon had other ways to reply. The ground between the two fiends rippled into a glassy pool where phantoms danced. Five demons cavorted there—two female, three male, the misfit outcasts of Hell— but not for long. Winds of change and battle swept across the pictured sands. Against all that was infernally natural, the five cast off their hellish allegiances to side against the pow- ers of darkness.

Again Murakh had to witness his own defeat, his foes' rewards: A mated pair, male and female, were transformed into angelic guise. A sulfur-colored incubus with one eye sank into blissful, wished-for dreams beneath the sand. A tusked and tailed blue demon regained his more than mortal station as guardian of the legendary Valley of Cloud, where sages and heroes sleep.

The last was a female, golden-haired, and she shed her bat wings willingly for a mortal life, a mortal love, a child. . . . Of the five, she had chosen the despised path of humanity, and for that, Murakh hated her most of all.

"He's grown now, Melisan's whelp," Murakh growled. "The only one of the five I can reach, and she's most vulnerable through that brat of hers. Your sister said she'd find him, snare him, steal his soul. . . ."

"Bingo." Raleel made a gun with his fingers and cheerfully fired it at his sire. "And a soul's just what you need to blow this bunghole, right? You're trapped here until you send one down thataway." He posed like a hellbent hitchhiker. "Woulda been neat, getting that soul *and* revenge on Melisan at the same time." His smile twisted small and taunting. "Only Lysi blew it."

"She fell in love. With *him!* A mortal, even though something more than human clings to him . . ." Murakh's teeth grated against each other like millstones. The sound penetrated the desert floor. Silence is not absolute, nor enchanted sleep invulnerable.

Someone stirred down below.

"Magic," Raleel said. "The kid's got sorcery he ain't even used yet. Well, hey, old man, I'm not here to rehash Lysi's snafus. She's so far gone, she's not even one of *us* any more. I'm here to make you an offer."

Murakh was suspicious. "What kind of an offer?"

"Straight business. I get you a soul—*the* soul you want: Melisan's brat. You get your exile ended, your freedom back, and you head home to our principality."

The elder demon's back stiffened. " 'Our'?"

"Parvahr. It ain't Hell, Daddy—shit, it ain't even Limbo—but it's the next best thing. I get the kid's soul for you, I get a share of Parvahr for me. Deal?"

"How big a share?"

"Seventy-five per cent."

Murakh said a very basic bad word.

"O.K. Have it your way." Raleel turned to go.

Murakh leaped onto his son's back, bearing him to the ground. He yanked the younger fiend's head up by the hair as he crouched atop him. "Wait," he said—an unnecessary request, considering. "Fifty-fifty."

"Sifthy-vorthy," Raleel returned, spitting silica.

"Deal."

Raleel got up and brushed himself off. His dapper threads had not been proof against Murakh's repeated assaults. The young demi-demon studied his rags while his father assumed a contrite expression.

"This was an eight-hundred-dollar suit," Raleel said.

"Shot to Hell. Too bad."

"Oh, I don't mind. I'll get it back, and more. I'm in the sweetest damned business you ever heard tell of, big daddy mine. It's alchemy made simple, gold out of dross, blood from a turnip—Hell, a whole flock of turnips."

Murakh pricked up his ears. "Do tell? You dealing dope? Gunrunning, perchance? Pimping livestock?"

"Better." Raleel licked his lips and linked arms with his sire, steering the elder demon up towards where the white limo waited.

A thought froze Murakh. "You haven't gone into *politics*, I hope?"

"Chill your chassis, Pa. I may be damned, but I've still got *some* class. My card."

Murakh read aloud from the shiny pasteboard rectangle. Within a border of black and gold drapery of stylized fig leaves supported by two bloated cherubs, the embossed red lettering said:

"SOMETIME" JOSEPH LEE
BLESSED LAST TABERNACLE MINISTRIES
NEW YORK   STATION WDIS   LOS ANGELES
YOUR SOUL IS MY CONCERN

While Murakh was still shaking, crown to Christmas, over the appalling cunning of his American-spawned son, Raleel sprang at his sire from behind and slammed him to the sand. They churned up several bushels of desert before Murakh lost his temper and vanished with a roar, but not before Neddy-boy leaped from the limo, camera ready, and snapped a photo of Raleel pinning Murakh to the grit. Printed eight-by-ten, the full-color blowup of "Sometime" Joseph Lee triumphing over Satan was suitable for inspirational framing but not for sale.

However, if the viewer sent in a suitable sincerity-offering to cover postage, printing costs, and incidentals . . .

Very few recipients of this lovely keepsake examined it closely, or else they might have noticed a third face in the picture. Because his natural coloring blended so well with the sand, he was hard to see. Even seeing him, most people would not call that a face. A face usually had more than one saucer-shaped eye.

He had been born a demon, but what he was now was anybody's guess, including his own. All he knew was that he wanted some sleep, and with Murakh's kid running loose he wasn't going to get it. He set out to remedy the situation.

1

Where Can I Get the Crosstown Rapture?

DWAYNE KNOX DRAGGED his feet all the way from the Holiday Inn to the television studio, rubbing the toes of his sneakers raw on the sidewalks of New York. His mother decided not to pay the boy any mind. New sneakers could always be bought when they got back home, away from these godless New York prices; the boy's soul wasn't going to be so easy to replace.

"Stand up straight, Dwayne, you want folks to think you're a hunchback?" she demanded.

Dwayne stuck his lip out even farther and thrust his hands deep into the pockets of his good suit. It was too short for him at the wrists and ankles, but Ma said it was the best he had and it would have to do him for one more year. *For as much as you go to church these days—why, I can hardly hold my head up in town when Elmira Wiggins asks me where you are, and her your Sunday school teacher ever since I can remember, you oughta be 'shamed—you don't need 'nother good suit. That one's scarce been worn.*

He snorted derision at his ma's mental voice. For what she'd spent on this trip to New York, he could've had a dozen new suits, and not just K-Mart stock, either! Heck, he could've bought something at Montgomery Ward's. But no, it wasn't enough she kept sending a dollar here, a dollar there to the Blessed Last Tabernacle Ministries. Now she just plain *had* to be in the studio audience, and it *had* to be this week. She never thought that her boy would be missing the Homecoming game, and the parties before, and the parties after, and Alma Jean Schneider in that short cheerleader skirt of hers and the tight sweaters she wore so the big Fremont High School *F* was always pooching out at a man, giving him these *ideas*. . . .

"Dwayne! Will you wake *up?* Goodness, you'd think you been taking drugs or something, the way you go around in a daze like some kinda *zombie*." Mother and son were standing at the aggressively Art Deco entrance to the WDIS studio. They had come early, but already there were some folks drifting in, handing their tickets to the thick-necked guard at the door who stood beneath a frieze of gamboling nymphs. One and all the attendees wore expressions of relentless holiness. The nymphs wore nothing, period.

"Huh?" Dwayne replied. His thoughts had wandered from Alma Jean's *F,* to contemplation of the nymphs, to remembrance of those fascinating wares he'd seen displayed in one of those funny stores they'd gone by down 42nd Street. He wasn't sure what most of those things were used for, but he'd be willing to bet it was something pretty darn good or Ma wouldn't've hustled him past so quick. Would Alma Jean know? He had promised her a souvenir. . . .

Mrs. Knox sighed deeply, as befitted a martyr. "Don't you hear me asking you where our tickets are?"

Dwayne patted his pockets as every drop of blood in his body sank into his feet. Now that it was too late, he remembered his ma handing him the treasured tickets to the *Heading Home* show, video voice of "Sometime" Joseph Lee's BLT Ministries. She didn't want to carry a purse in New York because it was just temptation to all the drug addicts who were looking to knock down respectably dressed women and snatch their purses and call them names in foreign tongues. He'd been on his way to the john at the time, and he told himself he'd stick them in his pants pocket when he was done.

He hadn't. The tickets were still on top of the commode back at the Holiday Inn, and he was in the toilet, figuratively speaking.

"Oh, *Dwayne!*"

"Ma, I—" Dwayne's protests were cut short.

"Is anything wrong?" A young woman appeared at Mrs. Knox's right hand. A young woman to some, but to Dwayne Knox the lady's advent was proof enough to still a querulous soul that had once dared to doubt the existence of Heaven.

She was just the way she'd looked in all his dreams, and the memory was at once titillating and embarrassing. Automatically, he folded his hands in his lap, even though he wasn't sitting down. No sense in taking chances. She was tall, blond, slim as a Flex-Straw at the waist, blessed above by the bounteous hand of Nature with a pair of the biggest Hefners Dwayne had ever seen. Alma Jean's *F* dwindled to lower case in his mind and heart.

"Any trouble, ma'am?" the lady's companion asked Mrs. Knox. Until he'd spoken up, Dwayne hadn't even noticed he was there. Now that he saw him, it was hate at first sight, immediate and absolute. Heck, the kid didn't look like he had more than three years seniority on Dwayne, though he was dressed like Old Man Hoover down at Dan-Dee 'Luminum Siding. How did he rate standing within inhaling distance of that gorgeous woman? Dwayne plotted to murder him as soon as he learned how the little weasel had done it.

Meantime, Mrs. Knox was explaining her predicament. The blonde continued to smile and respire in a way that left Dwayne feeling like he'd chugged a six-pack. With an effort, he averted his eyes from Paradise I and II and noticed that his ma was talking to the young man as if she knew him. That was weird. Normally Mrs. Knox regarded anyone from outside of Springfield as trash, to be mistrusted first, discarded later. The young man mentioned he was Canadian on his father's side and Mrs. Knox just giggled. That was weirder. She never had any use for foreigners. She wasn't even sure about people from Ohio—"Effete Easterners," she called them.

Canadian half-breed or not, the young man dropped a pair of fresh tickets in Mrs. Knox's hand, asked her blessing, and sailed away, taking Dwayne's bonbon with him. Mrs. Knox watched him go, her face flushed and beaming. Returned to the land of the conscious, Dwayne asked his ma who that little twerp was.

Mrs. Knox's beaming switched off cold. "You'd know *that* if you didn't waste your life running after sin every chance you get. If there's any justice in this wicked world, I woulda had a boy like *that* for my son."

"Does *that* have a name?" Dwayne snapped.

"Barking like that at your own mother. Just like there was only nine commandments, and no number five." Mrs. Knox got a great deal of satisfaction out of yet another proof of Dwayne's damnation. "*That* was a young man with more on his mind than driving all over creation in a cruddy car, and drinking beer with a gang of worthless, trashy 'friends,' and sniffing after every little tramp that comes wiggling down the pike! *That* was a young man who knows how to respect a mother, and knows the agony I went through to birth you, and the thanks I don't get, and the help I might's well whistle for as see. *That* was a—"

A slender girl with long black hair stepped from the phone booth where she'd been hiding. Lissome as any of the carven nymphs, she edged past Mrs. Knox and Dwayne, making for the studio entrance, then paused and said, "*That* was Noel Cardiff." She handed the guard her ticket and vanished inside.

Mrs. Knox was becalmed and Dwayne, grateful, resolved that if the studio seats were not assigned, he was going to move heaven and earth to sit next to his impromptu savior. The big blonde was all very well and good, but she was an epic, a symphony, a major novel TV miniseries! The brunette was an episode of *Dynasty*. He could handle that. A man had to hold onto reality.

'Sides, the dark-haired girl looked like she had some pretty spectacular realities for a fella to hold onto.

Noel knocked on the door of his mentor's soundproofed dressing room. "They're ready for you now, Mr. Lee."

The door was opened by a cautious, well-manicured hand. "Hymns all done, Noel?" Wearing a blue suit with the subtlest of green tattersall patterns, Raleel peeked out.

"Yes, sir. They just whipped right through them with Dix—I mean, with Ms. Dominus leading the singing. I guess everyone's all excited about the big announcement. Will you make it before or after your sermon?"

Raleel stepped into the hall and threw a bear hug around Noel's shoulders. On his own time, the boy still dressed like a fugitive Yalie—which was exactly what he was—but for all *Heading Home* shows, he wore the outfits Raleel picked out for him. With his thickly curling golden hair and huge sea-blue eyes, he looked like a seraph from the neck up. From the neck down he looked like a used-car sales trainee.

"Son, you jes' betcha I'm gonna pick the right moment to drop the Big One. And I'm gonna want you to help. Feel up to it, boy? A little of the ol' razzle-dazzle?" His hands made flimflam passes through the air.

"I guess so." Noel was subdued. He snapped his fingers and a dandelion puff of sparkling red light danced in his palm. He blew on it and it changed into a Lilliputian angel that whirred away on dragonfly wings, singing hosannas.

Raleel cast off a shiver of discomfort. "Fine, jes' fine, son." He thumped Noel on the back heartily. "But I betcha you could do better'n that. Hey, I *know* you can!"

"But it feels so—*wrong,* Mr. Lee!" Noel spread his hands wide. "My magic . . . it's *sorcery!* It's black! It's the devil's work! The Bible says—"

Raleel's silencing hand shot up faster than the cost of living. "Son, you know my feelings 'bout taking the name of that Book in vain. And I'm not one of your fancy-dancy scholars. What I do, is I give forth the testimony of my heart, and pour out upon the bowed heads of the seekers a stream that may nourish them in the desert and be their refreshment in the vale of sorrow. Hey, any book-learned jackass can throw quotes at you from dawn to Doomsday."

" 'The devil can argue Scripture,' " Noel quoted, looking very sober-solemn and wise.

Raleel gave a quick, sharp smile. "You don't worry none about the devil, son. He can look after himself. But you listen to me: Your power is a gift. You can sit on it until it hatches, or you can use it for *our* work. Wasting what you're given's a sin, you betcha. But if you won't take my word for it, the door's over there and the train back to New Haven's still running, they tell me."

Heading Home was broadcast from a state-of-the-art television studio whose interior had been artfully disguised to resemble a Depression-era movie theatre. When Noel first

saw it, he remarked that all that was missing was Bank Night.
His mentor only chuckled.

The audience sat on one side of the organ pit, gazing up at
the splendid gilt plaster representations of fruit and acanthus
leaves that graced the stage's proscenium arch. Cameramen
worked from the box seats. Several runs of curtains concealed
the stage proper from view. The foremost, a red velvet number, rose up to unveil a canvas painted with the more scenic
horrors of the Pit. This remained in place until the audience
was in a sufficiently religious frame of mind; then the hymns
began.

Dwayne Knox was hard put to decide where to keep his
eyes fixed. The dark-haired nymph of his more pragmatic
fantasies was indeed seated beside him. He'd spent the better
part of the audience warm-up session working on his opening line and the courage to use it on her. Alas, the warm-up
consisted of vigorous hymn-singing, led in brisk, athletic
enthusiasm by the blond vision. She had stepped out onto the
stage, introduced herself to the faithful as "Dixi, with an *i*. I
mean two. I mean the letters." Her titter was charming. One
look at her in that high-twirling skirt and clinging white rayon
blouse and poor Dwayne forgot his opening line, the hymn
lyrics, and his home address.

Mercifully, the music stopped. The canvas split right through
the middle of Gehenna and pulled back to either side. The
next curtain was painted the cool blue of airline commercials,
with lamblike clouds. A single mike stood center-stage, a
white-robed choir hummed in neutral at stage-left, and a sigh
of bated bliss rose from the audience as "Sometime" Joseph
Lee entered, stage-right, Noel after.

"Friends, I want to welcome you to *Heading Home*. Now,
some of you are old friends, and some of you are new. Some
of you—why heck, I jes' betcha that some of you're sitting
back home saying as how you only tuned in this show to see
what all the fuss was about and you're gonna turn it right off
again. You say you don't believe. You say you ain't no friend
of mine. Well sir, whether you're my friend or not, I *care*
about you. Sugar, yes. I don't even know you and I care: I
care who you are and what you want to be. I care where you
hurt and what makes you mad and how sometimes you jes'
feel so low you want to give up hope entire all and crawl off
someplace and jes' *die!*"

A murmur of agreement rolled through the audience.

"But you know what I care 'bout most?" Raleel clasped his hands. His right pinkie wiggled ever so slightly. Noel saw the signal, closed his eyes, summoned his powers, and waited for his cue. "I care 'bout your *soul!*"

Fiery white wings seemed to snap open across the breadth of the cloudy backdrop. The face of the sweetest, sincerest, most dewy-eyed little girl outside of a Dickens novel superimposed itself over them, and the daisies she held out to the audience came right off the screen into their faces. The fresh green scent of the flowers filled the hall, and viewers at home had to shake their heads a time or two before dismissing the evidence of their noses as merely the power of suggestion at work.

Dwayne was impressed. They didn't even give out 3-D goggles at the door and the F/X still worked slicker than owl shit. He sat up a little straighter in his chair and let his left knee press against the dark girl's right.

She pulled her knee away, then swung it back, hard.

Dwayne's yelp was covered by "Sometime" Joseph Lee's continuing sermon. Noel's conjured vision on the backdrop did an artsy fade just as a single photogenic tear trickled down the little girl's cheek.

The gist of the sermon was like many another: Holding the souls of others dear didn't come cheap. Mrs. Knox had heard it all before, but she never tired of listening to that man talk so pretty. She gave Dwayne a sidelong glance and was smugly pleased to see that her son was not fidgeting. Somewhere between nursing his sore knee and hoping that Dixi-with-however-many-*i*'s would return, Dwayne had fallen under the spell of the great televangelist.

"Sometime" Joseph Lee finished as his small platoon of collectors passed among the audience, bringing in the sheaves. His eyes twinkled as he watched the harvest. It didn't matter how piddling the take was this time; there'd be more later. He raised his arms for silence.

"Now friends, I got me a 'nouncement to make. You been hearing 'bout it for weeks, looking forward to it, and I sure hope it don't let you down none. Thanks to you—thanks to all of you good and faithful people out there—I am pleased to 'nounce that the Blessed Last Tabernacle Ministries are about to strike a blow against evil like'd set your head to spin!

Friends, where is evil loudest in your lives? Why does it have such pernicious influence on your young folks? Sugar, I'll *tell* you! *Show bidness!*''

Raleel steeled himself for the barrage of ''Amens'' the audience threw at him.

''Yes, *show* bidness! You tell your kids till you are blue in the face 'bout how wicked they're being, and then they take them four dollars of *your* hard-earned money and waltz down to the theatre and see all these other kids up on the screen, a-drinking and a-whoring and a-snorting and not once—not *one sweet time,* mind you!—not once do they ever have to suffer the rightful rewards of such low, vile, and worthless behavior. If there was any justice, every time one of those actresses took off her blouse, she get strick down with pregnancy, just to learn her! And those actors in their tight jeans, why, they'd take one puff off a cigarette and they'd—they'd lose their manhood right then-there!''

Raleel leaned into the mike and hissed, ''Why d'you think they call it *cin*ema?''

The ''Amen'' chorus was painful for him, but worth it.

''Well, friends, all that's gonna change. Thanks to your generous offerings, Blessed Last Tabernacle Ministries is going to fight fire with fire. Friends, we're gonna make us *our own* movie—a fine movie! A decent movie! A movie where sin gets just what's coming to it! A real *American* movie! And you know what else?'' He lowered his voice and told three thousand people a secret. ''Those of you who've shown your love and devotion the most generous to our cause . . . *you're gonna be in pictures.*''

2

Mama Don't 'Low

RALEEL BUZZED DIXI for the latest printouts.

"Now would you jes' look at that." He clicked his tongue as he reviewed the weekly finances. "Amazing how many more folks jes' kinda opened up their hearts ever since I made the 'nouncement 'bout the movie."

"Do you think they're just trying to buy their way into the picture, Mr. Lee?" Dixi asked.

"Aw, now, sugar, that's a heck of a thing to say 'bout our faithful supporters." Raleel looked truly shocked by the very thought. "Next thing, you're gonna tell me there's folks as think they can buy their way into Heaven." He grimaced. "Why, they jes' give outa the goodness of their hearts is all. And it hurts me worse'n you'll ever know that I can't have 'em all in this picture, but shoot, they'd tromp each other flat if I 'lowed that. Hey, let's ask Noel if he thinks we could do it different. Noel! Yo!"

"Hm? What—?" Noel was sprawled on the leather sofa in "Sometime" Joseph Lee's inner sanctum, reading a copy of *Stover at Yale* and daydreaming about his good old days as an Eli. All that had been pre-sorcery, and pre-Lysi. Dink Stover had a brief interlude with a totally unsuitable working girl before returning to his socially correct soul mate, but the sad situation was quickly and hygienically resolved and all was bliss. *Sic* Stover.

Not *sic* Noel. He tried to imagine himself, after Lysi, finding Ms. Right. Visions in denim and flannel, in sweatshirts and joggers' shorts, in pink and green and 'gator fluttered through his mind. It was discouraging work, for Lysi's face kept horning in, giving him impure thoughts. Stover never had that problem. Maybe it was something they taught you at

Lawrenceville; or something they used to add to the old Yale food.

Also, Dink Stover had never slept with a demon.

"I said, you got a better idea for deciding who gets into this here picture we're gonna make us?"

Noel snapped out of reverie. "Oh. No, sir." He could not picture himself ever presuming to have a better idea than his mentor.

"But where *are* you going to mark the cutoff, Mr. Lee?" Dixi inquired, a piquant frown-line appearing between her winged ash-blond brows. "How much in donations gets you a part, how much more gets you a *speaking* part. . . . We leave for L.A. tomorrow. People have to be notified."

"Honey, if you got a note in the mail telling you you'd been tapped for a part in a real honest-to-gosh movie, and it said you had to get yourself out to the Coast by next day or forget it, what'd you do?"

Dixi thought about it. "I'm not much for movies, Mr. Lee. I prefer television."

Raleel slapped his brow. "So O.K., a *television* role. But if I know people, I'm betting the nine out of ten'd haul it out to Tinseltown fast enough to leave skid marks on the sky. *Everybody* wants to be in the movies!"

Noel put *Stover* to bed on the Italian glass-and-bronze coffee table. "What if they can't afford it? You're not paying for their transportation, or lodging, or meals and expenses while they're out there."

"Son," Raleel drawled. "Son, they gave their hard-earned money to the BLT Ministries out of the pure love in their hearts. Now, don't you think it's 'bout time they spent a little of their cash on their own pleasures? 'Sides, we're picking up the tabs for you and Dixi and the three lucky folks whose ticket stubs got called right during yesterday's broadcast. Now, if we cover expenses for anyone else we gonna have nothing left to further the great works our organization is doing."

For the hundredth time since he had put his life into the holy hands of "Sometime" Joseph Lee, Noel Cardiff tried to find a tactful way to ask, *"What* great works?" When he'd first come into this office—weary, unhappy, disillusioned—he had never considered asking about the specifics of income and outgo behind "Sometime" Joseph Lee's operation. It wasn't his place, coming into the great man's care as a spiritual charity case.

Now that he was the gentleman's protégé, however, he was kept too busy to ask. The opportunity for a private chat never presented itself. If it did, Mr. Lee always seemed to have more than enough topics with which to fill the time.

He did tell Noel that using his inborn magic was a great work for the Ministries. That was consoling. And now there was the movie. That sounded like a pretty great work.

The phone rang and all but leaped into Dixi's slim white hand. "Blessed Last Tabernacle Ministries. Be on the winning side of Armageddon. How may I help you, please?"

She listened, then covered the mouthpiece and said, "It's that boy who won the all-expense-paid role in the movie. He's here with his mother. Can you see them?"

"Ahhhh, yes. Send them right in, Dixi." Raleel tilted his cowhide chair back and pressed the desktop button that opened the fruit-juice bar in the sideboard. A second button brought out a bottle of "Sometime" Joseph Lee's private stock of V.S.O.P. nerve tonic. He poured himself a good jolt and asked Noel, "Want to see how we handle this, son?"

"What's there to handle? The boy won—"

"—but his mama didn't. And what she'll say . . ." Raleel sipped his drink and gave Noel a sly smile. "Hmm, no; never mind. You got things of your own to see to today, now don't you, son?"

Noel lowered his head. "I have to say goodbye to my parents. I promised I'd visit them today, before we go to Los Angeles." He did not sound at all eager to renew family ties. In a more hopeful voice he added, "I'll be back by seven, the latest!"

"Take your time, son." Raleel could afford to be generous. "Must be hard on your mama, having to watch her boy grow up and go his own way."

"My mama . . ." Noel was bitter. "If you only knew." He trailed out of the office just as Dixi led the Knoxes in.

Raleel made a big show of offering them watered-down hospitality. Mrs. Knox was in a dither, obviously torn between conflicting emotions. Her expression changed more times than a traffic light, from prim self-righteousness over forbidding her son to go to L.A. unchaperoned, to gushy thrills at being in her spiritual hero's private lair.

There was a third emotion too—one that Raleel exulted to see: Envy, one of the Biggies. He stretched out the social preliminaries the better to savor Mrs. Knox's burning green grudge, and all directed right smack at her own son.

I know just what you're thinking, you old ragbag, Raleel gloated inwardly. *"Why him? Why not me? I was the one sent in all that money! I was the one who never had any fun! Why should he luck out and get a free trip to L.A. to be in pictures? Damn his worthless acne-pocked hide, that should be me!" Well, it's not you, babe, but you can't blame me. Blame your son instead. Make his life a misery for having the dumb luck to do better than you. Envy can bring along Wrath for company, and let's not forget your wounded Pride, while we're at it! He got first and ten, but the game's not over yet. Put him down every chance you get from now on, compare him unfavorably to other people's perfect children, belittle his every achievement as more dumb luck. Hate him. Teach him to hate you. And he'll pass it on to his kids, and they'll make sure their kids learn hate, too. Generation against generation, unto the end of time, and all for the price of a trip to L.A.! Oh, sweet Dis, that's what I call a big return on one smart little investment!*

Raleel proceeded to explain to Mrs. Knox that BLT Ministries had already picked out a fine chaperone for her son, but could not possibly pay for her to assume that role. She balked, but a strategic parable ending with the stubborn and selfish female protagonist roasting over slow coals brought her around. She left in a cloud of suppressed rage, already honing her tongue on Dwayne's ears.

Dixi followed the departing pair with her eyes. Distress only made her look more delectable. "Oooh, I hope that poor boy's mother won't take it out of him forever. Do you think she'll see reason, Mr. Lee?"

A thin grin tugged one corner of Raleel's mouth. "I'll pray over that, honey." *Hell I will.* "Don't fret. Ain't no one in this world more reasonable than a boy's own mama."

"It's all your fault, Atamar!" Melisan shouted. "It's your fault that I've lost my son!"

"Melisan, you're not being reasonable." Atamar crossed his legs, revealing precisely the acceptable expanse of black silk sock. "I am an angel—Noel's guardian angel, to be precise. My work is to save the boy, not lose him. If any-one's at fault—''

"Then you're making a damned big hash of your job!'' Melisan replied hotly. She pointed at the empty black-lacquered tray on the low table between them. *"Who ate all the sushi I made for Noel?"* A few pathetic grains of rice accused the defendant.

Atamar was unruffled. Beings of his sort were usually imbued with divine calm, but in his case there was the added self-tranquilizer of knowing that he was one of the most exquisitely beautiful creatures brought to being since the world began. Though he didn't like to recall past mistakes, this was his second hitch as an angel. He had made the error of siding with the losers during the great Revolt in Heaven, and his flawless face had remained unchanged when he tumbled down with the rest of his ill-counseled comrades. He'd still been beautiful even as a demon, but bat wings and an eternal stench of dung distracted from the overall effect.

He shifted his weight on the futon sofa. He disliked recall-ing those times. "While we are on earth, nothing stops us from having some of the same hungers as you.''

"That's true, Melisan,'' Lura said. She was dressed as impeccably as her mate, her thick black fall of hair bound into a chignon. "You should have made more. You remem-ber from our desert days how Atamar always liked his meat rare.''

"Atamar was a lizard-sucker like the rest of us,'' Melisan growled.

From the red leather Chesterfield chair, sole Western *objet du décor* in the room, Kent Cardiff looked at Melisan with mild inquiry. "Now, Marguerite,'' he said, calling Melisan by the name she'd adopted along with her chosen mortality. "Don't you think you're making a bit much fuss over a few slivers of raw tuna?'' He spoke in those tweed-and-leather-patched accents which had made him an irreplaceable institu-tion on PBS. The nearest Kent Cardiff had come to England in his formative years was London, Ontario, but few viewers ever suspected.

"Am I?'' Melisan sprang from the futon opposite the angels, no mean feat. "Didn't you hear what Noel told us? He's going to California with that—that greasy soulmonger! This was my last chance to win him back, make him see how

foolish he's being. I wanted everything perfect, which was
why I made it a point to have his absolutely favorite dish.''
Her eyes glowed dangerously, slued towards Atamar. ''Whoever said 'When pigs have wings' must have met you.''

''That's unfair.'' A little of Atamar's old demonic capacity
for quick anger had carried over into his second angelhood.
''Lura and I only came by to see if we could help out. Did we
get thanked? No! We got shoved into the kitchen and told to
turn ourselves invisible if your precious baby boy took one
step in our direction. Since when is it shameful to be an
angel?'' His mouth, chiseled by a greater Master than Praxiteles,
looked tempting even when he pouted.

''You know how Atamar gets the munchies when he's
feeling slighted,'' Lura accused. ''The tray was just sitting
there.''

''Why you had to turn proud about it . . .'' Atamar
muttered. ''You were the one asked us to be the boy's
guardian angels in the first place—an eternal commitment!
—and now you won't let us do our jobs. Did you expect to
win him over by stuffing him with tidbits? Ha! Nothing gives
a child more power over his parents than refusing to eat. *I*
could've talked some sense into Noel.''

''Afraid not, Atamar, old chap,'' Kent put in as he went
through the ritual of lighting his briar. ''The lad's been rather
off you and your lovely lady''—Lura simpered—''ever since
before he left Yale. You were a bit too attentive, if you
follow me; too ready to do things *for* him rather than letting
him muddle through on his own.''

''A nice muddle.'' Lura spoke sharply. She took all attacks
on her mate as personal affronts. ''Do you know who this
'Sometime' Joseph Lee creature really is?''

The walls of the Park Avenue apartment boomed and shook.
The legs fell out from under Kent's armchair. In the niche
where the fireplace had been plastered over, at Melisan's
Japanomanic behest, the *ikebana* arrangement exploded into a
Catherine wheel of fiery red roses. Floating cross-legged in
the midst of these sat the dark-haired girl of Dwayne Knox's
second-string lusts.

''They know,'' she said as the roses sputtered out one by
one. ''I told them. He's my brother Raleel.'' She swept down
from her smoking perch and restored the apartment to its
former state with a gesture and a sigh. The sleeves of her

green-and-gold silk robe lent her a dragon's wings. The veritable dragon embroidered across the back lifted his stitched head from the cloth and spat flames.

"I say, Lysi, is grandstanding necessary?" Kent asked, a trifle shaken by his chair's ups and downs and by the dragon's excesses. He cast an uneasy eye at the sprinkler system overhead.

"Doesn't matter, does it?" Lysi shrugged, making the dragon vanish along with the robe. She was now dressed in a decorous skirt-and-sweater ensemble and looked like a refugee from Miss Porter's. "I still have demonic powers, though there's not a demon in all the Underlords' realms who'd acknowledge me as such. I might as well use what I've got."

"Lysi popped by earlier than you," Kent explained to the angels. "She's been keeping a keen eye on our Noel ever since they parted."

"As have we." Atamar folded his arms.

"No one's accusing you of slacking off, old fella. Lysi was merely the first to tip us wise to the Lee chap, is all. Raleel, hmm? Possible Sanskrit roots there, you think?"

Melisan couldn't have cared less about the derivation of Raleel's name. "Can you prove to Noel that 'Sometime' Joseph Lee is your brother?" she asked Lysi.

"I guess. My word wouldn't be enough for Noel, so I'd have to make Raleel show himself. It'd take some work—the scum-truffle's pretty smart, but I'm sneakier. I got in to see his broadcast today and he never suspected I was there. When he gets going he becomes so wrapped up in his own show that he turns careless. Yeah, I can prove what he is." Lysi sniffed the air. "Do I smell sushi?"

Melisan had to hold in a full-throated crow of glee. "Excellent! Oh, bless you, Lysi." She embraced the girl with a warmth impossible some months ago. "When Noel comes to his senses, I do hope he realizes what a treasure you are."

Lysi's mouth twitched. "Sure." She didn't sound convinced.

"I say, Marguerite, it won't wash," Kent said. The angels bobbed their heads in agreement.

"Why not?" Melisan was fierce when contradicted. "Noel thinks that video pimp's so pure, so wonderful! If we show him the truth—"

"He might abandon Mr. Lee, only to fall prey to Raleel at the next turn in the road. My dear girl, Raleel is a demon, is he not? He has time and ingenuity to lay new snares and adopt new personae. Our task is not so much to make our son reject 'Sometime' Joseph Lee as to convince him to accept us again.''

"Something you won't get after a big revelation scene," Atamar said. "The temptation for I-told-you-so's is too much for any mortal, especially a mother. No other words are more guaranteed to make a child cut and run. You won't get him back that way either."

"Then what's the use?" Melisan cried, sinking back into the padded cotton ticking. "I've lost him!"

"There, there, dear." Lura traded seats to pat her old buddy on the back. "You're too mercurial. If one ploy won't work, it doesn't mean you must surrender entirely."

"Marguerite's given to wild swings," Kent contributed. "Witness our home. She found that charming sushi tray in Azuma one day, and the next day she redid the entire flat as a set from *Shōgun*. Sheer pluck alone let me keep my favorite chair." He patted its red leather flanks smugly.

"Don't give up," Atamar counseled. "Look at Lysi. She's in a worse situation than you."

"That's right," Lysi said. "I'm not mortal, I'm sure no angel, but I'm not a demon, either. It's not too comfy, being the world's biggest square peg."

Melisan did not view it so. "Maybe you're neither fish nor fowl, but at least you've got your powers. You're not helpless. But what do I have?"

Atamar stood and walked over to the phone. He made a series of whistling noises into the mouthpiece, followed by a battery of clicks, then listened. He hung up the receiver and said, "You have the spirit not to surrender your son's soul without a fight, you have us to help you, and you have enough in your bank account for plane fare to the Coast and expenses in L.A."

"You don't mean—?"

Atamar was serious. "We're going Hollywood."

3

No Business Like . . .

THE NEW YORK offices of Blessed Last Tabernacle Ministries were a mere bud on the body politic of Raleel's holdings. The main office—the Tabernacle itself—was in L.A., not two blocks from the Farmer's Market. It was an edifice that combined high tech and low taste to an astonishing degree. From the outside, all you saw was reflective golden glass going up and up into two thirteen-story towers. The base building between them was fronted by blue-green double doors with mosaic reproductions of the Ishtar Gate of Babylon.

Inside, after passing through a huge lobby arboretum, the visitor entered the Hall of Murals. Here were figures of Biblical mien, though not one of the scenes depicted could be ascribed to a specific Scriptural tale: Wild-eyed men out of the desert, possessed by visions; placid, self-satisfied merchants, surrounded by the material rewards of their holiness; white-bearded, stern-faced patriarchs, all dressed in robes heavy enough to give normal folks heatstroke after a half-hour in the streets of the Holy Land. These painted titans did not feel the heat, nor did their hatchet-visaged female counterparts. They were having too much fun chastising the naked sinners who cowered under their unforgiving gaze. In one of the murals, a helpful old harpy was already distributing hefty, suitable-for-casting stones to the rest of the pickup jury.

The naked sinners were all young, healthy, blooming—in brief, everything that their critics were not. Some of them were still engaged in the carnal misdemeanors that were about to purchase them a pounding. The casual passer-by could not avoid noticing every creative detail in the foredoomed disporters' interactions. Black marble benches were thoughtfully disposed opposite each of the murals, a public service of BLT

Ministries for any of the faithful who wished to study Evil in detail, up close, the better to know it when next they saw it.

High above the Hall of Murals, on the thirteenth floor of the west tower, was Raleel's private office suite. At the moment, the inmost chamber was occupied by Noel and Dixi. The boy paced around the room, stopping at times to gaze out at the panoramic view of L.A. At the circular rosewood desk, Dixi's fingers danced over the computer keyboard, her labors punctuated by small, rodentlike exclamations of distress over misstrikes.

"Noel, lovey, would you mind taking a look at this for me? I can't get this icky old machine to do one 'ittle thing I want it to and I'm sooooo peeved."

Noel did as she asked, most reluctantly. He didn't like being left alone with Ms. Dominus—it made him antsy. He wished Mr. Lee would get here already.

He hadn't seen much of his mentor since their arrival in L.A. "Sometime" Joseph Lee had a full schedule of personal appearances which had gotten backed up faster than a grease-plugged drain in the months since he'd taken off for New York. Now he had to make up for lost time.

"What's the problem, Ms. Dominus?" Noel asked, trying to keep it cool and professional.

The able secretary did not vacate her chair. She merely reached behind her, grabbed a hunk of Noel's seersucker jacket, and yanked him forward so that he had an unobstructed view of the CRT and her deeply scooped neckline. Both displays were impressive.

"I do wish you'd call me Dixi," she said, her breath a tingle in his ear. "It's my name, see?" She pointed to her personalized coffee cup as proof, the two *i*'s in *Dixi* dotted with hollow hearts containing smiley faces. "The problem is, I can't get it up. Can you?"

Noel croaked. "Gha—?"

"Mr. Lee's schedule for today. I have to get it up on the screen. I have to see if I can squeeze in the lecture against sex education in the schools. I thought he maybe had time after the rally to ban AIDS victims from public transportation, but then he's supposed to have these two visitors up here." She pushed her chair back, pinning Noel against the inner curve of the circular desk. "I don't know how he does it." She tilted her head back, blue eyes giving him what had to be a come-on look even if it was upside-down. "Do you?" Her lips invited more than a polite reply.

Antsy was not quite the right word for how Noel felt when left alone with Dixi. It was more like the inner buzz an incredibly moral child would feel on being left alone before dinner with an unguarded candy dish. The candy was tempting just by virtue of its candyhood, and who would ever find out? Dixi wouldn't kiss and tell. She hardly seemed able to kiss and remember.

No, Noel didn't feel antsy with Dixi; he felt human. His own lips began to tremble and purse. They weren't the only part of him with independent ideas. He leaned closer.

"Oooh, Noel, you are just so *cute!*" Dixi crinkled her nose and patted his cheek as she rocketed back into an upright position. No bucket of Arctic sea-water was more disheartening than the word "cute" tossed at a man at a romantic nexus. The nose-crinkle took its toll too, and when Dixi added, "I wish I had a little brother just like you," it was all over.

By the time "Sometime" Joseph Lee returned to his aerie, Noel was back at the windows and Dixi was filing her nails over the keyboard.

Raleel opened the door slowly, as if he had been expecting a surprise of some sort. He was visibly deflated by what he did find. *That kid been neutered or what?* he wondered. *I gave them enough time alone to—Maybe I did wrong, firing Patty-Jo. She looked like a mud fence next to this babe, but maybe she woulda had more luck frying Noel's circuits. Looks aren't everything. There's no substitute for a real slimy mind.*

"Mr. Lee!" Dixi arose from the desk like Aphrodite from the foam. Hell had its share of history's beauties, but Raleel still felt his breath catch whenever sight of Dixi took him off guard. "I am *so* glad you're back. Your first visitor's due *any minute.*"

The demon grinned. "Relax, sugar. I'm here now, and he'll be on his way up real soon. Saw his limo pull up outside. Dang thing's big enough to host a Harvard home game. Why'n't you go out front to say hi to him when he hits reception, hm?" He tried to pat her fanny as she teetered past him, but somehow missed an easy shot.

"All right, son." Raleel turned to Noel. "This here man

comin' up to see us is someone we need if we're gonna save the souls of America right between Beelzebub and buttered popcorn.''

''How's that, sir?''

''Can't make no movie 'thout we get us a studio to shoot it at, costumes, sets, film, cammers; little things like that.'' He clicked his tongue. ''We need us a connection, and this boy's it. Now, I want you to use them powers of yours to help me. He's gonna be a tough nut to crack, you betcha. Son, you tap into my words and make him *see* what I'm saying, savvy?''

Noel nodded. He'd done this stunt before. It was illusionary magic, fairly easy stuff.

''And soon's he sees it, boy, I want him to *feel* it too!''

''Sir, I'll try, but my magic can't affect a person's emotions directly.''

''Shoot, that ain't the kinda feel I got in mind. Follow 'long of me and you'll catch on.''

The intercom buzzed. ''Donald Swann to see you, Mr. Lee,'' Dixi cooed. She sent him right on in.

Oh, brother, Raleel thought. *This is one of the mortal pups who shot Big Dad down in flames?*

Don Swann did not look like much. In this, he was consistent: He had never looked like much, except in his own mind. There he had cherished gratifying fancies of self-importance, irresistibility, and merit that made even his adoring mother beg him to come out of the clouds.

Don liked it in the clouds, so he went into the one career field where they paid you more the higher you soared. Donald Swann Productions started small, with teen-gutting maniac-in-the-woods movies. They should have stayed small, but the Muse of Whimsy always was the patron goddess of L.A., and she decided to make Don successful, just for grins.

So it was that Noel saw a tall, skinny man dressed like a *haute couture* scarecrow. Between blinding flashes of gold at neck and wrist and eyeglass frames, Noel caught hints of wild beach-prints. The stuff looked like quality goods, but it was loud.

Then Don started talking, and there was something louder.

''I'm a busy man, Lee. I said on the phone that I could give you ten minutes. That was before I knew I'd be taking lunch with Steve.''

''Allen?'' Noel asked innocently.

Don gave him a withering look. "Did I say *Woody?*"

"Mr. Swann, sir—" Raleel purred, "what I got to say ain't gonna take more'n five. You'll be glad you heard it."

"Well, hurry it up." Don tapped the crystal of a watch that did everything but drive you home. "I'm only here because my exec assistant got zombified by one of your broadcasts— Girl's got shorthand where her brains should be—and she threatened to burn-bag my whole file system if I didn't agree to see you. So I'm here. So make with the words. Fast. I promised George we'd talk numbers prontoroony this P.M. *Not Burns,*" he snapped, seeing Noel open his mouth.

"Jetson?" Noel inquired, smiling pleasantly. This time it wasn't innocent, just calculated to gall.

"Mr. Swann, I mos' certainly do appreciate you takin' time offa your schedule to see us here at BLT Ministries. I promise you, you won't lose nothin' by hearing me out. I got me a business proposition to give you."

"If you're talking business to me, you gotta mean pictures." Don had a laugh harder than a week-old bagel. "Mister, I can see it didn't take peanuts to back a setup like you got here, but I'm telling you, that's zoo dirt next to what it'd cost you to do a movie. Hell, you'd have to bleed every one of your BLT turkeys bone-dry, and that's just if you're doing a short subject!"

"Well, sir, my—faithful turkeys weren't 'zactly the blood bank I had in mind. . . ."

Don Swann tried to laugh again. The sound cracked on his lips. There was something unusual about this televangelist creep. Don had tuned in on *Heading Home* maybe once, on a hung-over Sunday morning when he needed something to drown out the pounding in his head. Even then, he'd thought the man was a loon, but a hypnotic loon. Don noticed the way Lee swayed his audience; he noticed the way Lee used every cheap and stupid trick in the book, but made them work; he noticed the way Lee always had this shavetail kid hovering somewhere in the background, the perfect note of youthful artlessness to back his grown-up greed spiel.

Why hadn't he noticed that the man had glowing red eyes with twirling black pinwheel pupils?

Why did he feel so lightheaded, staring into them, hearing words that normally made him laugh: *Hell . . . lost . . . torment . . . eternity . . . agony . . .*

Why was he alone in Hell?

It wasn't your common tour of the Inferno: It was an eyewitness account with the garrulous native guide, no details left unsaid, every horror blazing up firsthand inside Don's own skull. Raleel spoke on, and Noel's magic wrapped Donald Swann in a curtain of fire, a whirlwind of ice. Scorpions stung him, nameless aches wracked his bones, and the only company he had in the ashes and the dark were people he'd always thought were good. If they were here, he surely belonged. There was a short, poignant mention of what might have been—Heaven just beyond the horizon—enough of a hopeful hint to make the victim lose all hope entirely.

By the time "Sometime" Joseph Lee had finished expressing his concern for the state of Don's soul, the producer was a crumpled wad of tears and trembling.

"You won't regret this." Releel smiled as Don put his signature to their partnership agreement. The demon almost wished he'd stuck in a clause giving him title to the poor zhlub's soul while he was at it. No way was this patsy in any shape to read fine print. "Thank you, son."

"I should be the one thanking you! Oh, Reverend Lee—"

"Hush up, son. I don't go round answering to highfalutin titles I never earned. You jes' call me 'Sometime' Joe. Earned *that* fair and square. See, you're not the first scoffer who's come before me in your pride. I seen 'em all. I ask 'em, 'When you gonna stop all this piddly sin and *really* get your soul where it's going?' And they all say to me, 'Oh, sometime, Joseph; sometime.' " He crushed Don's limp hand with sincerity. "Well, I guess I don't gotta tell you, there ain't no *sometime* in Hell."

Don groaned and clung to Raleel's hand like spinach to a front tooth. He showed no sign of moving out of his new guru's office. It was Raleel's turn to check his watch and look impatient.

"Noel, son, whyn't you escort Mr. Swann down to his car? Fact, you might's well start working with him, so's we can get this flick of ours going soon's ever."

Don blathered a hundred assurances that he would move heaven, earth, and all relevant suburbs to get the picture into production yesterday. Noel grabbed a clipboard and a Biro before guiding the broken man back to the elevators.

As they got into the limo, Don turned doleful eyes to Noel

and whimpered, "I usually throw a party right before every new project. It's kind of my trademark in this town, a good luck ritual. Do you think Mr. Lee would mind if I did it this time too? Nothing too sinful, of course: Turn off the Jacuzzi, give the masseuse the night off, nothing but decaf . . . I wouldn't even order those funny-shaped hors d'oeuvres from Fleurs de Mal Deli."

Noel reassured him that salvation and celebration did not have to be mutually exclusive. The limo pulled away just in time for a battered but game little Subaru to nab a third of the vacated parking space.

A sensibly dressed young woman stepped out, planted her oxfords on the pavement, her hands on her hips, and stared up at the looming façade of BLT Ministries HQ.

"Holy shit," Faith Schleppey exclaimed.

4

Alexandria's Ragtime Band

"THE REPENTANT COURTESAN?" Faith's eyebrows went up. "Don't you think that's a little—well—smarmy, Mr. Lee?"

"Smarmy *sells*, Ms. Schleppey." Raleel wished he could shuck his evangelical disguise for just a moment and give this outspoken female the full effect of his 360-degree smile. One big mouth deserved another.

From the moment she'd shaken hands with him, Faith Schleppey had disagreed with everything "Sometime" Joseph Lee had to say to her. She'd always reminded folks of a wirehaired fox terrier—bouncy, yappy, scrappy, and too damned smart for her own good. Raleel just thought she was a bitch.

A smart bitch, he thought. *The worst kind. Praise Moloch, we demons don't have to deal with jumped-up females. A succubus knows her place. Even Lilith follows orders. But these mortal brood mares . . .* He did the mental equivalent of a scornful spit. *I fear the day when human males stop following our example and start listening to the feemies with more than half an ear. We'll never get anywhere then.*

Faith leaned back in her chair and crossed a pair of surprisingly good legs. "I don't know, Mr. Lee. I'm flattered that you chose me as your technical advisor, but—"

"Who better?" Raleel's voice oozed melted butter and warm maple syrup. "Your credentials are something else: Archeology degrees from Princeton, Harvard, already a top name in your field, *and* curator of the *Splendor of Alexandria* exhibit down to the L.A. County Museum of Art." He leaned over his desk, hands pressed together as in prayer. "If'n you ain't the only one I'd have checking out how downright authentic *real* the Alexandrian scenes in this here picture, then may I shake hands with Satan himself!"

"Those are pretty strong words coming from you, Mr. Lee."

"Mean every last one of 'em."

"Don't make too much of my exhibit. The *Splendor of Alexandria* isn't that big: some jewelry, some statues, a few scrolls, a really fine sarcophagus with—"

"No ma'am, I believe as it's not so big. But something don't gotta be big to pack a wallop." *Like the wallop you packed when you helped bring my daddy down, you runty apple-nabber. And what's gonna bring you down lower than he ever hit? I don't know yet, but I'm gonna keep you where I can watch you, long as it takes for me to find out.*

"I hope the exhibit does well. Ancient Alexandria's always been a pet topic of mine. I guess you could say I was an expert on the site." Faith was wavering. "The fee you propose is very tempting . . . and the time schedule wouldn't interfere with my duties at the exhibit. . . ."

Raleel spun his Rolodex like a carny sharp with a rigged wheel. "We're more'n willing to work around your needs, sugar."

A momentary chill knifed the air. "Mr. Lee, my name is not 'Sugar.' Nor 'Honey.' Nor anything else that might cause cavities. Would you keep that in mind?"

"Why, sure enough, Ms. Schleppey." His disarming smile relaxed her. *How 'bout I call you 'Kaopectate'? You're stuffy enough.* "Now, like I was saying, your time is our time, and the money's not too poorly. We got us a deal?"

Faith shook hands with the man. "Now tell me more about the movie."

Raleel buzzed for Dixi, who floated into the office with a dictation machine in her palm the size of a pocket transistor radio. She perched artistically on the edge of her chair, finger poised above the ON button. "Ready."

Faith frowned. "That's how your secretary takes dictation?"

"Ain't she a ball o' fire at it, too! Ain't never lost a word of what I said yet."

The frown deepened. "Couldn't you just use the machine yourself?" Raleel allowed that he could. "Then why call her in?"

The demon turned a smirk into a look of earnest concern. "Why, Ms. Schleppey, I do believe I been the victim of a miracle here. Yessir, I do believe I have been vouchsafed the temporary ability to read minds. I can tell you 'zactly what you're thinking. You're thinking that I'm one of those two-faced men what keep theirselves surrounded by ladies who got nothing in their skulls and everything in their sweaters. You're thinking I keep Ms. Dominus here as my secretary solely because she got a face and figure fit to make a badger howl for mercy. You think there's enough hanky-panky going on behind closed doors here to fill a year's worth of *People* magazines."

"Amazing, Holmes," Faith muttered.

"Well, ma'am, might be I can't prove you're wrong. Might be I got enough satisfaction just *knowing* you're wrong. But I'll tell you something else. While you're a-sitting there, handing out your moral judgments like they was Gummi bears, I'll tell you that for all your high-sounding thoughts 'bout equality, *you still think any woman as beautiful as Ms. Dominus has gotta be a bimbo with Spam for brains!*"

He saw the blush rise to Faith's cheeks and went for the kill. "Dixi, get your file in here." Ms. Dominus did as requested, and before long Faith Schleppey was paging through the personnel file of Dixi Dominus, B.A. Radcliffe, M.A. Yale.

"But—but then why are you working as a secretary?"

"Whyn't you say *just* a secretary?" Raleel sneered, making Faith go a richer shade of crimson. "Whyn't you confess

as how you ain't prejudiced, but you still got 'bout as much
respect for women with clerical jobs as you do for the nearest
wastebasket?''

Dixi answered while Faith's cheeks burned. ''I majored in
Comparative Literature, Ms. Schleppey. And a woman has to
eat while she's working on her novel.''

''Read me the first ten pages and I didn't understand a
word of it,'' Raleel said with some satisfaction. ''*That's*
literature! Now, can we talk 'bout the movie?''

Faith was meek as a neurasthenic lamb after that. She
heard ''Sometime'' Joseph Lee outline his plans for the moral
epic he would make, with her help.

''See, trouble is most Americans don't never see sin as she
is spoke. Not less'n Geraldo Rivera does him a special on it,
and shoot, even that boy can't give you wide 'nough coverage
of every vice under the sun. But in this film, see, we're
gonna take us a stroll through all of Sin's faces and more'n a
sprinkling of her other parts. And artsy? Relevant? Ding-dong
redeeming? Hoo-eee, Ms. Schleppey, we're gonna intercut the
whole Alexandria side of the story with a plot 'bout a New
York City teenage hooker. We're gonna show Sin Past, Sin
Present, and Sin Yet-To-Come and leave Mr. Charles Dickens a-licking our dust!''

''If you think it will work . . .'' Faith sounded dubious.

''Trust me.'' Raleel smiled. ''It's all gonna be in the
special effects. Got me a boy who's a regular wizard.'' *I'll
say he is!*

''Well, I'll be happy to do my part. Not that I'm for
censorship or abrogating freedom of speech, you understand,
but I do think we could use some decent entertainment in the
theatres these days.''

'' 'Course we could. We'll be in touch. Addy-os.''

Dixi escorted Faith from the suite before returning, a look of
puzzlement on her face. ''I didn't know you'd planned the
picture out in so much detail, Mr. Lee. The part about the
New York girl—''

''Pure ad lib, honey.'' Raleel's chair pushed away from the
desk on noiseless casters as he put his feet up. ''Sure did
sound good, though. Guess we'll keep it. Yeah, show 'em all
the sins they got way back when, and how to go 'bout doing
'em, and then show 'em Sin with all the modern conveniences.''

"And redemption for the repentant," Dixi prompted. "The courtesan repented, in the story. So the hooker will too?"

"Huh? Oh, yeah, I s'pose. On their deathbeds, and we go for this real marshmallow fluff dissolve effect, make 'em look better when they're buying the ranch than they ever looked alive." He linked his fingers behind his head and leered at the ceiling. "Yeahhhh. Sin all you want and get off scot-free at the last minute." *If you can guess when your next-to-the-last minute's on you, that is. And who can know that?* "Show the folks all the fun they could be having, do it boldface with footnotes, and then tell 'em not to do none of it, in the fine print."

Dixi's lovely face was not coming out of all those nasty wrinkles. "I think it needs work, Mr. Lee. In the real story, the courtesan spent several years doing good works before she died."

"Sweetie, people in the boonies ain't gonna pay squat to see a Girl Scout pageant. But modern New York! Ancient Alexandria! The painted harlots, the luxuries of the world, the bazaar where every desire can be satisfied and every lust has its price!" Raleel spread his arms to the winds. "Now, where they gonna find anything like that this side of dreams?"

"Oooh, Melisan, wait up a second. I just want to pop into Giorgio's!" Lura shoved her bundles and shopping bags into Melisan's arms and sprinted back up Rodeo Drive.

Melisan let her get right under the yellow- and white-striped awnings before she dropped the Tiffany's bag. Despite careful packing, the crystal vase within was never meant to take such cavalier handling. The smash was magnificent.

A very angry angel asked, "Was that necessary?"

"Is this?" Melisan's gesture encompassed the immediate vicinity of Rodeo Drive and surrounding Beverly Hills streets.

"I thought a little spree might cheer you up. You used to adore finery."

"My son's soul is in peril and you think picking up a new tube of mascara will help? I *hate* shopping!"

"Oh, dear." Lura put two fingers to her lips. "You're worse than I thought. As I always say, when a person's tired of shopping, he's tired of life."

"That was Dr. Johnson who said that," Melisan said, good

and faithful PBS spouse that she was. "And he said it about London, not shopping."

"I've shopped in London too, and Harrods is almost—"

"My God, I hope Atamar's doing more for Noel than you are."

Lura took umbrage. "He's on shift right now, tracking the boy. Excuuuuse me for using *my* time off duty to try to cheer *you* up. The last thing he told me when he touched base was that Raleel's got a producer for that film of his, and you'll never guess who."

"Try me."

Mischief glittered in Lura's eyes. "Donald Swann." She got no reaction from Melisan. "*You* know: He was one of the kids on the Marmota tour with Dr. Hack; the ones who found us. Kind of a zod, but harmless. He used to wander around the camp fooling with dime-store Satanism books, junk like that. I almost felt like materializing in front of him once, just to see how fast a boy can run with wet pants."

"So Donald Swann's producing the movie. What's that to me, or to Noel?"

"So this: Atamar told me that Don's got a rep for giving a big party right before he starts shooting a picture. Don't ask me how, but Raleel managed to scare the man out of his Reeboks. He pulled enough strings to strangle Pinocchio, and the movie's going to start shooting within a week."

"Impossible."

Lura became very knowledgeable. "You just don't know the industry. Anything is possible, under the right circumstances. But we're not concerned with the shoot; we're interested in the party. You wanted another chance to reach Noel? This will be it. And Atamar and I will do everything we can to help you—under discreet cover of invisibility, if you insist."

The next thing Lura knew, she was being dragged up Rodeo Drive by Melisan, in search of that eternal Holy Grail, the perfect dress for an L.A. party.

5

Teen Angel

THE GIRLS WEREN'T in the top ten per cent of their class, but they were bright enough. None of them was married, none of them was getting any younger, and all of them had decided that since no one had asked them to the long-past Senior Prom like that slut Maybelle Purvis, at least they'd have the satisfaction of going to Heaven and spitting in the floozy's eye for all eternity. Now their faith had been rewarded: They were going to be in a movie. Wouldn't that just make Maybelle Purvis drop dead!

More than that, they had been specially chosen from out of the throng of extras. Letters of summons from "Sometime" Joseph Lee himself had been delivered to their motel and hotel rooms only this morning, bringing the great news. One of them would get the coveted starring role of the Repentant Courtesan. All that remained to be seen was which one.

"No way any of them's gonna play the teenage hooker," Raleel remarked to the scruffy demonling standing at his right hand. They observed the ranks of seated hopefuls through a one-way mirror in the third-best auditorium at BLT Ministries HQ. "Makeup can work miracles, but that'd take a *real* miracle."

"Not our line of work, Raleel." The demonling made a wry face and peered through the glass. "Now I know why they call 'em cattle calls." His chuckle rasped like sandpaper on plastic. "How come you got 'em all in there together? Trying to make a Dull bomb?"

"Put on your Brother Beau face, Brazlyp, follow me, watch, and learn." Raleel entered the auditorium.

"Morning, ladies. Let's get down to it. The letters I sent y'all are pretty self-explanatory. Y'all were asked here 'cause

I felt one of you had it in her to really *give* of herself on screen so that others might benefit. It wasn't easy, let me tell you. Simplest thing would've been to hire one of these loose 'n' low-living Hollywood starlets to play the big role in our picture.''

Murmurs of justifiable outrage fluttered up from many a modestly covered chest. Some of the ladies fanned themselves with their letters of summons in order to remain cool in the teeth of such an opprobrious suggestion.

"Yeah, that's the way I saw it too, ladies. Why hire us one of those sinners, who'd as like take her pay—what came from *your* hard-earned money—and throw it away on one of them big, blond, tanned L.A. beach boys with thighs like a pair of young oak trees''—the letters rattled faster—''when we could pick a true daughter of the Blessed Last Tabernacle to do the 'zact same thing? I know it's a grievous burden I'll be asking the one we pick. You'll have to play a woman of no morals, a frail vessel into which the princes and potentates of lewd *and* lascivious Alexandria pour their every fleshly *lust!* Covered in silks, decked with gems beyond price, waited on hand and foot by slaves and fawned over by comely youths who would *die* for your faintest smile, who would *slay* for one sweet taste of your ruby-red *and* luscious lips—!''

The bosom-fanning achieved gale-force winds, and several of the letters disintegrated into damp, sweaty wads of shredded paper.

One lady, bolder than her companions, stood up to speak for all. "It's a nasty, wicked, immoral person you're asking one of us to be," she said, "but somebody's got to do it."

"Love you, Sister." Brother Beau glowed with approval.

Raleel went on. "Your willingness to sacrifice yourselves is truly heartwarming. 'Spite of that, I still cannot find it in my heart to say to one of you, 'Go and put on the veils of a fallen woman.' And so, ladies, I have delegated the task of casting the Repentant Courtesan to my able assistant''—all eyes fixed hungrily on Brother Beau—''Noel Cardiff. What I'm gonna do is have you go on up to see him right now. No formal interviews, no stuffy introductions, just go right up to the eleventh floor of the east tower—that's this'n—and do what you will to persuade him as to the *right* choice. I thank you.''

One armrest was ripped off a seat at the left corner of the

back row as the ladies thundered out to find Noel. Raleel studied it thoughtfully. "Those older models just can't take the curves without clamping onto something. You see the *grip* on that woman?"

"Nothing more dangerous than a determined virgin," Brazlyp said. "That was mean, boss."

"Mean my ass. I want to get the kid damned, don't I? Lust's the fastest way to chute-the-chutes I know. Anyhow, he doesn't seem to be up for any of the other Six. Maybe pity'll get him to do what desire never did. Or maybe the ladies got their own methods of persuasion."

"I don't wanna know." Brazlyp shuddered. "Ever hear of the Bacchantes, boss?"

"*Any* big enough bunch of women's dangerous, 'less you give 'em plenty of coffee and cake. Hey, I'm a fair guy! I gave him his chance with Dixi and nothing happened. Maybe there's such a thing as too damned beautiful. It scares a man off."

"And a demon?" Brazlyp cocked a brow at his chief. It was an arch of green steel-wool.

"I've tried." Raleel didn't relish the memories. "Hell, yes. Tried it every honest way, and a few of the preferred underhand methods. No luck."

"Drugged her drink?" Brazlyp suggested.

"Do I look like a rookie? Of course I drugged her drink, and believe me, it's not easy finding a Mickey Finn that'll go undetected in a glass of Bosco. But either I goofed the dosage or she dumped the glass when I wasn't looking, because she went the rest of the day bouncier than before, and Belial, can that chick *bounce!*" Raleel shook his head. "Once I get Melisan's bastard parceled off to perdition, I'll be able to concentrate on Dixi."

The demonling's expression turned cunning. "There's more riding on the scales than one soul, boss, or I don't know you."

Raleel regarded Brazlyp with the proud look a teacher reserves for his special pet. "Right you are. Whoever says efficiency and fiendishness can't go hand in hand, lies. If I pull this off, I'll have not one, but *three* souls to break my sire out of exile, every one of them harvested in sweet, sweet vengeance. Melisan's brat is Job One, but if I can flak down two more mortals—"

"You're flakking down plenty more with this movie, boss," Brazlyp said. "I'm already getting feedback about domestic disputes busting out all over this town, every one of 'em in families who're just in L.A. to make your picture."

"Neat work, if I say it myself." Raleel actually had dimples. "The surest way to multiply damnations is to divide mortals. Fear's a great one for that—fear the stranger, fear the different, fear the afflicted—long as you can keep your pigeons so damn scared there's no room in them to even *try* to figure out whether there's anything *real* to be scared of in the first place. But fear's strictly mouse-pucky next to Envy."

Brazlyp bowed his head reverently. "A Biggie."

"Sure, you take a family and give one of 'em something the others would kill to have—like a speaking part when the rest are only playing stage-dressing—then you sit back and watch 'em do just that."

Brazlyp pursed his lips, full and supple as a pair of amorous slugs. "Sorry, boss. No fatalities yet."

"I've got time to collect on them. And there's an even bigger plan I've got in mind—" He noted his underling's interest and decided to change the subject. "But I want a quick return on Noel Cardiff, Donald Swann, and Faith Schleppey. She's gonna be the hard case. The men are on the brink already; all those years of Mama telling 'em they're guilty of *something* have a cumulative effect in the male. Swann's convinced he's pre-damned, thanks to my way with words and the kid's way with wizardry."

"And the kid?"

"That's the beauty part." Raleel conjured up a pair of Fuzzy Navels with which to toast the future. He and Brazlyp clinked glasses. "He convinced himself he's hellbent. Got a big dose of magic from his mama's side of the family, and being your typical dumb mortal, he's sure all magic's gotta be evil. Hell, he sure screwed himself up with it at college pretty spectacular, so *one* mistake with magic persuaded him that *all* sorcery stinks, period."

"It doesn't?" Brazlyp flickered his fingers and a fanged spider as big as a football sprang into being. It scuttled off in search of small poodles. "Wasn't *that* evil enough?"

"Brazlyp, you're new at this game." Raleel put an arm around his protégé. "What were you formed out of, anyhow?"

"The McCarthy hearings, I think."

"Boy, you *are* young. Then let me tell you, you can't always judge an action by its intent. S'pose that spider gets hit by a car that otherwise would've been in the right place and time to broadside a school bus? You do know why we've never had to blacktop the Hades Expressway?"

"Paving's done for us." Brazlyp grinned. "I get it. Noel thinks 'cause he's a demon's child and he's got magical powers, he's damned before the fact!"

"Right on the lip of the Pit." Raleel nodded. "And so I—as 'Sometime' Joseph Lee—wrote him a letter promising to show him the way around it." The demi-demon shrugged. "Can I help it if I dropped that banana peel right in front of him? And that shove—just trying to grab hold of the poor boy's shirt and jerk him to safety, Officer, honest! I *meant* well." He snickered. "The first word in all the best curses, Brazlyp, is 'Oops!' "

He produced another Fuzzy Navel for himself and drawled, "Brother Beau, whyn't you sashay up to see how our boy's doing with the ladies?"

"You can come out of the closet now, Noel," Dixi said. "They're gone." She was even lovelier than usual in a dress of rainbow sequins. Her golden hair was a sparkling cloud that floated past her shoulders.

Noel opened the door a crack. He was all set to go to Donald Swann's party, dressed in his finest suit, the green polyester number he'd worn on more than one broadcast of *Heading Home*. His hair was swept back off his forehead and gelled into a modest replica of the Elvis pompadour. He had just been putting the finishing touches on his expression of polite disapproval when the women had come charging in.

"Are you sure they're not here?" he croaked.

"I told them you'd see them at the party."

Noel came out of the closet and sat down right in the middle of the Bokhara rug. "Darn, I was looking forward to that party! Now I can't go."

"Sure you can." Dixi knelt beside him and tried to run her fingers through his hair. The gel fought back, then succumbed. "If you'll let me do what I want with you."

"Dixi . . ."

The lady giggled. "Really, Noel, you have the most *active*

imagination. All in one area. I think you need a girlfriend."
Her tone left no doubt that she was not on the list of candidates.

Noel became prim. "I've got enough to do, working for
the Blessed Last Tabernacle Ministries."

"Don't we all. It's all I can do to keep on top of what Mr.
Lee's trying to accomplish. But you—you're a healthy young
man. Your life should be your own, and part of that life
should be someone special. Didn't you have any girlfriends at
Yale?"

Dixi's fingers continued to comb through his hair, a soothing sensation that let out a little of the tension in his bones.
Noel gave a gusty sigh. "I had one. A girlfriend—" He was
bemused by Dixi's quaint way with words. Anyone else
would have said *lover*, but Dixi spoke fluent Mouseketeer.
"Lysi was more than that. I thought she really loved me . . .
as much as I loved her." He hadn't spoken of Lysi to anyone
for a long time. Dixi's fingers strayed to the buttons of his
jacket. As she deftly removed first his jacket, then his tie, he
found himself wanting to tell her everything, even if she did
think he was crazy.

"Dixi . . . do you believe in demons?"

She chuckled deep in her throat and undid the first button
of his shirt. "Have to. I've met enough of them in my time."

"No, I mean *really*." Another button surrendered, and
with it went all Noel's inhibitions. By the time Dixi had him
down to his underwear, she knew the whole story. Noel sat
motionless on the rug, staring at her exquisite face. He didn't
know whether the knot in his guts was fear or anticipation.

"Now, Noel"—anticipation rose—"let's get you dressed
for the party."

Noel's face fell. He was disappointed on more than one
count. Surely the tale of his doomed love for a succubus was
worth at least some passing comment, even if only *You are
out of your fucking mind!*? Only Dixi would never say the
dreaded F-word.

Dixi didn't appear to be concerned with his mental health.
She was burbling on about disguise and costume and Purloined Letters and the party. "—right in front of their noses,
but they'll be expecting a miniature 'Sometime' Joseph Lee.
I swear to God, when I get through with you, your own
mother wouldn't know you!" She dragged him away.

• • •

"Have you seen Noel?" Melisan whispered to Kent.

Her husband craned his neck, trying to peep through the field of multicolored heads surrounding them. "Not yet. This Swann fella's got a *pied-à-terre* the size of Shropshire. Perhaps if we asked the angels—"

"No." Melisan was firm. "I don't want them anywhere near him. I can handle this myself."

"Now you sound like Noel," Kent said. "Always asking us to let him do things on his own. We should have listened." He buttoned his Ralph Lauren polo shirt up to his chin. "Damn, but I miss my tie."

His wife grimly unbuttoned him again, so that the gold chain with its ankh was plain to see. "Don't blow our cover. We have to blend in until we find Noel."

"Need a ruddy native guide to find the loo in this house," Kent groused, shifting his prop-copy of *Thinner Thighs Through Reincarnation* from hand to hand. "If you'd let me ask the angels, they could tell us where he is. He's never out of their ken."

Melisan was obdurate. "If you're that keen on finding them, I told them to stay with the overflow from the cloakroom—in the master bedroom, I think."

"With what would a cloakroom overflow? Who'd bring a coat in this weather?"

"You'd be surprised."

"I think I should rather like being surprised." Kent stiffened his shoulders, bent over, and hiked up his leg-warmers. "It would be a decent change from being conscientiously superficial."

"Darling, it can't be that bad," Melisan wheedled, cozying up to her mate.

At that moment, a hollow-cheeked woman in silver and hot pink homed in on the couple. "Oooh," she gushed, margarita sloshing all over Kent's white slacks. "*I* read that book too! Did you ever read anything so mega-major *vicious* in your life?"

"Which one?" Kent inquired coolly.

The lady rested her elbow on his shoulder and confided in his left ear, "*I* was Nefertiti."

"Impossible, my good woman," Ken replied with regal hauteur. "I was her first. And now if you'll excuse me, I have an appointment with Catherine the Great and Cleopatra in the little boys' room. They tell me they've actually found someone who was never a king, queen, noble, warrior, artist, or genius in any of his previous lives. Which makes him rather a celebrity in this one, don't y'know. Ta-ta.'' He escaped from the woman and Melisan with one slick bit of broken-field running.

He did not stop until he located the auxiliary cloakroom. Don's master bedroom was all it should be, a paean to physical fitness, dramatic excess, overpricing, and Art Deco chromework. The waterbed floated atop a frame girdled by stylized lotus blossoms. A gilt and cobalt-blue Bast-cat at the height of a center forward for the L.A. Lakers gazed down at it with goggling crystal-ball eyes that held live goldfish. The Tunturi cycle on the other side of the bed was prettily concealed behind the false façade of a Ramessid chariot, and the set of hand-weights on the wall rested on enameled lion's-head brackets. That one room was the perfect pad from which to launch Tutankhamen and Jane Fonda to the Great Beyond together.

''Hi, Kent!'' The grand old man of PBS jumped when the Bast-cat yodeled at him by name. Lura peeked around the blue and gold feline's right flank, wiggling inch-long fingernails. One side of her hair had been scrunched, frizzled, shorn, and tinted chartreuse. ''Is this a fun party or what?''

Kent came nearer, within range of the angel's breath. He recognized the tang of tequila. ''Madam!'' His hands jammed themselves onto his hips. ''Your behavior is not quite what I expect of an angel. You are potted.''

''Oh, poo.'' Lura still looked divinely gorgeous, though her lipstick and nail polish matched the color of her hair. ''No preaching, you old fuddy-duddy. With a single thought, I can neutralize the effects of every margarita in Tegucigalpa, so why can't I enjoy the effects while they last? You wouldn't even be here if Atamar and I hadn't used our powers to get you *on-tray*. And are we thanked? No, we're sent off to mind the wraps!'' She gestured at the mountain of satin gang-jackets and suede capes littering the bed. A single sable cloak lay to one side, a shunned anachronism. Some fastidious guest had slapped a Greenpeace sticker on it.

''Marguerite only wants—''

''Your Marguerite and I are old friends. I know exactly what she wants. She wants the same thing she wanted when

we were demons together back in the Egyptian desert: everything her own way. We thought we were so smart, our
assignment would be a piece of manna. The temptation of a
saint! *Everyone* was going in for it in those days. Kind of like
buying a skateboard.''

"A saint?" Kent despised misinformation. "I don't think
Quintus Pilaster was ever recognized as such."

"Quintus." Lura gave a tiddly giggle. "Quintus was a
huggy-bear. We didn't succeed in our schemes against him.
We got the blame for that from the Underlords—and I guess
our hearts weren't really in deviltry even then—but I wonder
whether we'd have succeeded even if we wanted to? He was
such a *good* man. He tried so hard to do good works, and he
did succeed, by and large. If he didn't have *something,* then
why would a bunch of grown men follow him off into the
wasteland and set up a monastic community under his
direction?"

"I recall thinking the same thing when I researched Quintus'
life for PBS. The historical record has left certain lacunae.
Marguerite told me that the real brains behind the community
was a mysterious young Alexandrian monk who called himself Ambrosius Minimus. Quintus was just the figurehead."

Lura no longer looked so merry. After some hesitation she
asked, "Was that all Melisan told you about Ambrosius?"

"Apart from the fact that he was her lover," Kent replied
evenly, "not a peep."

Lura's mouth hung open like the legendary and extinct
two-dollar valise. Then Kent winked at her and her margarita-
fueled giggles came back. Soon both of them were laughing
so hard that they had to lean on one another for support.
Lura's heel caught in Kent's starboard leg-warmer and they
tumbled onto the bed. Being a gentleman, Kent contrived for
Lura to hit the sable.

The bedroom door had a sense of timing that a nascent
starlet might copy. It chose that moment to open.

"Excuse me, but is this the way to the ladies'—? Oh, my
Gawd!" Faith Schleppey was frozen by the scene she had
obviously interrupted. No one had to tell her what was going
on. *She* read *Cosmopolitan*.

As she groped for a sophisticated exit line, she could not
help pushing her glasses up the bridge of her nose to stare at
the couple. Shock gave way to recognition. A second "Oh,

my *Gawd!*'' followed the first. "Kent Cardiff! And—'' The face beneath the green hair was familiar. " . . . Lura?''

"Speak of the devil.'' The angel grinned. Then she hiccuped.

The bedroom door opened again and Atamar stormed in, dragging a slim young woman with jet black hair. She fought him like a Fury, despite wearing gold lamé jeans so tight that breathing must be problematical.

"Speak of the devil indeed,'' Kent murmured as the male angel flung Lysi down between the paws of the monstrous cat. "Lysi, what are you doing here? You were told not to come.''

"I'm shocked and appalled,'' Faith Schleppey said.

"*You?*'' Lysi scowled at the woman. "You don't even know me, so where do you get off being shocked and appalled?''

"Oh, not at you,'' Faith said. "At him.'' She turned to Kent Cardiff. "Leg-warmers over *slacks?* I am *mega* shocked and appalled.'' She turned back to Lysi. "I'm also Faith Schleppey. Who or what are you?''

6

Auld Lang Sin

ATAMAR FINISHED THE introductions. Lysi was mollified. "So that's why you said *or what.*''

"Experience.'' Faith grinned. "No offense.''

"None taken. It's kind of nice to meet someone who doesn't soil their pants when they hear I'm a demon.''

"If that is what you are,'' Kent commented.

"What the heck else am I, if not that?'' Lysi spread her hands wide, waiting for an answer that did not come.

Faith sat on the waterbed between Lura and Kent, mulling over what she'd just learned from Atamar. "So the preacherman is Murakh's get. And your son's joined him, Kent? Does the boy *know?*''

"Would the boy believe it even if he were told?" Kent returned. "Not only is the truth about Mr. 'Sometime' incredible on the face of it, but Noel would not accept it if one of us did tell him. He does not trust us quite so much as I'd prefer, these days. Atamar's told you why."

"Still, the direct approach, honesty, being upfront about things—"

"Honesty bites it." The bedroom door slammed behind Melisan. She glared at the assemblage, her eyebrows going up slightly when she saw Faith. "Isn't this Old Home Week," she mumbled. "What is it about L.A.?"

"The Great Cosmic Belly Button that attracteth the spiritual lint of the universe," Faith replied, just as grumpily. "Say hallelujah."

Melisan chose to say something measurably less pious. She flopped hard onto the mattress, wedging apart the two women already there. The bed rocked with tsunamis and Lura's face achieved a shade that complemented her green-dyed hair.

"I'm sobering up before I toss up," she announced, and did so. The ghosts of multiple margaritas were exorcised in a moment. "Now what is eating you, Mel?"

"An educated guess," Atamar said, "is that she found Noel."

"Fat lot of good that did." Melisan hugged herself into a shivering ball. Her gruffness turned to misery. "When I saw him, I had hopes he'd become his old self again. He didn't look anything like one of Raleel's holy clones." She cast a short, apologetic look at Lysi before adding, "He even had a woman on his arm."

"That was no woman," Lysi growled, leaning back against the Bast-cat. "That was 'Sometime' Joseph Lee's private secretary."

"Still, he seemed to be the Noel I knew. So I went right up to him and started talking." The ball clenched itself even smaller. "He froze me out. He turned me away. He said"
—her voice caught—"he said that 'Sometime' Joseph Lee was a saint, and what right did I have to criticize a saint when all I'd ever done most of my life was try to drag saints down?" Helpless sobbing took her.

Faith regarded Melisan for a time, then said to Atamar, "If I had your angelic powers and your demonic experience, I wouldn't be standing there like a ninny. I'd find this Murakh and blast him to half-past Dante.''

"Combat? Just like that?" Atamar found the suggestion risible. "Then you've forgotten how it was in the desert when angel met demon. The one we thought was just another mortal fought Murakh himself, and he belonged to a higher order of the Heavenly Host than Lura and I. Yet for all his powers, he would have been defeated without the help he got from mortals and fallen demons alike.''

"Being mortal's no help," Melisan said so softly that no one heard her. "We're cannon fodder. Without some extraordinary force like magic in our hands, we're powerless.''

"But Raleel isn't a full-blooded demon like Daddy," Lysi piped up. "He's half mortal. Don't you have enough oomph to off him?''

" 'Oomph,' is it?" Atamar registered dry amusement. "No, I fear my 'oomph' rating is low, even when joined with Lura's. It all comes down to power.''

Melisan nodded knowingly and shook off her husband's attempt to comfort her.

"Can't I link mine with both of yours? Or won't they mix?" Lysi asked.

Atamar rubbed his chin. "An interesting question. We might try an experiment. Here, Lysi, Lura, let's join hands and see if we can't change this oversized tabby into a refrigerator.''

"A refrigerator?" Faith inquired as the two angels and the succubus formed their little circle. "Why that?''

"Oh, anything will do for a test," Atamar said. "I just feel like a cold drink. Ready?''

The three mortals watched as the three supernatural beings concentrated their divers powers on the Bast-cat. The phantom outline of a Westinghouse refrigerator rippled over the huge statue, faded to the ghost of a big man in football togs, went back to the appliance, and exploded with a loud report as a jagged crack split the Bast-cat's breastbone. Spools of videotape spilled from the wound, unreeling madly.

"That answers that," Lysi observed. She sat down cross-legged in the nest of tangled tape just as Donald Swann burst into his own bedroom.

"What in hell's going—? Oh-oh." One look at the gathering in his sanctum was enough. He appeared to know them all, and to garner no comfort from that acquaintance.

"Donald! So good to see you again," Lura said, sweeping her trendy looks away as easily as she'd cast off the effects of the tequila. She assumed her most angelic aspect, short of full winged regalia, and offered him her hands. "Don't fear us. Atamar and I aren't demons anymore."

Atamar inclined his head courteously in Don's direction and followed his mate's lead. His heavenly semblance was awe-inspiring. He assumed that a benevolent, fully angelic bearing would set Don at ease. It only made the producer back away. His foot struck something.

"Watch where you're going," Lysi said from the floor.

Don leaped for the ceiling and nearly made it. He came down on his knees in front of the angels, wringing his hands desperately. "I never touched her, I swear I didn't! Oh, please, please, I'm not ready to die yet! I still have so much to atone for, so many sins! I have seen the depths of the Pit, and I know that I deserve to be plunged into the deepest, blackest recess of Hell for what I've done, but please, I've seen the light! I'm turning my life around! I'm using my powers to help other sinners get onto the right road! All I did was offer her the part of the teenage hooker—a straight offer, no 'favors' asked for it. She's a natural for the part! I mean—" He saw the poisonous look Lysi shot him. "I mean she's a great little actress, and—".

Faith took matters in hand by hooking Don under the armpits and hauling him upright, then dragging him over to his own bed and unceremoniously shoving him down beside Melisan.

"I know this is going to be a great disappointment to you, Don," she said, "but you're not damned yet."

"I'm not?"

"You don't have to sound so dashed about it, old boy," Kent told him. "You're young yet."

"And you sure wouldn't be damned for seducing me even if you did do it; which you didn't," Lysi provided. "I'm a demon myself. So is my blasted brother."

A little while later, Donald Swann sat watching his fingers twist through each other in his lap. "Your brother is—?" he asked Lysi, wanting to be sure he had it correct.

"A fraud, a charlatan, the biggest chunk of dog-whomp in all Tartarus."

"And I am—?"

"A little excessive, but not guaranteed hellbent quite yet," Lura said, her voice musical balm. "You do get carried away. If you were truly wicked, you wouldn't have to work at vice so diligently. It's like when you were a kid in the desert, fooling around with those paperback Satanism pulps."

Don's cheek flushed. "I still have them. In my den next door. Not that I try spells out of them or anything," he was swift to add.

"I doubt you have enough desire for the weakest of those spells to work," Atamar told him.

"I don't really want to be evil," Don said, eyes downcast. "It's just that this is Hollywood and—and I've got the neighbors to think of, and my reputation, and the tourists, and all that P.R."

"Hollywood Babylon does sound more entrancing than Hollywood Brooklyn." Atamar turned off the angelic F/X. "However, take it from an eyewitness, the original Babylon at its most sinful was nothing to write home about. The dirtiest thing its typical citizen ever did was ask one of the sacred prostitutes how a nice girl like her got into that line of work. The answer was just as dull then as now."

"Look, Don," Faith said. "You can either sit here bitching about how evil you'd like to be, or you can do something constructive for a change. This Raleel creep had you suckered pretty bad—an embarrassment, in fact. Wouldn't you like to pay him back?"

"But doesn't vengeance belong to—?" Don pointed upward.

"This isn't vengeance," Lura told him, returning to her party-girl guise. "This is a direct call from—" She mirrored his skyward gesture. "We need your help, Don; and yours, Faith. An innocent soul is at stake. Atamar's right: It all comes down to power. We haven't enough between us to challenge Raleel, not even when we combine ours with Ly-si's. We need yours too." Her eyes touched all four of the mortals present.

"What power?" Melisan laughed bitterly. "Mortals *have* no power! What can we do?"

"Make a path for power to travel." Lura was in earnest. "An angel can't call for aid, because we're supposed to be the source of help. But mortals can always call, and if the call comes strongly enough, if it comes from the heart—"

"Prayer?" Melisan's incredulous question cut in.

"It has been known to work," Atamar said.

"It's worth a go, my dear." Kent gently squeezed his wife's hand. "I'm game."

"So are we." Faith grasped Don's wrist tightly. His consent came as a squeak. The four all stood together and closed their eyes. A warm silence grew among them.

Melisan opened her eyes first. She looked around and saw nothing different. Lysi was trying to tuck the spilled videotape back into the ruined Bast-cat, but that was the only change.

Not unreasonably, she demanded, "Well?"

"You might keep trying." Lura suggested

"Why? Did we get a busy signal?" She threw up her hands. "Good Lord, what was I expecting to happen—a miracle? I haven't the right to it. All the centuries I was a demon weighed against the few years I've been mortal—and not the most perfect of mortals—How can they count for anything?"

"Melisan, there's no scale to—"

She would not listen. "My prayers do nothing."

"Maybe not," Don said, his voice going thin. "Look there. The jackets. On the bed."

Green satin with purple piping, fuchsia trimmed with gold, midnight-blue piped with black and silver—the small mound of gang-jackets humped up, wriggled, and gave birth to an ascetic, sun-browned face with vague blue eyes and a scraggly chestnut beard. Limb by sackclothed limb he pulled himself free of the garments piled atop him and dragged his skinny body off the quaking waterbed to the stability of the floor. Long fingers, roughened by manual labor, raked through his thinning brown hair.

"Dear me," he said. "I feel woozy."

Everyone stared. Then the three who knew that face the best—Lura, Atamar, and Melisan—all said in unison:

"Quintus?"

"*Ave.* May I please have a cold drink?"

Then his eyes focused on them. "I know you," he breathed. "You're—" He gasped. "*Demons!*"

With a shriek, Quintus Pilaster bolted. Atamar moved to block the door. "*Apage, Satanas!*" Quintus hollered in the angel's face.

"Now, just one minute, friend—"

Quintus fled the devil and all his works, but since one door was obstructed, he darted for another. Lura could not move fast enough to cut him off. He seemed possessed of other-worldly speed, if nothing else.

"After him!" Kent cried, leaping forward.

Don put out a languid arm to restrain the man. "Don't sweat it." A loud splash sounded from beyond the open door. "That's the way to my private bath. Sounds like Quintus found the hot-tub."

7

O, When the Saints

"AH," QUINTUS PILASTER said as he sank up to his chin in the bubbling water. "This is very nice, once you get used to it. I think I may believe you when you claim it is not a form of penance." He reached over the edge of Don's hot-tub for his Perrier. Twin pink-and-green neon palm trees bent their fronds above him as he sipped. The view of Los Angeles by night was likewise soothing to the displaced soul's frayed nerves. "Please go on. I can hear perfectly. You say you're not demons any longer?"

Atamar answered him from beyond the seven-panel silk screen which Quintus had insisted on setting up, for modes-ty's sake. "We are angels now, Lura and I. You had no reason to run away once you recognized us."

"Forgive me, Blessed One. The sudden return to this world was a jarring experience. I should have known."

"I'm surprised he didn't know," Kent remarked for Atamar's ears alone. "I was under the impression that sainthood brought certain—er—supernatural perquisites."

"If you can accept the fact that there are various ranks of

angels, with powers differing accordingly, why not assume the same for saints?''

"Is that how it works?''

"I don't know," Atamar admitted. "At my present rank, still so close to the things of Earth, there are many things hidden from me. So you see . . .''

"Psst. Did you tell him about me?" Lysi's whisper came from the doorway. Quintus stipulated that the females were not to enter the bathroom while he was immersed, screen or no screen, mortal, angel, or whatever.

"I hear you, Lost One!" Quintus called. "Yes, I know you for what you are, but I do not fear you. I see into your heart and sense goodness. You have called for aid, and I have been dispatched to give it. All will be well.''

" 'All will be well,' " Melisan echoed under her breath. "Was that the best our prayers could summon? *Quintus?*''

Lysi's ears perked up. Little escaped the succubus. "What's the matter with Quintus? Now we've got a full-fledged saint on our side. Not even Raleel and all his lieutenants can stand against a major power of Heaven!''

Melisan didn't know whether to sneer at Lysi's gung-ho optimism or pity it. "Wake up and smell the incense, little one. Quintus was never officially recognized as a saint, and for plenty of good reasons. Most authorities say he's apocryphal. I know he's not, but his miracles sure are. Anything positive he ever did came out of pure dumb luck! If this is the 'saint' we've drawn to help us save Noel, it's about what I deserve. I'll say it again: Mortals have nothing." Gloom descended on her spirit. "At least when I was a demon, I had a fighting chance.''

"If you're so hot for a fighting chance, try giving one to your son!" Lysi snapped. "I'm in worse shape than you, but you don't see me dragging my dustbin all around, whining that nothing's any use, nothing will work, we're all doomed, Fate sucks rocks! You act as if you're the only one who can save Noel. What are we—your faithful Indian companions? Together we can—''

"Together we still don't have enough power to put an end to your brother. What's the use of being on the side of the saints and the angels if one demon's too much for them all?''

"Well, rah, rah, Hades!" Lysi curled her lip. "Why don't we find Noel and tell him we're all joining the Blessed Last Tabernacle because we'd rather be winners than be right?''

Melisan pushed past her and left the room.

Lura did not see her go. The female angel kept fluttering up behind Atamar, trying to add her mite to the orientation lecture the men were giving Quintus. It was highly unrewarding work. To most everything he was told, the former abbot responded, "Yes, I know."

Atamar gave up trying to tell Quintus anything. Kent had been right in his surmise, apparently. "Does omniscience come automatically with sainthood?"

"Oh, please, do go on, Blessed One. I don't know *everything*, and it would be a shame to overlook a vital detail. I am deeply flattered that you would have me be the instrument of this false prophet's downfall."

"My son believes 'Sometime' Joseph Lee to be a saint," Kent said. "Deuced good idea to have the real thing in our corner, what? Show up the bogus article all the faster."

Atamar laid plans. "We'll do it tomorrow, in Raleel's office, with Noel standing right there. A few words from you, and a miracle or two, and it will all be over for Raleel."

"Blessed One," Quintus said timidly. "We ought not to take miracles so lightly."

Don Swann smacked his forehead. "Wait! Hold it! Oh, man, this is choice. I mean, it is beyond bitchen and all the way to supreme. Noel's not the only soul this schmuck is leading down the primrose path. This movie alone's sucking in more fish than a Hoover. We have to torpedo Raleel's operation big time. I mean not just in front of Noel. I mean in front of the whole freaking mondo *mundo!* I mean on the set, on the air, and on Wisconsin!"

"Ah," Quintus said. He rose from the hot-tub. His soaking wet sackcloth robes weighed down his frail body as he shuffled around the side of the screen. He peered at Donald Swann with a recluse's practiced intensity of contemplation. "Omniscience is not comprehension, my son. What in Heaven's name did you just say?"

Atamar stepped in suavely. "He said that you need a change of clothing and a place to stay until you unmask Raleel before his entire television congregation. We can arrange all. Kent, would Melisan mind if Quintus shared your hotel room?"

"Seeing as how they're old acquaintances, she shouldn't object. Marguerite, dear!" No one answered Kent's hail. He went into the bedroom and returned looking worried. "Lysi tells me she's gone, but she doesn't know where."

"Don't be concerned." Atamar comforted him. "Don can have a look around the house for her, but I'll bet she's just gone back to the hotel."

"She couldn't. I have the car keys, and we're in the Middle-of-Nowhere hills up here."

"Then she's definitely in the house. Have a quick look-see, Don."

Don obeyed the angel's direction, only to return with word that Melisan was not to be found on his property. The security guard at the gate had checked out more than one car containing women who matched Melisan's description.

"So she's hitched a ride back to town." Atamar was not disposed to worry about it. "You'll find her waiting for you in your room. It's not as if she's missing."

He bundled Quintus up in one of Don's thickest terrycloth robes and asked whether he preferred to travel by angelic means, by car, or via a miracle of his own manufacture.

"Oh—ah—heh—I think I should like to make as little fuss as possible. Save it for this Raleel creature."

In the goodbyes that followed, Don never did find the proper opening to ask Atamar about something that was missing besides Melisan. While searching the house for her, he'd noticed a gap in the den bookcase, just to the left of the Aliens Visit Earth section, where his old Satanism books should have been. The tattered paperbacks were gone, as well as two or three really beautiful hard-bound numbers that friends and co-workers had given him as gag gifts.

Don wondered if he should bring it up at all. It was such a minor theft—likely to be a goof too. Mention of Satanism might rile the angels, and saints were always letting off righteous wrath. He would keep still.

Don wasn't damned, but Don wasn't dumb.

At the hotel, Kent discovered that his wife had not returned and that his guest's omniscience did not cover locating her.

8

The Latter Has the Largest Congregation

KENT HUNG UP the phone. "I have to wait," he said, his voice straining to stay level. "They say she hasn't gone missing long enough yet for them to consider her a missing person. When will that be, Atamar? If they find her body in a ditch somewhere before the time limit's up, will they decide she's a missing person *then?*"

The angel leaned against the hotel room window frame, watching streams of cars pass by in the hazy L.A. sunlight. "I can't understand it," he said. "Why can't Lura and I find her? Why can't Quintus?"

"Shouldn't you be calling him *Saint* Quintus?" Don asked from the armchair.

"No formalities," the angel replied. "His request. Frankly, I'm relieved that it's reciprocal. I was getting tired of being called Blessed One."

"Where is she?" Kent stood beside Atamar and pressed his forehead to the glass. "Where is she?"

Atamar embraced the man. "She'll be all right. Melisan may be mortal, but she has centuries of street wisdom at her command. She was a predator too long to become easy prey now. And we'll keep trying."

"I'm hoping she's only gone off to be alone with her thoughts for a while," Kent said. "I tell myself she'll be back before I know it." His momentary jauntiness crumbled. "Has Lysi tried to locate her?"

Atamar affirmed this. "She did; she failed. Why can't we find her? If my rank were higher, perhaps I'd know for certain. As it is, I can only venture a theory. A time comes when a soul believes so completely in its own alienation, its own isolation and hopelessness, that it cuts itself off from those who seek to comfort and cherish it most.''

Someone rapped on the door, only a courtesy knock before Lura and Faith barged in, bearing Quintus between them. The ladies' cheeks were bright with exertion and they could not stop giggling. Quintus looked discomfited. His monastic robes were gone, replaced by khaki twill slacks and a white knit sports shirt with the predictable reptile over the left breast. A glance at his feet showed that the women had permitted him to keep his rough leather sandals.

"He tried to convert an automatic teller machine!" Faith whooped in lieu of greetings.

"Atamar, it was the funniest thing!" Lura exclaimed, between gasps for breath. "It was one of these *talking* autotellers, and this man was ahead of us on line and it wouldn't give him back his card.''

"So *then*"—Faith took up the thread—"he started cursing it out, and Quintus got upset.''

"Profanity is well worth my agitation," Quintus said, folding his hands on his bosom. "He took the name of the Lord in vain.''

"Also several bodily functions. Then he turned on Quintus and told him to butt out, and that was when Quintus told him to step aside.''

"I had to freeze the man's hand on the backswing," Lura said. "Otherwise he would've decked the poor dear." She gave Quintus a maternal squeeze that made him jump.

"Lura, if I am to be 'decked' in the name of doing what is right, so be it. Do not interfere." His chin came up as he addressed the men. "I laid my hands upon the offending creature and spoke to it of patience and forgiveness and love. And although the being was one such as my eyes had never seen, still it was amenable to God's sweet message, and it rendered up that which did not pertain to it and requested that I remove my card.''

"I released the man's hand, he grabbed his card, and he ran for it." Lura finished the report by saying, "He *did* admit that getting his card back was a miracle.''

"Then we got our money and took Quintus shopping," Faith said. "Like the look?''

Don eyed Quintus up and down. "The preppy priest," he mused. "Set you back much, Faith?''

The archeologist shrugged. "It wasn't my bank card."

"Angels have bank cards?" That made him sit up. "Why?"

Lura plucked a blue wallet from her purse and let the plastic card-holder accordion down to the floor. "Because we like to pay cash sometimes. Then we don't have such a big American Express bill at the end of the month."

"*Credit cards?* You carry credit cards?"

"Our sort do," Atamar said. "Who has better references?"

"But money is the root of all evil!"

"That's the *love* of money. We don't love it; we just use it as necessary."

"Yes, but where do you get it from when the bills come due? Where do they *send* the bills? How——?"

Atamar raised his hand, parrying further questions. "These are holy mysteries, my son."

Lura bent to Don's ear and whispered, "Ask me later. I handle the finances. Males just don't have a head for numbers."

Quintus contemplated his own image in the mirror above the dresser. He pressed the alligator experimentally, then flicked at the plastic buttons on the shirt placket. His hair and beard were still as wild as the Egyptian desert, but from the neck down he was ordinary enough.

"We'll comb him before we take him over to the television studio," Faith announced. "We may have to trim that beard some."

"Woman, you will not touch my body!" Quintus' words and stance were icy. "If it were not that my joy is to serve, and that this female is of the Heavenly Host, you would never have compelled me to part with the correct garments of my calling."

"You can't go on national TV dressed in a sackcloth robe," Lura said. "This is America. Looks count."

Quintus drew himself up even taller and prissier. " 'Consider the lilies of the field. They toil not, neither do they spin. Yet——' "

"Consider Vanna White," Faith countered. While Quintus was demanding yet another translation, they hustled him out the door.

The television studio for L.A. broadcasts of *Heading Home* was in the same massive BLT Ministries complex as the rest of the operation. On broadcast days, the line for tickets formed before dawn and was usually around the corner before the first seats were assigned.

This day was different. There was only a limited number of seats made available to the general public because of the large numbers of out-of-town faithful packed into L.A. to take part in the big picture. It wouldn't be fair to deny them seats. Some of them had even been tapped by ''Sometime'' Joseph Lee himself to pass among the throng of would-be audience members and decide which of them merited the few remaining tickets.

It was perfect, by Raleel's standards. The choosers were especially selected for their otherwise inconsequential histories. They became puffed with Pride at having so much power for once in their lives, and the ranks of the potential chosen seethed with Wrath over being at the mercy of some jumped-up hick yahoo's say-so. Those chosen for admittance lost a little of their resentment, but the Envy rearing up among those rejected made up for it.

''You won't need a ticket,'' Atamar told Quintus. They watched the milling crowd from across the street.

''I won't?'' Quintus didn't look too sure.

''You can create your own, or enter without benefit of any mortal passport. What barrier can stand against you, a saint? They could as soon keep me out!''

''Why don't we go in together, then?''

Atamar was puzzled by the suggestion. ''Raleel would be able to sense an angelic presence and avoid the confrontation. He won't be expecting a saint, though, and despite your exalted status, even I can't perceive any difference between your soul and that of an ordinary mortal.''

''Atamar . . .'' Quintus plucked at the angel's tanned forearm. ''Would you mind reviewing what I am to do just once more?''

Atamar's puzzlement deepened. ''Go in, sit down, wait for the proper dramatic moment, and show Raleel up for what he is while everyone's watching.''

''Everyone . . .'' Under the knit shirt, Quintus' heart beat faster. He looked up and down the street, which was teeming with cars that raced by faster than the Emperor's finest chariot. On the sidewalk he saw more people hustling past him every minute than he had seen in an hour's time in the heart of Alexandria's great bazaar. The peace of heavenly rest was no great change for a man who had fled into the silence of the desert, but this—! And where were the beasts that had churned up so much dust? The air was foul and gritty with it. It stank in the nose and stung in the eyes.

"It's time," Atamar said. "Go. We'll be watching."

"But you said you wouldn't come near!"

"On television. We'll be watching at the hotel."

He was gone before Quintus could ask another question. Alone, the one-time monk crossed the street without benefit of traffic signal or crosswalk. Brakes squealed, horns honked, drivers took the Lord's name in vain, but Quintus came through unmarked. As he set his sandaled foot upon the opposite curb, a young man in the ticket hungry crowd remarked, "Boy, if *that* ain't a miracle . . ."

Brother Beau was the one to fetch Raleel from his dressing room when the BLT Ministries shifted to the West Coast. "Hymns all done, boss."

"Good. Everyone in place?"

"The broad's still conducting the Joyful Noise Singers, but they're doing folk songs now. The kid's on his mark, ready to beef up your sermon with a little fancy wizardry." Brazlyp chortled. "As if you needed a punk thaumaturge like him to do special effects for you! Shit, that's like having one of the Little Rascals give acting lessons to Lord Olivier."

"Don't scoff, Brazlyp." Raleel tugged his bow tie. "If I do have more power than Noel, that doesn't mean I'd scorn linking my gramarye to his."

"Team up with a mortal?" Brazlyp was repulsed.

"With whom else can I pact? Not with other demons. Cooperation has never been our watchword, has it? With angels, then?"

Brazlyp guffawed so hard at the thought that he got a combined attack of hiccups, sneezes, and compulsive belching.

"Mortals are the link." Raleel held up one finger. "Mortals are the catalyst. Their gifts are as many, as varied, and—excuse the language—as blessed as all the miracles of Creation surrounding them. It is their gift alone to be able to link themselves and their powers with us, or with our enemies; their gift, and their choice. Mortals are the key to unlock doors more wisely left unopened, sometimes for our good, sometimes for theirs.''

"Doors—*hic!*—boss?''

Raleel wore a secret smile. *"As above, so below, nothing to impede the flow. From the Pit bid them rise to a world their rightful prize.''*

Brazlyp recognized the quote at once. He wiped a burning acid tear from his eye. "Aw, boss, the—*urp!*—the *Helliad*. That's—*yachoo!*—that's beautiful. I mean, that's poetry that really—*hic!*—lives, y'know?''

"It will live, Brazlyp.'' Raleel's voice shifted suddenly into "Sometime'' Joseph Lee mode. "Sure's you're a-standing there, Brother Beau, you're gonna see something fit to knock your eyeballs all the way to *I*-ran when I use Noel Cardiff's powers with my own. Hoo-ee, you betcha. Now, let's get out on that stage and flimflam us some suckers.''

Quintus saw nothing strange in the fact that a small yellow kitten kept rubbing against his ankles as he sat in the studio audience. In his day, before he left the cities of the ever-shrinking Roman Empire for the peace of the desert, animals had the same freedom of the streets as men. More livestock than citizens had listened to his impassioned marketplace sermons, and who could say which group benefited more from Quintus' speeches?

The kitten was afflicted, poor thing. It tilted its head to regard him out of its one good eye, and Quintus wondered whether he ought to take it up on stage with him when he went to confront the demon. Healing something would be dramatic enough, even if it was only a kitten. Before he could make up his mind, the little beast scampered away.

Now Quintus' attention returned to the stage. That pretty lady with the blond hair had just announced "Sometime'' Joseph Lee. Quintus sighed. His cue would come soon. Should he levitate from his seat? Should we call down a flash of lightning to herald his coming?

"No,'' he mumbled to himself. "Save it for the demon.''

"You too, brother?'' the lady beside him asked, her voice heavy with compassion.

"Please?''

"Got a demon in you.'' She managed a crooked smile and

tapped her temple. "Me, I've been a sufferer and a martyr to this incredible migraine for, oh, six weeks now. Know what I mean?"

"Indeed yes. I too have been a martyr."

"So then I said, 'Louise, you got something that's beyond those so-called doctors. Every time you want to do good works, or submit to your dear husband's marital demands, this migraine comes cropping up faster than chickweed. Louise, it's not your fault; it must be the work of the devil. You got an affliction that it'll take a miracle to cure. How many times you see that blessed Mr. Lee heal folks just like you, the pains shooting through their bodies like fire? Why can't he heal you, too?'"

"Actually, there is one very good reason why he can't—" Quintus' explanation was drowned out by the pounding applause that greeted the great televangelist's entrance.

The former abbot writhed through Raleel's opening remarks. He heard the underlying principles of faith twisted and contorted beyond rescue or recognition. A message of love was warped into a license to hate. The same God who had created the myriad life-forms of earth and air and water was now cited as saying that there was only one acceptable way in which to worship Him. Those who did not follow this way were damned, but it was not enough to let them go their own merry way to Hell. First they had to be trampled face-down into the dirt, or preferably have six feet of it shoveled on top of them.

It was amazing, said "Sometime" Joseph Lee, how much taller a man stood when his feet were planted in righteousness on his faithless neighbor's neckbone.

Then it was time for the healings. Quintus saw his seatmate leap up to get a good spot on line. The afflicted formed a long row across the stage, and the cameras panned over them as Brother Beau switched a few people from one position to another before retreating to his inconspicuous corner. Louise wound up Number One for Raleel's attention. She knelt at the demon's feet, he placed his hands on her head, and commanded the evil spirits within her to be gone.

"Poor woman," Quintus said under his breath. "A demon can never be a healer. Nothing will happen."

But something did.

A pea-soup green wisp of smoke poured from Louise's ear. Quintus heard no gasps, and reasoned that either he must be the only one to see it, or that such aural exhalations were commonplace, the modern body's natural way of cleaning all that filthy air out of the system. The issue was decided when Louise stood up and shouted that she was cured, which brought the gasps of awe.

With vision only he possessed, Quintus continued to watch the small green fog drift across the stage towards the one called Brother Beau. While the next sufferer knelt before Raleel, Beau-Brazlyp discreetly passed a folded wad of currency to the evicted migraine-fiend.

"Aha," Quintus said. He had lived within the decaying Roman Empire long enough to know a payoff when he saw one. The selfsame motions were gone through with every one of the people waiting in line for "Sometime" Joseph Lee's healing hands. Sprites and imps, minor cacodemons and puny will-o'-the-wisps in all shapes and shades departed from their temporary lodgings and picked up their pay on the way out. It was Professional Courtesy in action.

Brother Beau called an abrupt halt to the healing when the line got down to a man whose pain was not caused by Raleel's cronies. "That's all the time we've got. Y'all come back next week, friends, and keep on praying over your sufferings, and showing that you're sincere in your promise to help us help you, and maybe it'll be adjudged time that your own miseries depart from you." He tipped a sharp signal to the offering-collectors. The cameras zoomed after them as they passed down the line of the unhealed. All America could watch sincerity in action as the baskets filled up.

Quintus shuddered at the television cameras. He didn't know precisely what role those strange machines played here, but his innards didn't like them. They moved too smoothly, too swiftly, and dove at their prey too much like vultures. How could a machine seem so hungry?

He recalled the time one of his monks, Brother Maurice, had gone from his cell during a sandstorm. Days later the vultures had been the ones to lead Quintus to the body, with their horrid, graceful sweeps of the sky. He had been forced to chase the largest one away from poor Maurice. For a time the big bird merely stood on the open rib cage, gazing at Quintus' ineffective shooing motions with one cold red eye. It took wing at last, after one final peck at its prey's head. He could never see a vulture in flight after that without remembering Brother Maurice's body, and the dead monk's eyeless stare.

Organ music dripped from the white plastered walls as Raleel made a great deal of recovering from his spiritual exertions. The collar of his starched shirt was rumpled, his bow tie dangling by one clip, and he patted the sweat from his brow with a folded handkerchief. From his seat, Quintus saw Noel move carefully to a small *X* taped just below the big stage mural of Adam and Eve. The Snake was nowhere to be seen.

"Friends," Raleel thundered. The painted leaves of the Tree of Knowledge appeared to tremble in the breeze. The audience cooed. "Friends, there's been a lot of mail I been getting lately 'bout our picture—*our* picture, I call it, but it's really *your* picture. Now a lot of this mail's been kinda, y'might say, *critical* of your old friend Joe up here. Lot of it's been saying where do I get off telling other folks what's sinful and what's not, what's okay to do and what'll get you to Hell faster'n money goes through a liberal Congress."

Shouts of indignation rose up on Quintus' every side. He did not know what most of the crowd's words meant, except for 'godless' and 'freaks' and 'diseased' and 'heathens,' but he could tell that sympathy was with Raleel.

The demon raised his hands for silence. A Snake appeared in the Tree's lower branches, with an androgynous human face and a gloating look.

"Friends, this is America. They got a right to say all that they're saying—right or not, decent or not—just like they've got a right to print all kinds of filth and sing all kinds of songs full of unnatural lust and make *their* kind of movies. Yessir, they got that right because that's the law in this country, and until folks stand up and *change that law*, that's the way things are gonna be for decent people in this great land of ours."

An eerie sound drifted over the audience from the mural. Noel's eyes were closed in concentration. As near as Quintus could guess, those half-hissed, half-chuckled noises were the boy's best imitation of the Snake's laughter as Eve plucked a joint from the Tree, toked up, and passed it to Adam.

"But I didn't come before you today to tell you 'bout the

sad state we're in. I came to say that we will not be swayed. We will *make* our movie, and we will *show* our movie, and if we win over enough souls to our cause *with* our movie, then maybe we can get us the courage to band together for something even more important, and get a man who knows what is right and what is wrong by *revelation* to lead this whole fool country *out* of her foolishness and onto that one glorious road from which there is *no* divergence without utter *and* complete *ruin!*"

"Heavens," Quintus marveled. "What breath control."

By this time, the audience was hooting and stamping their feet and making the walls shake with their cries of approbation. Eve donned a fig leaf that turned into a square-shouldered gray business suit. She stuck a stogie in her mouth and goose-stepped out of the Garden one pace ahead of Adam, whose fig leaf had metamorphosed into a stunning evening gown. The Angel chasing them with the fiery sword looked a lot like Rambo. The Snake slithered out of the Tree and nested in a flame-shaped electric guitar that materialized just outside the gate of the Garden.

Quintus decided that his time had come.

"LIES!"

Paint exploded from the mural in a flurry of multicolored snow. Raleel and Brazlyp gaped. Noel's eyes snapped wide open as Quintus, splendid in his wrath, came slapping his sandaled feet up the studio aisle and onto the stage. He leveled a trembling finger at the senior demon. "INFAMY!"

"Cut to a commercial," Brazlyp hissed to one of the cameramen. The red filming lights winked out before Quintus was aware they had been on.

"Unholy creature, I am Quintus Pilaster! I have come in the name of righteousness to bring you low. I know you for what you are! Now I bid you reveal your true nature to these pitiful, unwitting fools your words have seduced!" His arm scythed over the entire studio audience. They heard his words clearly, even if the folks back home were presently hearing a pitch for Land of Love time-sharing vacation resort ("Evil never takes a vacation, but you've earned one.").

They didn't care for what they were hearing.

"Oh, my poor, ignorant children!" Quintus wrung his hands over the audience. "Turn back before you are dragged down into the Pit for your sins. You are blunderers and infants in this creature's hands, but you may yet save—''

Raleel tapped him on the shoulder. '' 'Scuse me, friend, but if you're gonna keep this up when the cameras roll again, you better stay on your mark.''

Quintus' eyes blazed with wrath. ''Unhand me, in God's name!'' Raleel unhanded him in jig time. ''Think you that I will brook . . . Uh . . . What mark?''

''Right there.'' Raleel pointed to another taped X on the floor, right near his own taped O. ''Y'see, friend, you got a message to give, but if you're off your mark when we roll, ain't nobody gonna see you giving it 'cept these fine people right here.'' He waved to the studio audience. They cheered him briefly, then glowered at Quintus. Growls were heard. ''Take my advice and go for the national audience, 'cause brother, you have lost this'n.''

''Lost?'' Quintus boomed. ''It is they who are lost! It is they who will be swept—''

''Five, four, three, two, one, and . . . *action!*'' Brazlyp shot Quintus through the heart with an index-finger Magnum.

The red lights above the camera lenses and Raleel's oily grin blinked on simultaneously. The demon began to speak, and Quintus had been too properly reared in his patrician household to interrupt.

''Friends, we got us a real *happening* here. Now, you know I'm a fair man, and *Heading Home* has never been one to turn aside responsible spokesmen for opposing viewpoints. *We* ain't got nothing to be 'shamed of. So here he is, a surprise guest speaker, let's give a really warm welcome to Quentin Plaster, President of the First Coven of Gay Mages and Sorcerers. Please go on, friend Quentin, so's our at-home audience can hear. You were saying 'bout how cocaine kinda *frees up* a person's inner ability to do magic . . . ?''

''I was *not!* And my name isn't—''

''Psst. Get on your mark,'' Brazlyp hissed, distracting him. Long adherence to the rule of Obedience made Quintus blush, then sidle onto the X. He tried to regain the full fury of his justifiable rage against the devil and all his works, but the storm within him had dropped to a squall.

''I was saying that *you*, sirrah, are nothing but a fake and a fraud and—''

''—and in the pay of Satan hisself?'' Raleel winked at

Camera Two, which always pounced on close-up opportunities. "Sound familiar, friends? Sound like what's been said 'bout old Joe before? Sugar, any you fine people out there want to believe it this time, go right ahead. It's a free country. Even free for people like—Son, you want to look right *into* the camera? Don't want the folks at home to think you're a-scared to look a man in the eye."

Raleel gave Quintus' chin a quick shove, before the man could protest. One cold red eye stared into his while the camera lens glittered as black as the empty socket of a dead monk's skull. Memories surged. Quintus uttered a strangled scream and covered his face with his hands.

"*Hallelujah Chorus,*" Raleel hissed at Brazlyp.

"But, boss—!"

"Grit your teeth and *do it!*"

Brazlyp shrugged, braced himself for the assault, and cued the Joyful Noise singers. The final tableau for that week's broadcast of *Heading Home* showed "Sometime" Joseph Lee wearing a rigid smile, triumphant above the quaking, huddled body of his foe. The choir pealed victory.

The audience went mad. Some of them didn't wait for the collectors to come to them, but ran up the aisles to meet them halfway. With all the shifting of seats and pushing of people, no one complained when a blond-haired woman got up and barged her way out of the studio. The pile of fat, leather-bound books in her arms made her into a human bulldozer. She only paused once, in the aisle, to cast a disgusted glance at the dark-skinned man still crouching at Raleel's feet. As she left, a small ball of matted yellow fur bounded after.

The cameras went dead. Raleel left the stage, followed by the cheers of his followers. Quintus stayed where he was, hands clasped, lips moving, ignored by the contemptuous demon. Brazlyp gave him a wide berth.

"Come on, mister. I'd better get you out of here."

Quintus raised his eyes. "I can—I can go myself."

Noel studied that ascetic face, trying not to let all the pity he felt for the man show. "Not safely. The audience'd like nothing better than to pay you back for what you said about them." He indicated the crowd. With the spotlights off and the houselights up, Quintus saw a host of faces that reminded him of the first time he'd been driven from the marketplace with rocks instead of cowpats.

"I only brought them the truth," he whispered.

"Truth's chancy. I know. Come on, I'll get you out the back door." Noel looped his arm under Quintus' and led him away.

In the audience, Dwayne Knox let his arm drop casually over Lysi's shoulders. He could hardly believe how golden his luck had turned, even with those daily phone calls from Ma telling him he was still a no-account bum. To think that one of the stars of the big picture had actually agreed to sit beside him. Something about what a powerful aura he projected, she said, a girl could get lost in it, goo-goo stuff like that. Heck, long as he got to be this close to her, he didn't care if she called him radioactive.

Damn, but he was glad he'd got religion!

"So how's about we get us a Big Boy?"

"Later, Dwayne." Lysi untangled herself from his embrace, scurried up onto the stage, and dashed out the way Noel and Quintus had gone.

Dwayne shrugged. He had time—the whole shooting schedule's worth. This was only Take One. Yeah . . . he liked the sound of that. Take One.

God, how he did love show bidness!

9

Devil or Angel

"YOU'RE SURE YOU want to go to the museum?" Noel asked, bucking the traffic on Wilshire. "Not to your home?"

Quintus smiled wistfully. "I do not think you could take me to my home, young man." He clenched his fists in his lap as a little red MG whipped around them and nearly climbed the back of the BMW ahead. "Although that person looks as if he is headed there momentarily."

"Uh-huh." Noel concentrated on driving. He liked this

weird guy, for reasons he couldn't name. It was just a feeling he had, like the one that kept telling him not to believe a word of what "Sometime" Joseph Lee had said concerning the fellow's affiliations. First Coven of the what? Noel had enough personal experience with sorcery to theorize that if there were such an organization as the Gay Mages and Sorcerers, they'd pick a spokesman with a bit more panache and a hog's load less stage fright than this guy.

But why would his mentor lie? This man didn't look like a threat. Why come down on him so hard, in front of a national TV audience? L.A. grew its own sun-ripened crop of religious nuts. Like garden toads, they were to be tolerated and sidestepped. Stomping them was too messy. Why reduce this poor man to the quivering lump of humiliation Noel had witnessed?

It didn't sit right with him, and he decided not to let it go until he figured it all out.

At the Los Angeles County Museum of Art, Noel found a space in the parking lot conveniently close to the four buildings. "Boy, there's a miracle," he mumbled as he locked up the car.

Quintus was staring at the sign in front of the Frances and Armand Hammer Building, announcing the *Splendor of Alexandria* exhibit within. Noel followed him as he walked up to the entrance.

It was past the five o'clock closing. Quintus made a face at the building's schedule sign.

"Looks like finding the parking space wasn't such a miracle after all. Can I take you someplace else, sir?" Noel asked. "They won't be open until tomorrow morning."

"I want to go inside," Quintus replied. So saying, he walked through the locked door. On the other side, he turned to look back at Noel and calmly asked, "Won't you join me? I would be glad of company." Without waiting for a response, he raised two fingers in benediction and Noel felt the cool passage of glass and metal trickling over his skin as he was borne through the solid substance of the museum door.

"Good Lord!" he gasped. "You *are* a sorcerer!"

"I am not." Quintus got huffy.

"Look, I don't mean you're a *gay* sorcerer—"

"*That* is one of your words I've heard hurled enough times

to understand. Hmph. I am not a sorcerer, and I am neither gay nor rectilinear—''

''That's 'straight.' ''

''*I* am celibate.'' Quintus' coarse eyebrows met above his nose. ''And I am a saint.''

The museum was filled with silence. Noel's own speech-less reaction merely added to it. In the awkward emptiness, Quintus' brows relaxed. He lowered his head.

''Or so I am supposed to be. If so, I am not a very good one.'' Fleeting hope lit his eyes. ''*Have* you heard of me? Quintus Pilaster? I flourished in the fourth century, in Egypt.''

''Sure.'' Noel's reply brought joy to Quintus' face. ''I heard all about you from this archeologist I met back at Yale. He said it came to obscure historical figures, it'd be hard to beat you.''

''Obscure?'' Quintus' smile crumbled. ''And . . . histori-cal? Not—not religious?''

''Well, yes, sort of religious. Apocryphal, though. There was a big to-do about you nearly twenty years ago, but it all died down. He said the stories about the dig were all killed.'' Noel's face hardened. ''That was one dig that should've been killed before it started.''

''Why? Because that was where your parents met and you were born?''

Noel's eyes flashed shock. ''How did you know that?''

''I'm a saint. Or so I always assumed. Perhaps I am merely one of the lower orders of angels, or perhaps the few powers I seem to command are standard issue for all blameless souls who return to Earth. However the circumstances, I know who you are, Noel, as well as I know what you are, and what I fear you may become.''

''You've got me at a disadvantage, then.'' Noel looked over his shoulder at the locked door. ''Also, trapped.''

''Not really. You could use your own powers to get out the same way I brought you in. You do have magic.'' Quintus sighed. ''Go, if you wish. I am used to solitude.''

Noel thought it over. A slow smile creased his face. ''I think I'll stick to using my powers to hide us from the security guards, O.K.? I want to talk to you.''

They wandered through the halls of the museum. A guard walked past them as if they weren't there. More and more, Noel found himself drawn to Quintus. The doubtful saint kept nothing back, reciting his life's history up to and including the demonic temptations he had undergone at the hands of Noel's mother and her comrades.

"I do not blame her," he said as they drifted into the large room where the prize of Faith's exhibition lay in cool marble majesty. "She was a demon then, though at heart unfit for that calling. I should have suspected her flaw the first. The other succubus—she who is now the angel Lura—was always trying to tempt me with the pleasures of the flesh. Your mother—"

"Yes?" Noel's tone dared him to go on.

Quintus leaned back against the old sarcophagus, feeling the lines of hieroglyphics pass beneath his fingers. "Once, before I heard the call of God, I was fond of hunting. My father would take me up into the hills surrounding our villa and let me shoot small birds with my bow and arrow. One day, we surprised a pheasant. He rose up like a streak of wildfire, a comet fleeing the sun. He escaped while I stood there, staring at how beautiful he was in flight.

"My father chastised me for that, of course. He called me a fool, a failure, a daydreaming girl."

"What does that have to do with—?"

"Indulge me, Noel." Quintus' smile mocked his younger self. "Well, I had been brought up in the best Roman fashion— too well brought-up to blame my father for the acid his words left in my entrails. And blame myself? Find me a grown man capable of accepting self-blame! Wherefore I cursed the pheasant, and swore that if I had another chance—

"It came next day. You might call it the first of my miracles. The same ground, the same pheasant startled into flight, but—ah!—not the same boy. Without pause or thought, I nocked an arrow to my bow and shot him. He fell, but I could not believe that one arrow was enough to secure such treacherous prey. I would not risk another of my father's scornful lectures if the bird escaped. I loosed another shaft, which struck him in mid-fall, and another, which hit him as he lay among the hillside brush, and another, and then another, and—"

"But why so many?" Noel asked. "Wasn't one enough to kill him?"

Now Quintus did not smile at all. "The first shaft slew the bird; the others were to slay the humiliation I had blamed upon the innocent creature. Not all the arrows in the world were enough to expiate that debt. The bird was a scapegoat for my pride. Poor thing, he was a mass of blood and torn flesh when I brought him home; no trophy, but meat for the dogs. I never hunted since. Wherefore, Noel, do not ask me for arrows.''

''Arrows?''

''You track the pheasant too. See that your hunt has a better ending than mine.'' He came forward suddenly and seized Noel's hand. ''Let her fly free, Noel; free of guilt, free of blame she hasn't earned. Let your mother go.''

Noel was silent. ''Go on,'' he said at last. ''It was centuries ago, and she was . . . different then. Tell me. I just want to know, not to judge.''

Quintus looked pleased at this. ''Did that tale truly reach your heart, Noel? I was never very good with parables. Usually I asked Ambrosius if he could come up with a story to illustrate some point I wanted to make with our brethren. Ambrosius was always the better man with words . . . as with all things.''

''Quintus, when my mother and the others were . . . tempting you, how did you resist?''

''I didn't. I fell. Why look so shocked? Didn't you hear that from that archeologist friend of yours?'' Quintus inquired. ''That Lura was quite persuasive, and imaginative too. I built my celibacy about me like a wall of stone, but she was the sweet, delicate blossom that insinuates its fragile root-threads between the cracks and brings the bastion down.''

''And so you, uh . . . ?''

''No.'' Quintus drummed his fingers on the sarcophagus lid. ''When the breakdown came, I ran screaming across the desert, filled with enough Lust to ravage several of the more voracious empresses. If I did not couple with Lura, it was because I still retained *some* sense, and feared a demon's damning touch. I did, however, stumble across some nomads, and made the mistake of accosting one of their wives. I got a thump on the head from the lady's husband that called quits to everything, Lust and life inclusive. So I died innocent of sin itself, though not of intent. Apparently it was one of those technicalities that count for something. I believe Ambrosius gave me a nice funeral, and then the whole monastic settlement went to—Noel? What's the matter?''

"I *did* touch a demon! I *am* damned!" The anguished words tore themselves from Noel's heart. "And I'm *part* demon. My mother—Lysi—Quintus, I loved them, and I still love them, but it's *wrong!* It's so wrong!"

"Wrong to love?" Quintus was perplexed. "That is, as you might say, a new one on me."

Noel was too wrapped up in his own presumed damnation to listen. "Please, you have to help me. If you are a saint, heal me."

"Heal you?" Quintus repeated. "Of love?"

"Heal him." A sweet voice spoke from the sarcophagus. Quintus did a *grand jeté* across the room. The carved marble shimmered as *Lysi* emerged from its side, looking pristine in a creamy drape of gauze.

"Heal him of love, and you'll answer to me, Quintus," she said.

"That's her!" Noel cried, taking refuge at Quintus' back and jabbing a finger at Lysi. "That's the one who tricked me, the one who seduced me! That's the succubus!"

"Is she?" Quintus squinted at her, shading his eyes as if gazing into a great light. He shook his head. "You must be mistaken, unless they've greatly changed the basic model. I sense nothing of Hell about her."

"Didn't you *see* what she just did? Just walked through that sarcophagus like it was air?"

"As I walked through the museum door." Quintus called up the strict tone he'd used centuries ago with froward novices who refused to tend the pigs. "Are you tarring me with the same brush?"

"You mean she's not a succubus? But she *was!* When I was at Yale, she tried to get my soul. I'm not lying!"

"Young man, perhaps she was a succubus, in the past. And what were you?"

"Fool enough to love her," Noel muttered.

"Will you deny the great mystery of change?"

"You expect me to believe *she's* changed? Sure she has. Come on, Quintus! The truth is, she's hellspawn, and the truth never changes."

"Noel!" Lysi tried to come to him, arms reaching out. He moved away, ignoring the yearning in her eyes.

The saint of the desert sidestepped, leaving Noel no place to hide. Raising his hands, Quintus declared, "If you wish to play hide-and-seek with truth, I'll give you a proper playground. Behold!'' His arms described two arcs of white light, twin gateways that sparkled open before Lysi and Noel.

"Enter, if you are so sure of yourself,'' Quintus commanded them. "Prove that you are the one person who sees things as they are. Within that gate, there is no past. Time stops at *now*. If nothing in all the worlds can sway you from what you alone can see as truth, enter.''

Noel peered into the light, uncertain. Then he turned slowly towards Quintus, resolute. "I was a fool to love her, but I learn from my mistakes. I don't repeat them. I'm not afraid to prove it.'' He passed into the shining.

At the brink of her own portal, Lysi gave Quintus a beseeching look. "I am afraid,'' she admitted. "What lies on the other side, really?''

The supposed saint smiled kindly encouragement. "Only your selves as they are. No debt of passion. No memory of pleasure. Only soul to soul.''

"Ah.'' Lysi raised her head to stare into the sparkling portal for a moment before she too stepped in.

Quintus whistled his relief, propping himself against the sarcophagus again. "I didn't think I could do that. Wonders *will* never cease. Good.'' His glance strayed to the lid portrait of the marble box's occupant. Such paintings were a frugal Roman affectation that had replaced the ancient Egyptian custom of carving the deceased's death mask there. Large, familiar eyes filled with the sorrow of the world stared up at Quintus.

"Oh, hello there, Ambrosius,'' he murmured to the box. "Fancy meeting you here. I'm not at all surprised. There is a pattern to being that goes beyond coincidence. If I've been summoned to serve in this city of madmen, you must be here too, the eternal *amen* to my every prayer. Even in death, you come following after, picking up the pieces of my mistakes and making them into something worthwhile. I know how that lad Noel feels, someone always hovering around, not trusting him to do anything right on his own. And what will you do if I've erred this time, Ambrosius? Not precious much, in your present state.''

The twin gateways stood empty, two glimmering, vacant eyes fixed on Quintus in perpetual *Well?* As he watched, they rippled gradually nearer to each other, the twinkling rims touching, blending, melding into a single door that held a paean of light too bright for ordinary eyes to bear.

Even Quintus had to shield his eyes at the moment when Noel and Lysi stepped out of the gateway together, hand clasped in hand.

" 'Blessed are the peacemakers.' Not bad for an old bungler, eh, Ambrosius?" Quintus whispered as the gateway crumbled to sparks. He went forward to embrace the reconciled lovers.

10

Trust Me

"AN ADVANTAGE LIKE that and you didn't follow up on it?" Lura couldn't believe her ears.

Lysi sat before the dressing-table mirror, a dreamy expression on her face. Faith and Lura lounged in a pair of moiré-covered armchairs in the angels' suite, waiting for her to reply. Lura and Atamar had checked themselves into the Beverly Wilshire Hotel. It was a step down from what they were used to at home, but a very small step indeed.

Lysi combed her hair from style to style, never able to leave well enough alone. "Change," she told her reflection. "Oh, I do like the great mystery of change."

Faith Schleppey tossed three quarters down among the perfume vials and lotion bottles. "There you go. End of mystery. Buy yourself a Coke and then explain why you didn't tell Noel exactly what your damned brother is!"

"I will," Lysi said.

"When?"

"When it's time!" Lysi slapped the comb onto the table-top. "He's just accepted *me* again. I thought one breakthrough was enough. Excuse me for having some sense of timing. I suppose if you would've been in charge of Exodus, you'd have pushed for all ten plagues in one day. If it's Tuesday, noon, this must be murrain.'' She ended with a sanctimonious: ''*Saint Quintus* didn't think I was wrong!''

''Well, Saint Schleppey begs to differ.''

''*Will* you tell him?'' Lura joined Faith in pressing the attack. ''Now that he believes you again?''

Lysi was smug. ''I may not have to. I told him about the movie—the *real* story. I've got my little ways, you see, and I managed to lift a copy of Raleel's master-script. Noel's not stupid. He read it, and it didn't take him long to see what Raleel's really doing with that picture.''

''Yeah, shouting 'Wowee, boy, all this sin sure does feel great, here's how to do it!' and whispering 'But maybe you better not try.' '' Faith did not approve of the demon's tactics. ''How did Noel react?''

''Shocked, of course.'' Lysi tried a feathered barrette in her hair. ''His idol of righteousness, actually leading folks down the path to fleshly whoopee? La! He's going to demand an accounting from Mr. 'Sometime' Joseph Lee. I'm betting it ends with Noel walking out. Next, Faith, you jerk your technical advice out from under him. Then Don can pull the use of his studio, spread a few choice *caveats* through the industry about BLT Ministries, and ta-daaah, my brother's left with his barnacles in dry dock. Back to strictly penny-ante perdition-mongering for Raleel.''

''But we can't just leave him as is,'' Lura protested. ''I don't like thinking about the harm he can still do with that Blessed Last Tabernacle Ministries organization. I'm surprised it got as big as it did, untouched. We're usually very good about tidying up messes.''

Lysi dismissed all discussion with a lift of her eyebrows. ''Probably someone in your department believes in the old 'enough rope' principle, Lura. If your higher-ups aren't concerned with sgcoshing BLT Ministries like a potato bug, why should we worry about it?'' Her tongue darted over her lips. ''What *do* you think I ought to wear?''

''For what?''

''The pre-shoot party tonight. Raleel's. *He* still thinks it's a go on the picture for tomorrow, poor sod. The whole cast's invited to the set tonight for his big pep talk. Elmer Gantry meets Cecil B. De Mille, and I wouldn't miss it for worlds.''

"I would," Lura grumped. "But I've got to be there. I'm on Noel patrol."

"Can't you drop the guardian angel bit? I'm watching out for him now."

"Atamar would turn my pinions into a king-sized order of Buffalo wings. Anyway, how can you watch Noel? Your brother would smell you in the audience a mile off, and he might decide to play dirty. He's a pretty powerful demon. You and I together might not be able to defeat him in an open fight, not even if Noel joined with us."

"What would he smell?"

"You know what I mean: your aura."

Lysi giggled. "Ever heard of supernatural deodorant?"

Lura was not amused.

"O.K., camouflage, then. One of the boys involved with the picture is so extraordinarily ordinary that my aura gets damped past detection by his. Raleel would have to be actively hunting me to find me while I'm with that one. And why should he want to?"

"I still don't like it. I'm going with Noel anyway. Atamar wants to try his hand at locating Melisan." A thought touched Lura. "Do you think her aura's being masked in some way, too?"

"By what? She's mortal herself now. She doesn't need to hide behind spiritual mediocrity when she's got her own supply."

"On behalf of us mediocre mortals, thanks heaps," Faith remarked dryly.

"Oh, no offense, Faith." Lysi anchored a twist of hair with a marabou-trimmed comb. "But you must admit, compared to demons and angels, mortals really don't have any imagination when it comes to things of the spirit world."

"In a previous life you were . . . you were . . . Nefertiti."

"That does it," Melisan announced, hauling herself out of the hot-tub. The sloshing broke her spirit-guide's trance. He blinked like an owl in daylight.

"Where are you going, O Queen of Queens?"

"Back to my true previous life, O Plucker of Turkeys." She rubbed herself down briskly with a towel, ignoring the hungry looks the hot-tub guru fastened on her naked limbs.

"But we have not yet finished the session. Your spirit wanders in the void. Do you want it back or not?"

"Only if there's a deposit. When it gets back here, tell it to meet me at Trader Vic's. This time, it's buying."

"I am still uncovering your life-path. We can't leave the quest half-finished. There are clear indications that when you were a priestess of the Druids, you were transported off-Earth by alien intelligences!"

Melisan tilted her head in his direction. "That I remember."

"Do you?" He rose partway from the water in eagerness.

"They were tall and golden-eyed"—he could not see her smirk in the dimly lit gazebo—"with no hair, no clothes, and unisex restroom facilities. Of course as a decent Druid priestess, I would not stand for such impropriety and I jumped ship somewhere in the Crab nebula. There is a planet full of my descendants there to this day, all of whom drink warm beer, eat boiled beef, and blame the Tories for everything. The aliens did give my priestess incarnation the secret of life, but it was excess spiritual baggage and was routed to Poughkeepsie. I am heading there as soon as possible to claim it. It ought to be good for at least four best-sellers. Good night."

The spirit-guide caught her in the robing room as she was fastening the last button of her rather street-worn dress. Since the night of Don's party, Melisan had only used her credit card and scanty cash reserves for food, lodging, and the purchase of a canvas backpack sturdy enough to tote all the books she had purloined from Don's study.

Though Melisan was not dressed to impress, the guide was less so. His midriff made a furry bulge above his blue terrycloth sarong. "Where do you think you're going?"

Melisan's hand dropped into the backpack's open top. One of the paperbacks inside began to oscillate on its own, then rose to meet her groping fingers. The first time it had happened, Melisan had been swapping problems with a *madre santa* in East L.A. She had gone to her to see if *santería* could help her regain some measure of her old powers. If residual magic from her demon days had been passed on to her offspring, couldn't she hope to have some too? Maybe it was dormant, just waiting for the right wake-up call. She had tried almost every avenue to the Otherworld that L.A. had to offer: Tarot readers, crystal healers, mushroom munchers, unionized haruspices, those who read the future by the pattern of sand-flea bites on surfers. When the book took wing, the old woman had screamed and run, seeing her potential pigeon turn into a falcon right before her eyes.

"None of your business where I'm going," Melisan snapped at her guru. "My aliens told me not to talk to strangers."

"Listen, I only give a course of six spirit-voyages—no singles!—payable in installments. You only paid for one."

"One was plenty."

"I don't care if your spirit winds up cleaning windshields on a galactic street corner, lady, but you better pay me for the other five trips, use them or not."

The man was taller than Melisan, and he looked like a former jock. The beer gut overlay muscle. He dropped his hands to her shoulders and gave her a persuasive squeeze.

The book in the backpack opened. A tingle of knowledge ran up Melisan's arm. It was the dime-store Satanism manual Don had first owned, the one he'd read cover to cover while on that dig in Egypt, searching for Quintus' tomb. Melisan had taken a look into it once, when Don was out of his tent.

She had a pretty good memory, and the words were catchy. She chanted them right in the guru's face, to the tune of "Fight for Your Right (to Party)."

The terrycloth sarong turned into steel wool, its temperature dropping to ten degrees Fahrenheit.

Melisan found herself alone in the robing room.

"Natural talent," she told the walls. "Just natural talent." She slung the backpack over her shoulder. "I wish that were enough—having these chintzy spells to use against Raleel. But it's nickel-and-dime stuff. I need more, and I'd better not waste any more time fooling myself. I'm going to have to make the Change."

The Change. She knew what it entailed. The big books in her backpack made that much clear. She didn't want to do it, but she had to, if she were to acquire the strength to save her child.

The yellow kitten had been waiting for her patiently at the iron gates of the guru's house. She nearly trampled it underfoot as she strode out. The tiny creature gave a hurt and offended mew as her shoe pinched the edge of its paw. Melisan stooped to examine it.

"No harm done, little one," she said. "Unless you count that missing eye, and I didn't do that. You'll be—" The kitten rubbed its matted fur against her hand. She could feel the ribs beneath the skin. "Hungry. Skinny. What kind of a life have you got?'' The kitten raised its one good eye, let her see the redness rimming it, the milky discharge.

Melisan's breath shuddered out of her. "Come on with me, baby. I'm going to do you a favor.'' She scooped up the kitten and held it close to her heart. Its single eye could not see her tears.

Raleel sniffed the office air. "You sure you didn't smell it?'' he asked Brazlyp.

"What?''

"When Noel was just in here, sort of like a residue.''

"After-shave?''

"Moron. The telltale scent of an alien aura clinging to him. Our little friend's been associating with the wrong element. My dam always said she could smell a churchgoer a mile off, and a secret sinner further away than that. My money says that the little scene we just witnessed wasn't Noel's idea. But where did he get that copy of the script?''

Brazlyp raised his hands. "Search me, boss. You did handle it beautifully, though. You really gonna let the little creep give a sermon at the pre-shoot?''

Raleel's lips broke their human boundaries and spread to the full limits of his demon-self smile. "The spotlight is the ultimate temptation. The chance to have the attention of the multitude fixed upon him will keep Noel on my side just a little longer. That is all I'll need. We move tonight, Brazlyp.''

"Move, boss?'' The junior fiend cast a longing look at the Los Angeles panorama below, sunset turning the buildings to gold, the streets to purple. "I like it here.''

"You would. Let us hope that the Underlords find this place as congenial as you.'' He laughed to see Brazlyp gape. "Yes, the Underlords, my friend! Didn't I tell you that I would make the *Helliad* live? Not on my own—I haven't the force—but my powers linked to a strong source of magic, what's to keep the gate barred then? They scorn me below, call me half-breed, taunt me for my mortal blood. This will teach them where my allegiance lies, and as I use a mortal to help me accomplish my ends—Oh, Brazlyp, in one move I'll free my sire, bring down souls by the score, secure myself the prince-dom of Parvahr, and even earn a dukedom in Hell itself!''

Brazlyp's scurfy green face shone with admiration. "Gee, boss, that sounds swell.''

" 'Swell'? The coup of the millennium, and it sounds 'swell'?" Raleel spat. The gob turned into a steel-jawed cockroach when it hit the carpet, and the vermin wasted no time in trimming Brazlyp's toenails up to the ankle. By the time the smaller demon stomped his assailant to smoke, Raleel was sniffing the air again.

"I *still* wish I knew what that scent means," he said.

Dixi came in with a pile of papers for him to sign. "What scent, sir?" she asked.

"Oh, somewhat like frankincense . . . a hint of myrrh . . . some sandalwood undertones . . . a garden enclosed . . ."

"Beats me. I always wear Joy." She whipped out a can of Lysol and sprayed away all Raleel's misgivings

11

No Doubt About It, I Gotta Get Another Hat

THE LIMO PURRED over the backlot road, leading a caravan of lesser vehicles, mostly vans. Inside, Raleel leaned over Dixi to get a look at the yellow legal pad in Noel's lap.

"Workin' with that suggestion of mine, son?" he asked.

"Mm-hm." Noel knit his brows and bit the end of his pen. Since dropping out of Yale, he'd gone too long without practice at organizing his thoughts. Here he was, on the edge of a golden opportunity to have his words really do some good, count for something, and he didn't want a raging case of *hysteron proteron* to botch it.

"Works in real good with the message you want to give 'em," Raleel went on. "Fine analogy. Real pretty figure of speech, 'specially if you use your talents to make 'em *see* how it was."

"I keep thinking of *The Ten Commandments*," Noel said.

Raleel winced. "Son, your sermon ain't gonna be taking certain *names* in vain all over the place, now is it?"

"I meant the movie. You know, with Charlton Heston."

"Oh." Raleel sank back into the leather upholstery. "That's just fine, son. You just keep thinking 'bout it, and when you get up there to give your speech, effects and all, I want you to know that ol' 'Sometime' Joseph Lee's gonna be right with you every step of the way."

Noel looked at him askance. When he'd been with Lysi, in that neverland of Quintus' devising, it was easy to believe anything she told him about "Sometime" Joseph Lee. He couldn't argue with the evidence of that master-script she'd shown him, either. Ah, but when you were in the great televangelist's presence . . .

Does he really want to make the picture that way? Noel wondered. *Is he a hypocrite, or worse, or just the victim of a bad scriptwriter? He claims he's letting me talk tonight to make sure our people don't take the movie's message wrong, there's that. . . . But who's going to watch over all the people who go to see it once it's released? I don't know, I just don't know. I wish Lysi were here. And Quintus. I wonder if he felt like throwing up too, before he gave his first sermon?*

The limo-led caravan came to a halt in the middle of a mock-up agora. A cut-rate replica of the Parthenon dominated the slope, with colonnaded buildings flanking it and a bunting-draped platform built onto the front. Cameramen were already there, riding booms in midair, seeking the perfect angle for shooting both the audience and the officiants. Over to one side, behind the set, a host of long tables had been set out in an olive grove. Hirelings passed among the trees, lighting the clusters of perfumed torches in their iron stands. There would be full tech lighting for the formal ceremonies on the platform, but the feast beforehand was consecrated to judicious sensuality, rated PG.

The vans behind the limo drove on to the olive grove, where they discharged their passengers. Lysi and Dwayne emerged from the fifth in line and hurried to get a good place at the tables. A coterie of caterers worked with serene efficiency to set up a sumptuous buffet that was a hymn to Gluttony. Dwayne's scrawny chest swelled with pride at the way his lady clung to him with every indication of devotion, especially when they passed close to the separate, screened-off section where "Sometime" Joseph Lee's private party was having dinner.

On the buffet line, Lura tucked her luxuriant hair under a silvered coif and doled out lobster bisque by the dipperful. When Lysi came down the line, she tipped her a wink. The two of them made excuses and stole away to confer.

Full night had not yet fallen, and the olive trees' shadow made for total darkness. Lysi's eyes glowed incandescent green in the gloom until Lura told her to cut it out.

"Oh, nuts. You never let me have any fun."

"You're having enough fun just being here, when you're not needed. This is just one big nyah-nyah at your brother, isn't it?"

"I have to be here." Lysi made a moue. "*I'm* one of the *stars.*" A mischievous smile lit the darkness. "But it is fun to stick out my tongue at Raleel, figuratively speaking."

"Your tongue won't be the only thing sticking out if he sees you face to face. Which he will, when the shooting begins."

"It won't come to that. Noel will leave him, just like I said, and so will Faith and Don. Not even a demon can make a movie without mortal help—not if he wants to maintain the illusion that 'Sometime' Joseph Lee is a mortal." A random thought struck her. "Say, speaking of Faith and Don, where are they?"

"The males are still searching for Melisan, and Faith is at the museum with Quintus. The *Splendor of Alexandria* exhibit has him all stirred up with nostalgia, especially that sarcophagus."

"If he's so homesick, you should go tell him how close he is to being done with this job. Noel's as good as saved."

Lura was not as ready as Lysi to believe that. "I'm not going anywhere. A guardian angel has to be particularly vigilant when her charge is in grave spiritual peril. All my senses are sending out warning signals about this party."

"Not more of your aura-sniffing!" Lysi moaned.

"I just don't know . . ."

"I know that *I* never expected to be chosen for this part, Mr. Cardiff." Noel's dinner partner leaned over to dip a suggestive asparagus spear in the hollandaise sauce on his plate. By torchlight, her mascara and eyeliner made her look like a fey raccoon, and Noel was her chosen garbage can. "You can't imagine how utterly grateful I am to you for selecting me to play the courtesan."

Her knee located his and nudged. His shifted away, but it wasn't quick enough to evade the hand that dropped beneath the table to squeeze his thigh lightly. He felt her gel nails through his trousers.

"I didn't," he said, wobbling the beleaguered thigh like mad to dislodge her questing claw. "Ms. Dominus did."

"Oh." The lucky lady showed no sign of extending her thanks to Ms. Dominus, who sat at Noel's other side and devoured her filet mignon with dispatch. "Well, Mr. Lee tells me that you and I will be seeing a lot of each other during the filming. You're to be my coach."

"There must be a mistake. I don't know anything about acting. Now, Ms. Dominus used to take some courses—"

The courtesan's mouth made a small, hard ball of Willing Wine lipstick. "My *spiritual* coach. I am *not* a professional actress, even if you were kind enough to notice any small talent I might have, to use for the greater glory of God. Mama always did say that there was something basically sinful about the movies. Of course, she couldn't say one thing about it when it's a picture made under the BLT Ministries' auspices, and when I got chosen to have all expenses paid, well, she did stir up a little fuss, but I just told her I'd hire a girl to come in and look after her every so often—all perfectly respectful, I said it, because when it comes to keeping the Commandment about honoring your father and mother, there isn't one person in Watling can even come close to touching me, sacrificing a decent social life and everything just to stay at her beck and call, not that she needs it, really, the pain's all in her head—and a real devoted mother, like she's always going on about how she's one, so ready to do anything to see her children succeed, grateful or not, well, how could she argue with the fact that here I've got the chance to become a star and her not come off looking like seven kinds of hypocrite? I ask you!"

"Could you repeat the question?"

"Later, son." Noel couldn't remember ever being so glad to hear "Sometime" Joseph Lee's voice. The televangelist beckoned him to rise and join him at the steps leading up to the back of the stage. "Right now we got us a message to give. Got everything you need?"

"Book, seven pieces of silver, iron bowl, knife, matches,

candle,'' Melisan enumerated for the yellow kitten's benefit.
''Yep, looks like I've got everything. Oh, yes . . . and
blood.''

The kitten sat at her feet and cocked its head to one side.
Its ribby flanks were already plumping out a little from the
feast of cream and designer cat-food Melisan had given it. Its
worshipful look as good as said that only death would take it
from its newfound benefactress's side.

Only death . . .

Melisan rubbed the kitten behind the ears. ''I have to do
this, baby,'' she said, her voice breaking. ''I don't want to,
but I must. The books all agree about the—the sacrifice part
of the ceremony. It's the only path left open to me. He's my
son, and you're only—''

The kitten mewed, then butted her with its head. She still
felt matted fur, a touch of the mange. Time and care would
cure that, for the miserable little creature; or a quicker cure.
Her eyes fell on the knife, lying beside the candle in its iron
bowl, both laid out neatly on her folded clothing. She was as
naked as the kitten, and shivering with cold in spite of the
balmy night.

Her bones shook as she kindled the candle, took a deep
breath, and by its light began to read the ancient words from
the opened book.

Noel skimmed the index cards with his sermon notes one
last time, then passed them to Dixi. ''Sometime'' Joseph Lee
never used notes or idiot cards for his speeches, so neither
would he. If the man was as bad as Lysi claimed, Noel
wanted to go into the final confrontation with a moral advantage.

The stage was bare, no backdrop but the fake Parthenon.
The agora was filled with the cast for the movie. The BLT
Repentent Courtesan picture didn't even have a working title,
as far as its would-be actors knew, though they referred to it
as *God's Vengeance* among themselves. Dwayne called it
Bimbo II: First Blood. Lysi thought of it as *The Search for
Schlock*, but no one asked her.

It was eerie, standing up on the platform, staring out over
the audience. When Noel helped Mr. Lee during studio broadcasts of *Heading Home*, the kliegs dazzled him so thoroughly
that the faces out front looked like no more than a box of
assorted marbles. There was plenty of lighting for the camera-

men to shoot by here, but it didn't seem as bright. Noel could look right through it to see every face in the crowd, every feature, every upturning glance of hope and hunger and anticipation.

He took a deep breath, and began.

"O.K., cat. Come here."

The kitten hadn't moved. He'd made no attempt to escape even when Melisan's chanting reached its highest pitch, even when she threw the silver into the iron bowl with a startling clang. When she called, he came to her hand. She held him to her, cradled in her palm, her fingers under his tiny forelimbs. His heart beat against her skin, his purr rolling up from calm contentment to a nervous rumbling.

The knife was a half-moon sliver reflected in his single eye.

" . . . And so we now find ourselves at the shore of our own Red Sea. Behind us, the chariots of evil and sin and vice are all bearing down." Noel summoned up an illusion, and on the air behind him the Children of Israel stood waiting while Egyptian chariots that looked a little like bumper cars drawn by the Budweiser Clydesdales came hurtling on. "The waters of perdition are hungry, ready to drown us. The far shore of salvation beckons, but how are we to get across?"

Brazlyp refolded his arms and from the corner of his mouth told his senior, "The kid stinks. Well, maybe not that, but he doesn't have your moxie, boss, and never—Boss? Boss, you okay?"

Raleel did not reply. He sat with his eyes closed, the mask of "Sometime" Joseph Lee hard and immobile as a porcelain shell. Brazlyp surreptitiously nipped his master's thigh with quickly retracted talons. No reaction. He recognized the signs.

"Trance. But where . . . ?" The junior fiend was devoured by curiosity. Since his spawning at the McCarthy hearings he had been possessed of a passion to investigate everything, especially matters that were none of his infernal beeswax. There was a way for him to find out where Raleel had gone, and not just by waiting for him to return for questioning.

Brazlyp closed his eyes, gritted his teeth, and thought of Avernus.

The darkness from which he had come, a formless afterthought of far greater evils, welcomed him easily home. He was spirit, melding into a world of spirit, sailing down the great currents unseen in their infinitely splaying branches beneath the earth, beneath the skin, beneath the stars. In the shadows of his inner path hellward, he spied a kindred ember falling far and fast ahead of him.

Raleel, he thought, and the passing entity's aura left a trail of scent from which Brazlyp's own spirit snuffled recognition. *Going where? Parvahr? He could get there faster if he went shell and all. And anyway, why'd he want to do it? The kid stinks, but I'd rather be up there suffering through his soul-spiel than in Parvahr.* The junior fiend shuddered at the thought of Murakh's realm and all its unspeakable horrors.

Then he became aware that he and Raleel were not the only lights among the shadows. A shaft of brightness was there too, a clear light that burned without the sooty, somber glow of demonic spirits. It lanced down towards the deep sources of power, drawing up strength, shining with the force it already had of itself.

The kid! Brazlyp's ember sizzled with mockery. *Scaring up what it takes to toss a few special effects at the rubes, see if that'll wake 'em up. The Red Sea, huh? It's been done, but this might be worth watching. Gotta see how he wrassles it all togeth—*

A growl from the very bones of the earth shook Brazlyp's spirit. The ember hissed and fizzled angrily at the jouncing it took, and so close to home! Not three *yauranis* below lay the gates of Hell itself, the adamantine gateway built to keep the great ills and the great demons in. Only the minor evils could escape: War, death, hate, holocaust. The worst that Hell could hold, Hell still kept close.

Who's the wise guy?

Then he saw Raleel's spirit turn, shoot a hook of crackling fire that clawed into Noel's channeling magic. Demon's power and mortal's sorcery seemed to fuse into a single blazing spearhead that plunged into the earth's own heart, knifing through to the purely physical region where plates of land rocked and drifted atop the molten sea and sometimes . . . touched.

A final word, and the knife hovered above the kitten's belly. The creature squirmed in her hand, now frightened. It mewed and struck at her uselessly, its tiny claws unable to reach any mark, incapable of doing real harm if they did.

It was a scrap of nothing, a rag of hunger and sickness and pain, but still it fought to survive. It hissed defiance of death itself into Melisan's face. One stab of the blade, and there would be an end.

"Oh, the hell with it."

Melisan put the struggling kitten down and instead stabbed her own thumb with the knife. Blood dripped down onto the candle flame.

The night sky screamed with scarlet comets, and the web of the world tore wide.

"And I say to *you*"—Noel pointed vaguely at the back of the mob as the words of his own speech gave him momentum— "that if we are to do any good with this movie, we must be *firm* in our purpose, and *believe* in our cause. And so, like those before us, we may pass through dry shod, as we witness the doubters and the denouncers who oppose us torn asunder, even as the waters do *part!*"

The Red Sea split right down the middle. It made an awfully loud noise for water, and Noel was almost positive he hadn't commanded the ground to shake that way. The platform bucked like a bent saw. The Parthenon crumbled behind him. Plaster dust sent him into a sneezing fit until the stage did another bump-and-grind. He was thrown over the top of his lectern, down among the groundlings.

"Noel!" Lysi screamed his name when the ground gave its first big lurch. She would have run to him, but Lura was there, a hand clamped around her wrist. "Run!" the angel ordered.

"Run? From what? Noel needs me! He—"

Her protest lost them any time for escape they might have had. The waters of the illusory Red Sea surged towards the heavens, twin crests of hungry foam that crashed down onto the shrieking crowd, sparing no one, demon, angel, mortal, or mix. Waves of sea and waves of land lashed against each other as the stars streamed past. The winds roared with the pain of a strange birthing, gusts of salt air echoing with Raleel's laughter.

Then the earth was quiet.

12

California Split

NOEL HELD HIS head to make sure it still had all its component parts. A cloud of plaster dust billowed out of his hair. Dixi damped it down with the same wet cloth she'd been applying to his brow.

"What happened?" he asked.

"An earthquake."

"Oh, my God, not the big—?"

"I don't know what you'd call big," Dixi told him, "but I think we passed Catalina on our way out here. I could be wrong, you know. I was never a whiz at geography."

Noel was on his feet instantly. The light of early day bathed the wrecked set. Cameras swung upside-down from their booms, wires dangling like lianas. The platform lay crumpled, wood and bunting an indistinguishable mass. High above, sea gulls played stand-in roles for the traditional vultures. The shock of the scene blew Dixi's mention of passing Catalina completely out of his mind.

He was alone with a gorgeous blonde amid the aftermath of disaster, and like any normal man, one question burned within him:

"Where is everyone?"

"Getting settled."

"Where? In shelters? Did the Red Cross get here?"

Dixi's expression was hard to interpret. "I think that's one agency we won't be dealing with for some time. No one was hurt, Noel; not really. They're all at the theatre, waiting for Mr. Lee's morning address."

"Theatre? What theatre?"

"Mann's Chinese. We were almost there before Brother

Beau recalled that you hadn't been accounted for. He sent me back to pick you up. It's only a couple of blocks away."

Noel didn't know what to object to first. *Mann's Chinese a couple of blocks away?* Was Dixi crazy? It had taken hours of driving to get to this studio from downtown L.A. And what was that about picking him up, like he was an old coat to be recovered from the Lost and Found? His sense of self-love was almost as injured as his sense of logic.

Dixi took his arm. "Most of the damage is localized at the epicenter, but that's all right. We agreed that the ruins are so much more inspirational. Ooh." Without warning, she staggered against him. Laying a hand to her bosom, she smiled apologetically. "I'm a little dizzy. I haven't felt entirely myself since the quake hit, so would you mind—?"

From the lee of the unearthed root-ball of one of the olive trees, out of hearing range, Lysi watched Noel slip his arm around Dixi's waist. They walked from the ruined agora like the quintessential pair of young lovers.

"I'll kill her."

"How? With a rock?" Lura pulled Lysi well out of Noel's line of sight as he and Dixi stumbled down the road. The angel wiggled her fingers and a chunk of rubble airlifted itself halfway to her hand before stopping dead in midair and falling back down. "And how are *your* powers this morning, dear?"

"I haven't tried . . ." Lysi concentrated on the same rock that Lura had failed to levitate. It wobbled *in situ* but didn't even gain an inch of altitude. "Shoot. What's wrong with me?"

"More important, Lysi, what's wrong with *us?*" asked the angel. She cast worried eyes all around the disaster site. "Whatever forces caused this, they were strong enough to cut a chunk out of reality. I'm not what I was."

"You mean we've turned mortal?"

"No. I think I'd feel that big a difference. But the powers that go with our callings have—well—gone."

"But *why?*"

Lura looked determined. "I don't know, but I'd say we'd better get back to the others and see if they're affected too. Meantime, let's keep to the brush. I don't want to run into your brother when I'm in this condition."

Angel and succubus plunged downhill into the undergrowth, taking their direction from the angle of the sun. The cover of thick scrub didn't last forever. They broke through the branches at a narrow strip of tarred road.

One lane out, the road itself broke off. Lura and Lysi stood at the edge and gazed down at foaming breakers crashing against a sheer cliff face.

Across a relatively narrow expanse of Pacific, the towers of L.A. were backlit by the young sun.

Noel and Dixi stood on the western slope of the same hill Lura and Lysi had descended. The one-time Yalie stared at an imposssible vista.

"No."

"See?" Dixi stepped into the part of guide. "There's a good section of Bel Air over there, and Rodeo Drive, and a fine stretch of Hollywood Boulevard—can you see any of the stars?—and the BLT Ministries HQ, of course, and—"

"It looks like a New Yorker's idea of L.A.!" Noel cried, slapping a hand to his brow to keep it from falling off.

"The person or the magazine?"

"Both. None. One. I don't know. Good Lord, Dixi, is that really Mann's Chinese next to the La Brea tar pits?"

Dixi squinted. "Mmmm, nope. That's Mann's Egyptian. The Chinese is next to the Hollywood Bowl, see? Just a couple of doors down from Frederick's of Hollywood."

Noel sat down on the grass. "What happened?" he croaked. "I got a concussion, right? Did I die from it, or am I still in a coma?"

"Let's hope not," Dixi replied. "I like to think I can still tell the quick from the dead, though nothing's certain these days. And if you were injured, you'd be out of luck. We don't have any hospitals. Also no museums, no schools, no libraries, and no—"

"No water, no electricity, no communication, no food?"

"No way. Come on, I have to get you to the theatre. Mr. Lee doesn't like to be kept waiting."

Inside the theatre, the cast and crew of BLT's first feature film sat in quaking terror. They had been through as much hell as any of them wanted to see for a long time. They gained no confidence from the fact that after a cataclysm of such magnitude, not one of them was injured. They felt no

reassurance in the fact that all the lights and the air conditioning system inside Mann's were working smoothly, or that the
water fountains still ran fresh and clean. Brother Beau and his
assistants had been forced to herd them into this building like
so many sheep, and like sheep smelling wolves on the wind,
they waited.

The houselights dimmed. Someone screamed, but it was a
halfhearted effort, more of a loud gargle. Noel and Dixi came
in just as a spotlight struck center-stage. The curtains parted,
and the big screen filled with "Sometime" Joseph Lee's
beneficent face.

"Now isn't this something, friends?" The familiar voice
laved the audience with waves of tranquillity as warm and
thick as Cream of Wheat. "Isn't this just *something?* Here
you been telling the doubters and the naysayers all around
you 'bout how *we* were the only ones to know the one *true*
path, and they been mocking us and scorning us and saying
how all our offerings just been going down the one hundred
per cent genuine copper plumbing for *nothing,* and what
happens? *What happens?*"

No one knew, so he told them. "We had us a miracle."

Immediately, the televangelist's face was replaced on-screen
with an aerial view of the L.A. area. Just off the coast, not
really past Catalina at all, a new islet rode the tides. A
gigantic pointer thrust through the smog to touch its summit—
the wreckage of the pseudo-Parthenon—scattering the clouds
of curious, disoriented sea gulls wheeling above the fluted
pillars.

"See, friends? Here we are, safe and sound. Out of the
mouths of babes you heard it: the splitting of the Red Sea, of
the sea of *iniquity* that rose up to overcome us, but could not
stand against our flagrant *righteousness!* The wicked are to be
brought low, but were we brought low? Were we? I say unto
you, *no sir!* The earth shook, the very substance of the world
was *torn asunder,* and were we harmed? Was any man,
woman, or child among us hurt?"

Dwayne Knox stood up, intending to testify to the fact that
he'd bitten his tongue when the quake first hit. A glimpse of
the suspicious faces turning towards him made him reconsider
and sit down.

" *'Course* we weren't hurt!" Raleel's voice was everywhere. "Instead, we have had us our *reward,* and I don't mean what's waiting for all of us in the hereafter, no sir! I mean the *here* and *now!* For we are the elect. We are above the common run of humanity for what we believe in, for all we're willing to do to *defend* our beliefs, for how we know just how to handle anybody damfool enough to try convincing us we might be *wrong!* We would not be led astray from our firmness, our fixitude of purpose, and now we shall *reap* what is ours by *right!*"

The image on the screen turned into a closer overview of the islet. The audience gasped to see so many of Los Angeles' most famous attractions all marvelously translated to this small patch of ground. Everything that made the City of Angels into the tourist's Holy Grail was there, most of it within easy walking distance.

A shot of several streets revealed enough Cadillacs, Mercedeses, BMWs and Lincoln Continentals ready to serve the faithful, and to make "walking distance" just a formality of speech.

"Now what more can I say to you, friends?" Raleel was seen full-length, spreading his hands wide. In the background, Brother Beau led a pickup group of singers in "Memories," this being one of the two slow songs they could all get through without hitting a screecher. No one in the audience knew from where the screen projections were originating, but that question didn't make "Sometime" Joseph Lee's latest broadcast any less absorbing.

"Our merits have given us a separate land, a land uncontaminated by the wrongheadedness of our detractors. Anybody got the worm of Doubt a-gnawing at his gizzard 'bout how maybe this wasn't any miracle, just a freak accident, check the evidence: We got us running water, electricity, gas, oil, food, and *not one* computer's gone down yet! If that ain't miraculous, tell me what is?

"Now, I want us to enjoy this gift. I mean really *enjoy* it, not waste time looking it in the mouth . . . less maybe you don't have the *faith* to accept it as your due."

Everyone muttered that his faith was as strong as the next man's; maybe stronger.

Raleel was pleased. "Fine, just fine. I don't want to see any glum faces, I don't want to hear tales 'bout how you're spending a quiet evening at home—and wait'll you see the homes I got for *you!*—and I don't want to hear any talk 'bout how you're not making yourselves happy *any way you like!* Because what have we learned this day, by reason of this miracle? Sugar, I'll tell you: We weren't none of us entire-all free of sin before it happened, now were we?''

Many a shamefaced mumble of assent came from the audience. In the fifth row, Corey Hudson of Haffley took out his wallet and surreptitiously tore up a photo clipped from *Playboy*.

"But if that's so, why were we spared? Because our spirits, friends, are *greater* than what counts for sin among normal folks! Because our being spared was both a measure of our innate goodness, no matter what we do, as well as proof that everything that happens on this earth happens for a reason that men can understand! And if that's so, the way I understand it is we'd be damned ingrates—and I do mean *damned*—if we didn't turn our lives in this new land into living, breathing examples of the above-mentioned principles and our abiding faith therein!''

There was a hush. No one in the audience registered comprehension, although some of the older folks bobbed their heads up and down and sprained their necks trying to act wise.

"Double-talk," Noel said. He turned to Dixi. "What does he mean?"

She answered just as Raleel's voice boomed in to join with hers: "DO WHAT YOU WANT, AND DEVIL TAKE THE HINDMOST!"

In a softer voice, Raleel said, "Now that we're all saved, we are gonna have us some *fun.*"

Corey Hudson of Haffley picked up the scattered bits of his clipping and asked his neighbor where he could get some Scotch tape.

Melisan studied one cloven hoof, then the other. She posed her goat-legs in the style of a pantyhose ad, then whipped her tail with its arrowhead-point around for inspection. The yellow kitten stared at her taloned hands, extending and retracting his own minuscule claws for the sake of comparison.

The transformed woman stood up and teetered wildly until she got the hang of hoof-walking, then lurched into a jacaranda. She clung to the trunk for support.

"Where the blazes am I?" she asked the kitten.

Got me. The reply came in her head.

"Oh, goody. You can talk. Maybe you can tell me how hard I whacked my skull to conjure up *this* pretty little hallucination?" She waved a hoof at him.

Why are you so sure it's not real? You performed the rites of transformation. As for me . . . Doesn't every demon need a familiar with whom to communicate? Maybe it was a package deal.

"It's witches who get familiars."

Sue me. I didn't ask to be cast in this role, although— Melisan thought she heard a mental sigh—*now I don't know how I'm going to be able to get out of it.*

Melisan pushed herself away from the tree and stood steady. She looked down the length of her body, past bare breasts to a hairy belly. Her skin tone had deepened to a ruddy chestnut, and her claws were formidable.

"Transformation, my Aunt Simony! I *never* looked like this when I was first a succubus."

Yeah. You should see your hair. The kitten chuckled.

"My—!" Melisan's hands flew up and woke a knot of very testy serpents. "Not my *hair!*" she moaned.

You wanted to be a succubus again. You didn't specify what kind. You still have a good figure, and your face is the same. A lot of men are willing to overlook unshaven legs, and they do say that the tousled look is in.

"Maybe some styling gel . . . " Melisan considered. The snakes hissed their objections to being spiked, scrunched, or finger-waved. "Oh, shut up," she told them. "I've got my old powers back again—that's the main thing—and if I want, I can turn myself baldheaded. Being a succubus is like riding a bicycle: You never forget how."

Saying this, she attempted to pop a wheelie with her appearance, trying to change herself into something a little less *Wild Kingdom.*

Nothing at all happened.

"What's wrong?" Melisan demanded.

Search me. The kitten wasn't happy.

"Was all that—that spellcasting, a risk of my soul, the iron, blood, and silver—all for nothing? What good can I do if I only *look* like a demon?"

Believe me, I know exactly how you're feeling. The kitten rubbed against her hairy hocks. *But let's feel sorry for our-*

*selves somewhere else. You don't exactly blend into the crowd
now, Melisan.*

Following the kitten's lead, Melisan tottered out of the
trees. She was so intent on cultivating a graceful goat-footed
walk that she never questioned how the kitten came to know
her name.

13

Down and Dirty in
Beverly Hills

DWAYNE KNOX FELT like a burglar, even if he did have the
key to the mansion in his hand. The carved mahogany door
opened noiselessly, admitting him to the Spanish-style foyer
where a tiled fountain leaped and splashed. Air conditioning
countered the heat outdoors. Potted plants with leaves shaped
like spears and feathers and elephants' ears added to the cool,
placid atmosphere.

The girl who appeared from a side doorway, wearing a
frilly French's maid's apron over her suntan, sent the temperature soaring right back up there.

"Uh-oh. Um, I'm sorry, miss. I guess they must've given
me the wrong key down at BLT HQ. I thought this was my
house."

The vision giggled. "Are you Dwayne?" His name became an endearment when she said it. The boy nodded.
"Then there isn't any mistake. I'm your housekeeper, Tivoli."
She wagged a feather duster at him to confirm her appointment. She hadn't been carrying anything a moment ago, and
her costume had no pockets. It barely had any cloth.

"Well, gee, uh, how come you have to do that, Tivoli?
Take care of my house and all? I thought we were all supposed to just sit back and enjoy ourselves."

"Silly." The feather duster tickled Dwayne's chin. It dropped
from Tivoli's hand, but there was no sound of its hitting the

tiles. Dwayne didn't think that was odd. With Tivoli's exquisite body adhering to his, he didn't think at all. Her breath smelled of cinnamon, and she did the most commendably tingling things with her lips on his ear.

If he was too distracted to notice the feather duster's passage into oblivion, he was less apt to mark the unfathomable way in which his housekeeper's hands seemed to be all over his body at once.

Gee, like an octopus or something, he thought, eyes closed in bliss.

For her part, Tivoli was thankful that Dwayne's eyes remained shut. She didn't have eight arms—merely six—but it was so much simpler when a succubus could go about her business in her normal form.

"Now y'see that, Laurabeth?" Avery Kimball remarked to his wife as they watched Dwayne and Tivoli frolic across the screen of their mansion's rear-projection television set. "We was back home, watching that sorta thing, you'd be steaming worse'n a big ol' Indian pudding and marching your ass down to the Seven-'leven to make sure they still didn't have any of that filthy porn stuff on their shelves. But now—" He humped himself back on the down-filled divan and took another swig of Vouvray right from the bottle. "—Now we know we're okay with the Powers that Be, isn't any harm in us watching it for just a little-bitty second longer. Might learn something. Something *never* to do, I mean," he finished, and burped piously.

"Where's this coming from, Ave?" Laurabeth asked, glancing up from painting her toenails orchid pink. On the screen, Tivoli did something very innovative with a potholder and Laurabeth spilled her polish all over the Karastan. She blushed the same shade as the slowly spreading puddle of Estee Lauder's finest.

"Dunno, honey. We don't get any other channels but this'n. Kinda too bad. I miss *Monday Night Football*." The Vouvray paused an inch from Avery's lips. Tivoli was being incredibly creative, now. "Wonder where'n hell they got them a six-armed woman?"

"This is Hollywood, Ave. Nothing you can't get here, for a price. I read so in the *Enquirer*."

"Latest issue?"

"Uh-uh." Laurabeth sounded sad. "Can't find me a supermarket here to save my life. No real need—the pantry's chock full, and so's the fridge—but I surely do miss my reading. Only magazines they got down to Schwab's are the same ones I sweated blood to get out of the Seven-'leven back home. You know, I just kinda picked one up and read it a little. Got some pretty interesting articles . . .'' She wriggled her toes to dry them, then slipped on her shoes. "Well, see you later."

"Where you going?"

"Hank Bevis from down Beaufort way—you remember him from the last big BLT rally we had near the capital?" Avery allowed as he did. "Well, he mentioned to me kinda casual that he's been lusting after me in his heart, and he got assigned the next house over, and so I thought I'd kinda drop in on him and let him do what he wants with me, seeing as how it *is* my duty and proof of my continuing faith, 'cording to Mr. Lee.''

"Give'm my best, honey. Oh, and see if there's a can of Bud in the fridge on your way out?"

"I checked. Nothing but champagne. There's hard stuff in the liquor cabinet."

"Naw, I don't want that. Makes my head ache."

"Maybe not here," Laurabeth suggested. "Maybe now that we're special, it'll be different."

"Honey, the devil hisself can't stand in the way of a hangover. You go on to Hank's place and have yourself a good time, y'hear?"

The man at the big desk didn't have a hangover, but he clutched his head as if he were suffering from the Founding Father of them all. "What else is gone?" he asked the desk blotter.

His aide read a list of L.A. properties and landmarks, fresh off the printer. When he finished, he added, "At least they didn't take Disneyland, sir."

"*They*, Cartwright? Who is this *they* you're accusing of— of—of Grand Theft: City?"

Cartwright looked injured. "How do you want me to phrase it, sir? All of those places are gone. Nothing around the sites was wrecked, or even touched. Nothing but empty land where they used to be. It's very strange."

Another groan broke from Cartwright's superior. "That's

all this city needs, Cartwright: more strangeness. California's the punch-line of enough jokes as is, and when they want a real yock, they mention L.A. Valley Girls! Granola! Hot-tubs! Sunbaked zanies and Kleenex religions! And *I* had to get a job running P.R. for this plastic paradise!" He laid his head down in his arms and sobbed.

"There, there, sir," said Cartwright. "With the new com-puter, we can rewrite and reprint all the brochures in a fraction of the time. There's a real up-side to this whole incident, you know."

"There is?" The P.R. chief sought comfort in Cartwright's surfer-blue eyes.

"For sure. The Big One hit and we didn't fall in the ocean. One shudder, nothing happens but a lump of real estate pulls a Kon-Tiki, and it's kiss my San Andreas Fault all over. California stays *el rock solido.* How's that for Sunnybrook Farm City?"

"But *how* did all those landmarks get transferred with the land-mass?"

"Hey, who knows? 'The fool is insatiable. He devours wisdom in a sauce of questions. The wise man accepts the meal of ungarnished truth set before him and merely browses.' "

"Who said that: Jerry Brown?"

"Nah, my girlfriend. In a previous life, when she used to be Nefertiti. I was a captain of chariots, but I fucked up at Tel-el-Amarna, so she had me lashed to death. She says she's sorry about it now. I'll get on the brochure rewrites." With a toss of his sunbleached hair, he jogged out.

Alone at his desk, the P.R. chief commenced composing a letter of application for a similar post with the North Dakota Bureau of Tourism.

The network news shows covering the bizarre circum-stances of the California quake were all intercepted, over-ruled, and boarded with a jaunty yo-ho-ho by the smiling face of the televangelist known as "Sometime" Joseph Lee. No anchorman or woman was steady enough to do more than gawp at the message beaming from every picture tube in the nation. The theology Mr. Lee outlined wasn't orthodox by anyone's standards, but it all boiled down to the fact that you could deify anything you damned well pleased if you had the clout to back it up.

"Sometime" Joseph Lee's clout was neatly contained in the phrase: *You can't stop us*.

"Now that we got a veritable and *un*refutable proof of our *favored standing* above all the common sinners of this earth, we're not about to get it all messed up by a whole passel of freethinking tourists. And so we do hereby decree and *declare* ourselves to be beyond the reach of your laws even as we are beyond the reach of your poor *and* pitiful moral code. Hey, not to say we ain't *friendly*. Sugar, sure as I'm sitting here, I bet there's plenty more folks still trapped and *fuming* on the mainland who'd fit in real nice with our lifestyle out here. We're not just a new idea, we are from this day forward a whole blamed new *country*, and we're out for blood. Fresh blood. Pioneer blood. Your blood. You got it, we want it, sooooo . . . c'mon DOWN!" Raleel's lips stretched halfway to his ears. "The demonocracy of Los Angeles Caídos wants *you*."

"Did he say 'democracy'?" one reporter asked another.

"Says he's calling it Los Angeles *what*?" a third demanded.

But when they re-ran the videotape they'd made of Raleel's broadcast, it was blank.

"Boss, that was bitchin'!" Brazlyp handed his commander a Planter's Punch as the senior demon entered his private office by the back door. "I watched it on the set here."

"As did all our subjects, Brazlyp."

"How do you know for sure? Our subjects have been kind of *busy* lately, know what I mean, nudge-nudge, wink-wink?"

"I preempted all regular broadcasts of in-house Lechery. I also put a temporary hold on the Lechery itself by calling off the incubi and succubi, and by putting a minor saltpetrification spell into effect on the mortals. No one felt like doing anything except watch TV."

"Gee, boss, the Nielsens could really use a man like you. By the way, can we talk about the scabs?"

"Scabs?"

"The incubi, the succubi, the damned *competition*, man! How come we're up to our alligators in other demons all of a sudden? Poaching on our preserves, muscling in on souls that *I* want to—oops—I mean that *we* ought to keep all to ourselves. What gives?"

"What gives soon, my dear Brazlyp, is . . . the Gate."

The lesser demon's eyelids made a chinking sound when he

blinked. "The Gate? You mean like in the *Helliad? That* Gate, boss?"

Raleel closed his eyes and recited from the demonic epic: " 'Hell below, Hell on Earth, nothing shall impede the birth. Evil past mortal ken, brought forth by the hands of men.' You know the rest. If one nation on earth gives way entirely to the great evils—the evils that will reduce all other mortal sins to mere mischiefs—then the Underlords themselves will feel the way opening for them. Los Angeles Caídos will be that nation. The Gate will open, the path will be clear, and the Lords of Hell will rise to claim a new realm for themselves."

"And for the guys who made it all possible?" Brazlyp said slyly.

"A dukedom. At the very least. Oh, it won't be a long reign the Underlords will have on this world—how could they, when humankind can hardly survive the minor ills Hell's been dishing out all these years?—but it will be a fire that burns short, hot, and bright. And when it burns to ash, there will be other worlds."

"First fiend in space . . ." Brazlyp looked dreamy.

"These incubi and succubi are here on my sufferance, mere migrant workers to be used and dismissed as needed. I have already had word from below. The Underlords approve the audacity of my plan. No help offered, of course—the major demon lords do not concern themselves with the petty karma account—but they are looking my way."

"Uh, boss, if they're perking up over this down home, you think maybe we're gonna draw us some flak from . . . ?" His eyes wandered upward, towards the traditional location of the real competition.

Raleel was devil-may-care about that possibility. "As above, so below; and so above that. We shall have no intervention by any angelic forces worth mentioning. Bush-leaguers, no more. Specifically, I'd expect the traitors who overthrew my sire."

"You sound like you want them to show."

"So I do." The senior demon's mouth twisted. "There's more to this chunk of rock than meets the eye, Brazlyp. It's in essence an outcropping of Parvahr, a region neither Heaven, Hell, Earth nor Limbo which will be my realm soon. Parvahr is no place for the indecisive."

"How's that going to save our heinies from the halo dollies, boss?"

"No ordinary angels, Lura and Atamar. They were demons, once, and Atamar was an angel before that. The mortal world draws them too. They have all the earmarks of Parvahr's captives: a foot in either camp, no choices made because they fear to choose. Oh, yes, I know they have chosen the side of the angels, Brazlyp, but that choice is still relatively fresh. The magic of Parvahr is strong enough to affect them because they have known choice and change so recently. The great mystery of change has its darker side too."

"Wow. Hauling up a hunk of Parvahr like that, gee, it's a wonder you didn't rupture something." Brazlyp got his leader another drink.

"It was a dearly purchased spell, but I did not have to pay the full price. Noel is a Joiner. I never saw one so strong. Link his power to another source and the effects are—well, the effects are all around us right now. His power, my direction, and here we are."

"No kidding? You did all that using *him?*"

"As I shall use him again, when the season comes for the great Gate to open at last."

"Does he know?"

"No. But I'm going to make sure he does." Raleel hit the intercom. "Dixi, honey, send Noel in."

The interview was short. Dixi was making a fresh pot of coffee when Noel stumbled out of "Sometime" Joseph Lee's inner lair, his face ghastly. She hurried forward to support him.

"Noel, what is it? You look awful!"

His teeth clattered slightly as he forced up a smile. "I'd say I look pretty good, for a damned soul."

"Noel Cardiff, you *are not*—"

"I used my magic with evil in my heart, Dixi! I was turning against the man who's done everything to help me, and look what happened! Ingratitude never goes unpunished. This whole cataclysm's all my fault, because I'm still half a demon and I can't do anything good unless Mr. Lee is there to channel my powers for me!"

"What cataclysm? The earthquake? Honey, you're a pretty good sorcerer, but alone you don't have what it takes to make a major move like that. Besides, you were there in the theatre. You heard Mr. Lee go on and on about how this split's one giant step for holykind. He said—''

''Dixi, three men died!'' Noel pulled three crushed and blood-smeared drivers' licenses from his inner breast pocket. He tossed them onto Dixi's desk. She recognized the faces.

''Jim Silver, Conrad Fisk, Ismael Martínez: The cameramen. But how can you be sure they didn't just lose these in the quake? People drop stuff all the time.''

''Mr. Lee showed me other photos in there. Photos of them on the set, lying crushed by fallen quake debris. The quake *I caused!* He won't say a word about it. He wants to protect me from what his followers might do if they knew. And that man—that *saint's* the one I was going to leave?''

Tears streamed from his eyes as Dixi tried to calm him. Noel shook his head and went on about how he'd been led astray, but no more. He would entrust his powers fully to his mentor's directing wisdom, and he'd be damned before he'd question ''Sometime'' Joseph Lee again.

Listening in on the intercom, Raleel whispered, ''Oh, you will, Noel; you will.'' On the desk before him, the photographs of phony dead men airbrushed themselves out of existence.

On a newly formed promontory above the Pacific, a snake-haired demon sat with her goat-legs dangling over the void and a yellow kitten in her lap. She had just traveled all around the islet, futilely seeking escape, and her hooves were killing her.

''Shit,'' she said to the L.A. skyline across the water.

Nicely put, said the kitten.

14

When the Devil Drives

''DO YOU THINK they'll make it?'' Kent asked Atamar.

The angel shaded his eyes and looked across the abyss toward the newly created land called Los Angeles Caídos. His mouth was set. ''I could not.''

"Ah, yes." Kent puffed on his pipe. Rings of sweet, bluish smoke rose into the air. Breezes from the Pacific scattered them with little puffs of salty spray. "Frightfully sorry about that, old man. Ever happen to learn why it should be so?"

"No." Atamar clenched his fists in anger and rounded on Kent. "How can you be so calm, so cursed *analytical* at a time like this? We still haven't found Melisan. For all you know, she's over there, in Raleel's power. Do you know what he'd do to her? He's Murakh's son!"

"So he is." Kent remained unflapped.

"Have you stopped caring, then? Are you stone?"

"Atamar, I know you're upset about Lura, but 'are you stone'? Great Scot, man, I'd view it as a personal favor if you'd reserve the Byronic posturings for another day. They complement a velvet cape better than chinos, in any case. Of course I care. I don't know where my wife is, which is bad, and I do know that Noel is most assuredly over there, in Raleel's new realm, which is worse. Moreover, so is your mate. Now, you've tried how many times to reach the isle?"

"Six." The angel shoved his hands into his pockets. "Every time I try to fly across the water, I feel my powers draining from me. There's something uncanny about that isle—uncanny and familiar. I turned back before I fell into the ocean. I'm a miserable coward."

"Rather not. Robert the Bruce's spider notwithstanding, I'd say you've given it a fair go. No sense being a bloody fool about it. Ergo, my feathered friend, if your powers desert on approaching yonder isle, we may assume that your mate's have fled in similar fashion. We are thrown back upon other remedies than angelic intervention, and I know that I always think best when in a calm frame of mind."

"How you can stay calm—"

"I wrote, produced, and narrated the in-depth *History of Cricket* for PBS. Better than Novocaine for erasing the nerves. Do attempt to calm yourself too. Your powers of detached observation coupled with mine might give us some useful information at this point. If those young chaps down there succeed, we must pay attention and note how they manage it. And if they fail, we shall have learned from their mistakes."

The gentleman of PBS finished his smoke and knocked dottle from his pipe into the sea-filled chasm. They were standing on what had been the San Diego Freeway, in happier times. The recent upheaval had not done a lot of damage to private property, aside from appropriating certain tracts outright, but it had played sweet hob with the transportation system. Those roads and streets still intact did not always take the driver to his expected destination. Aerial reconnaissance revealed more of the quake's effects than the mere filching of Frederick's of Hollywood.

A little to the north of where Kent and Atamar kept their vigil, the land had not broken off quite so violently. There were cliffs, but there was a beach at their feet. It was this beach that drew the attention of man and angel. Swarming across the sand were a host of aggressively healthy, superbly bronzed young men and women. Their smiles were so many miniature heliographs, and the churning colors of their swimsuits as they jogged towards the water looked like a parrot orgy.

Nearly all of them carried surfboards. It was every winecooler ad's Valhalla.

"They're nuts," the angel opined.

"They are mad, but not in that sense. While Raleel was juggling real estate around here, he should never have swamped Santa Monica."

"He only got the beach."

"The nearest beach to this city with any decent surfing." Kent got down on his stomach and observed the milling herd of golden youth. "No one minded when Marina del Rey took up some elbow room in Oxnard. No one uttered a peep when the airport went wandering into the San Gabriel mountains. They still aren't certain of what's become of Venice, but by all that's holy, it never pays to piddle in someone else's playground."

Down below, the surfers were forming up into orderly rows. Farther back from the sea stood a cobbled-up grandstand filled with indignant spectators, all expensively dressed. A lady of the media was passing among them with a hand microphone. There were more than a few faces in that crowd recognizable to anyone with the price of movie tickets. Those unwise enough to appear without their bodyguards were swiftly pounced upon by the foxhound of the Fourth Estate.

Her first victim was a craggy monument to rampant machismo, his eyes fixed in a perpetual squint as if from riding off into one sunset too many. To him she put the question, "Could you tell us what's happening here?"

"Yeah."

After a polite wait, the reporter rephrased the question. "Who are those people and what are they doing?"

"Surfers, ma'am. Gonna fix things. Sure's hell looks like nobody else can. Planes can't fly over. Coast Guard cruisers get turned away with extreme prejudice. No way to know whether they're receiving our radio and television signals, but we're getting theirs."

"But how can a bunch of surfers fix—?"

The reporter's arm was yanked back by a lank-haired youth wearing cutoffs and a Nirvana-bound expression. "Hey, dude, I mean, we're gonna, you know, *fix* things over there. I mean, first we gotta get over there, you know. Nobody's been able to do it so far, so it's like, you know, up to us, dude. A couple of small craft got over, full of those religious nutcakes that Gonzo Joseph Lee invited last time he was on the tube, but big ships can't make it. So we're gonna do it on our boards, 'cause they're plenty small, catch some tasty waves out there and find somebody to talk to, and then, like, if we *talk* to those dudes, maybe they'll tell us what's going down with them and then we could, like, you know, get them to chill out and put it all *back*, dude."

"Just by talking to them?" The reporter didn't bother to hide her skepticism.

"Hey, wow, whattaya want us to do, dude? Go catch a wave over to there with a couple M-16's strapped on our backs, maybe a coupla flame throwers? I mean, major uncool."

There was a momentary stir in the grandstand crowd as a short, over-muscled man with a prizefighter's face pushed his way to the front and whispered urgently in the young spokesman's ear. The surfer looked appalled.

"No *way*, dude. We don't *do* exploding arrows. *Bogus*." To the reporter he said, "Hey, trust us. It'll be awesome."

"It better be." A young woman whose platinum hair matched her mink spoke up between snaps of bubble gum. "We're paying you dorks enough to try this, y'know?"

The reporter started towards her, but caught sight of her escort and thought better of it. However, the lady wanted to be heard and photographed, for once, so the mink mountain came to Mohammed.

She wrested the mike from the reporter's hand and held it with professional élan. "I'd just like to say one thing, O.K.?

A lot of people would've gone to pieces if they went to sleep in their own beds, for once, and woke up in Griffith Park, but we didn't. I mean, so I had a little trouble catching a cab out to my other place in Malibu for a change of clothes, y'know, but I didn't fall *apart* or anything.''

She doffed the mink to reveal the lace-camisoled evidence that she was still in one piece. "I think I speak for all of us here today when I say we really grew from this experience, kinda. There's a whole lot being said about the homeless in America, and now all of a sudden when somebody just reaches in and *steals* some more homes—*our* homes—nobody says a word about it! All you hear is 'Thank God they left the Rose Bowl' and 'Thank God they didn't get Spielberg!' I mean, I always thought rich and poor got equal treatment in America, y'know? But has anybody offered us a nice hotel room since we lost our homes? Uh-*uh!* So I'd just like to say that I'm gonna donate the proceeds of my next movie to aid the homeless poor, and the same goes for the income from my next video to cover the lodging expenses of all my good friends from Bel Air who got shafted in this mess, O.K.?''

"Excuse me"—the reporter grabbed back her mike—"but don't you think it might be more equitable if you did it the other way ar—"

The leather-jacketed young man in the mink's shadow jabbed out a fist at the reporter, who took it as a warning shot across her bow and jumped out of range.

"Isn't he wonderful?" the mink demanded as she hugged her knight. "*Really* liberated; treats men and women the same." She got a growl and a snort in reply from Galahad.

Now the moment had come. The leader of the fleet scoped out the waves, tested the wind, scanned the sky, and gave the signal to hit the water: "BANZAI!"

Shoal after shoal of boards thundered into the surf. Foam churned up all around them as the determined dudes and dudettes paddled farther and ever farther out. They passed the breakwater, where a deceptively calm patch of Pacific lay midway between the mainland shore and the islet. Beyond, the waves did the oceanographically impossible: They broke in a counter-tidewise direction on the islet's shores as well as on the mainland.

The first line of boards drew up in parallel ranks in the calm water, their riders up. Hands stretched out from board to board, touched, linked. The islet-bound waves humped up under them, began to bear them towards the new land. As they prepared to ride the surf in together, the next row got into position, and the next. Properly spaced, they would form a veritable bridge of boards, and whatever spells kept large craft off the isle would hopefully wash right through their ranks to no effect.

In the executive suite of the BLT Ministries building, a talon touched the VIEW control on the world's only VCR-equipped crystal ball. Someone laughed, and dispatched a very commonplace sort of spell.

Seven feet out from the islet's beach, a comber the height of the purloined Hollywood Bowl reared up over the heads of the approaching surfers. They saw it coming, and instinct broke all their discipline, fractured their cool. They dropped hands, turned their boards around, and got ready to ride or die. The ranks behind them saw the monster wave too, and they lost no time in doing a fast reverse.

Some of them were quick enough to get out of the way.

When the wave hit the mainland beach, it sloshed surfers and surfboards all the way up to the grandstand. There wasn't a dry eye in the house, and both the platinum mink and its owner looked like drowned cocker spaniels. Hermit crabs and grunion were found in all the best places for weeks after, uninvited.

To the press, the surfers' spokesdude simply said: "We shot the pipe and it shot back. Bummer."

"Well, Kent, what did we learn from that?" Atamar demanded.

"That we shall have to find another route."

"Not by air, not by sea. Over land's impossible."

Kent got to his feet and reloaded his pipe. "Not when you've the makings of a miracle."

"But I *can't* perform miracles!" Quintus protested, pacing back and forth before the sarcophagus. The museum was deserted, closed for the duration of the declared state of emergency. Faith had no trouble getting in, in her official capacity, and she admitted Don and Kent without drawing on Quintus' powers. Atamar let himself in.

"You've been staying here undetected all along," Kent pointed out. "Doesn't that qualify?"

"Your son can do the same, and he is no saint."

"Well, I know the boy's sown a few wild oats, but—"

"You're the saint, Quintus. Saints do miracles all the time!" Don couldn't understand why the ancient Roman was being so persnickety.

"It's not that easy. I can do some things that aren't wholly natural, but if I could do miracles, would I have folded so abysmally on that hideous television show?"

"But you're a *saint!*" Don thought that saying the same thing enough times could change anything, a delusion carried over from his days as a poor-but-optimistic Hollywood newcomer with only one mantra to his name.

"Am I?" Quintus turned away from all of them. He could not bear the weight of so many eyes, all waiting for him to make everything well again. It had been like that in the desert. The monks had always come to him, demanding instant answers, healings, guarantees of salvation. *If I do this for God, He will do that for me. Won't He?* Won't *He?* He had tried to put them off, but they remained stubborn, insisting that he had the power and was only being selfish with it.

People never change, Quintus thought. *They come to that Lee creature for just the same things, only he gives them exactly what they want, whether it's possible or not. They come away from him smug, stuffed with promises like spoiled children are stuffed with sweetmeats; but they remain empty inside.*

"Am I a saint?" he repeated, looking at Atamar. "You would know."

The angel looked uncomfortable. "There's so much of Heaven and its workings that I don't yet know . . ."

"There you have it! Even an angel can not assign me a place in the great scheme. I was never canonized. No one has ever called me Saint Quintus with anything close to authority. All of my so-called miracles are unsubstantiated. Where does that leave me?"

"Where does that leave us?" Faith asked.

Atamar had no ready answers.

Quintus rested both hands on the sarcophagus and regarded the portrait on the lid. "Ambrosius," he said. "So this was your end, a death among your mysterious Alexandrian relations. You could help us. You always had more answers than questions. You could *prove* so many things with clever words—

things that I only believed without seeking proof. Your mind blazed so bright, leaving my poor flicker of faith in shadow. You always knew what to do in a crisis.'' He sighed. ''You ought to be here with me now.''

Faith yelped. Kent's pipe hit the floor. Don gurgled. Even Atamar lost control enough to flash into his fully angelic state.

''*Ave*, Quintus,'' said Ambrosius Minimus, palm up in the fashion of all the better senatorial statues. ''We who have already died salute thee.''

15

Valley Boys

''DON, MIRACLES ARE not magic.'' Faith felt as if she'd explained the same thing for the fiftieth time.

''But he brought this guy back! Look! There he is, standing right next to you!'' Don pointed wildly at Ambrosius. Tall and slender, the returned chronicler of Quintus' life viewed the jabbering contemporary man with a philosopher's impartial eye.

''I did, didn't I?'' Quintus sounded pleased with himself, though he quickly retreated to a more acceptable attitude of humility. ''That is, I was allowed to be the instrument.''

''You can be a five-piece jazz combo and it still won't change the facts,'' Don squawked. ''You *did* it! You can do *anything!*''

''Perhaps he can,'' Atamar said. ''But not with any reliability. We have already had the proof of that.''

''Why not?''

Kent decided to illuminate matters in Don's native tongue. ''You see, lad, magic is like room service at L'Ermitage, whereas miracle is more like getting an Oscar. It only comes to you when—''

"I assume I was brought here for a reason?" Ambrosius' words were curt and cutting. "Or is my reincarnation solely for argument's sake?"

"Oh, my dear friend Ambrosius, not at all, not at all. How could you think that I would subject you to such—?" Quintus went into a tizzy of oaths and assurances to his old companion, patting the younger man's tunic and toga until a cloud of fine white dust rose from the fabric.

Suddenly, Quintus grasped the material between thumb and forefinger, feeling the texture closely. "Ambrosius," he said, "this is somewhat finer array than you used to wear in the desert."

"My Alexandrian relations' doing, not mine." The younger man wore a sardonic smile as he too rubbed the scarlet-embroidered *clavi* bordering his tunic. "Silk and linen, and the banded toga of a Roman citizen; they sent me to the Otherworld in a style unbecoming my desires, if not my station. Even this sarcophagus"—he patted the stone box like a faithful war horse—"was not my idea of the proper conveyance to take a man to meet his Maker."

"But Ambrosius, when I died, didn't you—?"

"—seal you in such a grand lump of stone too? Yes, I did that. You merited it, Master. It would not do to have the desert devour your remains as if you were an ordinary man. What should your petitioners have done for relics?"

"Relics?" Don's ears pricked up. "Aha! See? I knew it! I said so. He *is* a saint!" In a more cautious manner he sidled up to Ambrosius and inquired, "Are you one, too?"

"Nonsense!" Faith Schleppey wedged herself between the two returnees and did her best to take over. She poked a finger at Ambrosius' chest and declared, "This man is Ambrosius Minimus, author of the *Life of Quintus Pilaster*. His own life isn't such an open book."

"Scroll." A cold glint lit Ambrosius' eye. Of Quintus he asked, "Who is this person?"

Faith would not be deterred. "When I brought this sarcophagus to the States, it was the big mystery item of the exhibit. The hieroglyphs go on at great length about how good you were in life and best wishes in your new location, but they don't tell a single concrete thing about you; not even your name!"

"How politic of them."

"Now Quintus recognizes you from your portrait, and here you are, but even he doesn't know you; not really."

"Why, I certainly do," Quintus protested. "Ambrosius was my right-hand man all those years in the desert. He—"

"If you had read the *Life of Quintus*, you would know that in the *prolegomenon* your pal drops some pret-ty complex hints that he's only adopted Ambrosius Minimus as an alias."

"Well, I didn't," Quintus responded. "I was dead."

"Why do we waste time debating my identity?" Ambrosius cast off his toga. "Or my mode of dress? You did not snatch me from sleep for that."

"Actually, old fellow, it's your mind we were after, not your body," Kent said. He extended his hand in greeting. "Awfully glad to meet you. We have a good deal in common."

"Do we?" The young man's swarthy features were basically Roman, modified by the finer lines of Greek blood and with hints of a still more exotic heritage. In combination, these made his supercilious stare devastating.

"Rather." Kent Cardiff declined to be devastated. "Melisan."

Ambrosius' face drained of all color except for two dusky red spots high on his cheekbones. With shaking hand, he made the sign of the cross in the air between them and in trembling Latin-salted syllables urged Kent to return to the fiery pit which had spawned him.

"Good Lord, man, that's no way to speak about Ontario!"

"This is no demon, Ambrosius." Quintus touched his friend's tunic softly. "Nor—nor is your Melisan, anymore."

A look of shame melted Ambrosius' haughty bearing. "Master, you know that she and I . . . ?"

"I knew then." Quintus shrugged. "Or I suspected. She disguised herself as one of us, did she not? Brother Parvulus, I think she called herself. It was not the last time an outer shell of holiness held a different sort of nut within. We were unduly beset by demons in those days, a horde, a swarm, a veritable plague of fiends."

"There were only five of us," Atamar said. "Lura, Melisan, Gerial, Horgist, and me. Don't exaggerate."

Now Ambrosius became fully aware of the angel. Atamar's glory had burst into full brilliance with the monk's return to life, but mundanity dimmed the resplendence almost at once, to say nothing of the effects of L.A. smog. Still, he was an awe-inspiring presence, and a sight that brought Ambrosius to his knees.

"Blessed One, how can you claim to have pacted with the demons that beset us?"

"Not that name again!" Atamar made a disgusted sound and encouraged Ambrosius up with a firm tug. "I am Atamar. Formerly of the demon-plague, presently employed elsewhere."

"Oh, I am doomed!" Ambrosius averted his eyes from the angel. "Now at least I know why I have passed the centuries in sleep, rather than in the company of the blessed! Punishment for the sins of my flesh, and so the flesh remained intact to be my burden again!"

"What's with him?" Don asked Faith.

The archeologist grew thoughtful. "What he's saying about the flesh remaining intact? He's right. When I put this exhibit together, he was the star—a mysterious sarcophagus in a unique Egypto-Roman style. But what was more amazing, the remains had been embalmed by a process we thought lost ages before Ambrosius died. His body was preserved to an astonishing degree." She gave the tall young monk an appreciative once-over. "Still is."

Ambrosius overheard her, and snapped out of his lapse of self-pity. "Woman, my flesh is not your concern, preserved or otherwise!"

"Scientific curiosity." Faith played innocent.

"By such curiosity was all mankind brought low! It was Eve who tasted first of the forbidden fruit, and then did deceive Adam so that he followed her on the path to sin!"

"Which proves," Faith replied calmly, "that it took the best Hell had to offer to outsmart a woman, but it only took one woman to outsmart a man."

Before the discussion could heat further, Atamar came between them. "Quintus told us that you were always the brains of the outfit, Ambrosius. You were brought back for a purpose: to help us now."

Ambrosius listened as the angel lay their predicament before him. When Atamar was done, Ambrosius said, "Why don't you ask the woman? Surely she could outsmart any poor solution I might offer."

"Maybe." Faith showed her teeth. "Especially since you couldn't outsmart your cousin Berenice and that plate of poisoned quail she fed you." Over the monk's harsh exclamation of surprise she added, "If your name wasn't carved on the box, hers was, over and over again, saying how much she was going to miss her darling cousin, light of her eyes, breath of her nostrils, marrow of her bones, something of her large intestine. I don't know art, but I know guilt when I smell it. The tests confirmed my hypothesis.''

"What tests?'' Ambrosius' eyes were iron.

"On the body.'' Faith waved at the sarcophagus. "There were still traces of arsenical poisoning. It's standard research procedure to—''

"*You profaned my body with your touch, woman?*'' There were no limits to Ambrosius' wrath. "In all my life since I came to conscious manhood, no woman ever dared so much!''

Coughing into his hand, Kent said, "Aren't you forgetting someone, old boy?''

"Melisan does not count.'' Ambrosius folded his arms. "She was not a woman, but a fiend.''

"Well, she's a woman now, and she needs your help. More on the mark, our son does. Will you pitch in like a good fella? We'd be most awfully grateful, really.''

"Your son?'' There was a shade of green in the young monk's eye now. "Yours and hers?''

"Oh, come along, old man, there's such a thing as carrying the torch a step too far, what? You'd been dead for ages before I touched the girl.''

Ambrosius measured the length of the hall several times, deep in conference with his own thoughts. He stopped in his progress only to glower at Faith each time he passed her. At length he stopped, took a noble stance and announced, "I have decided. For Melisan's sake, and to expiate my past impieties, I will help you.''

"Whoopee,'' slipped out of the corner of Faith's mouth and into Don's ear.

"Shhh!'' the producer hissed back. "Don't get him mad. I bet he's a saint too, no matter what he says. You want someone sore at you who can do that kind of stuff?'' Don turned a fawning look, usually reserved for investors, on Ambrosius and meekly asked, "And how will you do that, Your Sanctity?''

Still with the same gallant resolve, Ambrosius answered, "I don't know.''

"Oh, for—!'' Atamar smacked a peal of thunder out of the sarcophagus lid, then dropped to the floor in a sulky squat. His angelic attire fled, replaced by jeans and a Hawaiian shirt.

"But I do know where I would seek help," the young monk continued. "Where there is ignorance, demons revel. Where there is wisdom, demons flee. Thus, since you tell me otherworldly knowledge fails in this case, I would seek my answer at the greatest source of mortal wisdom."

"You have William F. Buckley Jr.'s phone number?" Faith gasped. Don gave her a vicious nudge.

"That name is air to me," Ambrosius snapped. "I speak of ageless wisdom. I mean none other than him whose learning allowed him to converse with angels, whose knowledge bound djinn and demons with a word of power: Solomon."

Quintus' hands came together as if in prayer. "Ambrosius, you can't mean that. I brought you back from death, but the wisest man of all—Solomon the King—I don't think I could muster enough might to resurrect him as well."

"If you brought me to wakefulness, you can wake him," Ambrosius maintained. "By the ancient scrolls I once studied in my *dear* cousin Berenice's villa, I know that the son of David is no more truly dead than I. For in death the soul departs the body, but in the sleep that comes to some it hovers nigh, awaiting whatever unfathomable purpose has kept it from true rest."

"What does he mean?" Faith bristled. "Dead is dead."

Atamar begged to differ. "You mortals and your dichotomies! Dead and living, good and evil, Heaven and Hell, all these are your inviolable either-ors. Yet you yourselves come up with more varieties of Coca-Cola than there were plagues in Egypt. I'm surprised at you, Faith. You, who walked the darkest paths of Parvahr, Murakh's realm, which is neither Heaven nor Hell."

Faith remembered that journey, and it gave her a little *frisson* of dread just thinking about the weird sights she had seen. Chief of these was a diner of the old Art Deco dogwagon design, an aluminum-and-chrome supernatural feedbag patronized by deadbeat abominations and run by a bizarre and beautiful being who called himself Honest Ariel.

"All right," she conceded. "Solomon's not dead, just sleeping, to quote a Victorian gravestone. So how do we get him here and wake him up?"

"We do not. His slumber is sacred, the place of it blessed." Atamar traced curlicues of vision on the air. They twined themselves into a scene of ineffable tranquillity, a seeing that all present shared. Tiers of snowy mist formed, their crests bright and sweet with banks of flowers. Poplar trees and cedars brushed a sky too blue to lie near the earth. Robed figures passed along paths whose gravel shone with the soft light of crushed pearl, their hands ever busy tending to the great marble tombs set back amid groves of blossoming apple trees, hedges of lilac bloom.

"It is called the Valley of Cloud, where heroes and wise men slumber, awaiting the day that their spirits shall be needed on earth again. There are treasures untold in the tombs of that place, tokens of power beyond belief. Blessed are the guardians of that sweet valley who keep their bonded word to ward and protect the sleepers; cursed the ones who violate their oath, tempted by greed. You knew one such."

"Gerial." Faith remembered the blue demon well. "But—he was forgiven because he helped us, wasn't he?"

"So he was." Atamar finished tracing the outline of one last poplar tree against a soft sunrise glow. He dropped his hand, but the vision remained. The Valley of Cloud was all around them, and the museum was gone.

"I always expected Heaven to be shinier," Don commented for Faith's ears alone. "You know, like a real estate ad."

"You heard the man. This isn't Heaven." She looked around, slowly inhaling the golden tapestry of scents, feeling the satiny touch of spicy breezes, letting the all-pervading glow of the Valley of Cloud seep through her skin.

Beside her, Don exhaled a longing sigh. "If it's not, then I'm sure going to try to make it to the real place when I die. If it's like everything else I do, I'll come in second-best. In this case, that's not bad."

The five visitors stood at the foot of a flight of rose-veined stone steps. Terraces of flowering cloud seemed to rise above them and fall away below them forever. A fountain of violet waters played on the terrace at the top of the stairs. In the near distance, Faith could just catch sight of one of the great tombs, of classic Greek proportions and design, with a frieze of horses galloping around it.

"Alexander's," a familiar voice behind her said. "We couldn't do anything about his keeping Bucephalus here with him, so the ornamentation was the least we could do."

"Gerial!" Faith wheeled and threw her arms around the cowled figure. His hood fell off under her enthusiastic assault and the one-time demon welcomed her warmly.

Eventually, Faith broke their embrace and considered her old pal at arm's length. "It's weird. I'm used to thinking of you blue."

"With tusks," Gerial amended. "And a tail, and filthy habits. You've grown up too, Faith. But who are your friends and what are you doing here? You never struck me as the heroic type."

"You've been out of touch. I'm supposed to sleep inside a ring of fire up here and to be awakened only when the earth is in danger of being overrun by Wagnerian opera."

Atamar gently moved Faith to one side. "The wise sleep here, my dear, not the wise guys. Gerial, have you nothing to say to me? How soon they forget."

"*Atamar!*" Gerial pounded his erstwhile commander on the back lustily enough to dislodge an entire trout skeleton. "Hey, it's been too long!"

"An eternity."

"So how's Lura? Kent! I didn't see you back there, behind that beanpole in the toga. Come here, you old PBS sonuvagun. How's Melisan? Mortality treating her all right? And the kid?"

"Frankly, Gerial, that's what brings us—"

"And who're those guys?" He indicated Don, Quintus, and Ambrosius. "They look like people I ought to know. Now, don't tell me . . ." He pinched the bridge of his nose in thought.

"I am Quintus Pilaster and this is Ambrosius Minimus. You attempted to debauch our monastic community over a millennium and a half ago."

"Donald Swann." The producer stuck out a hand. "I think you tried debauching me once, too. Unless it was one of the other demons."

Gerial nearly turned blue all over again. "Sshhhh! Not so loud. If my superior ever heard—"

"Doesn't he know what you were?" Atamar asked.

"All he knows is that I was a guardian of the Valley relieved of duty for a time on account of disciplinary problems. No one told him I was a—a—the D-word. You know these bureaucratic types. Give them one scrap of scandal to hold over your head and they use it forever. I'd be put to work scraping barnacles off King Arthur's funeral barge for centuries!''

"We're here about a different king," said the angel, and he elucidated.

Gerial's complexion went through a number of fascinating color shifts. He was shaking his head vigorously in the negative long before Atamar ended his tale. "No. Uh-uh. I can't. Not a hope. Mucking around with the tombs is what got me thrown out of here in the first place!"

"But that was for personal gain. This would be to help souls in peril, all aboveboard.''

"Get yourself another boy.''

Atamar turned to the others. "This may take some time. Why don't you wander around for a bit? I might be able to persuade him better if we're alone.''

"DON'T TOUCH ANYTHING!'' Gerial's shout followed Faith and Kent all the way to the top of the rose-veined stairs.

"Remarkable how the vista changes from up here," Kent said, resting his hand on the lip of the violet fountain. The waters spurted from the mouths of rampant lion cubs into a basin supported on the horns of five golden rams. Faith stood beside him, watching the ripples form over her reflection.

Kent sighed. "I wish Marguerite were here. She always did like gardens.''

The ripples meshed. A face not Faith's appeared in the water as she watched. Snakes curled about its ears, and a yellow kitten snuggled beneath its chin. Apart from the serpents and the scarlet skin, it was recognizable.

Faith's shriek brought everyone running.

"In there! In the basin!''

"Mercy on us, what manner of monster is that?'' Quintus cried, crossing himself. "How did such an evil vision enter this blessed spot?''

"All I said was how much Marguerite would enjoy seeing the Valley, and that—that—_that_ appeared.'' Kent pointed at the face in the water.

"Marguerite?''

"Melisan's mortal name,'' Atamar explained to Gerial.

The guardian gripped the basin's lip and sank to his knees with a groan. "This is a pool of Sight. The name calls up the vision.''

"Then that thing in there is my wife?" Kent was incredulous. "Impossible! How could it be?"

"The great mystery of change," Faith spoke low. "I don't like it. Oh, don't any of you *see?* She's found some way to turn herself back into a demon!"

"My books," Don mumbled, then hoped no one had heard.

"She wants to fight fire with fire, meet Raleel in a fair fight for Noel's soul!"

"If this Raleel is Murakh's son, as you tell me," Gerial said, "there won't be anything fair about it."

"Marguerite . . ." Kent reached out to touch the image on the water, and shattered it. Gerial saw his tears.

"That does it!" he announced. "Follow me."

They did so, single file, climbing up to the next terrace, partway down again to a sunken garden, through an alley of cypress trees, over a bamboo bridge, until at last they stood in the shadow of a grand building. It was squarely constructed, piled up of that dawn-tinged rock called Jerusalem stone. The bronze-banded cedar portals stood open, revealing the single huge chamber within.

Light from twelve tall, narrow windows in an upper dome lanced down to form a star whose center was a golden throne. Asleep, his body robed with Tyrian purple, King Solomon kept the state of ages.

16

Wise Guys

THE SIX SEEKERS and their guide Gerial stood outside the tomb of Solomon, too awestruck to take a single step over the threshold. The lines of sunlight from the dome above now picked out the gems set into the floor, a mosaic of rare and precious stones, the ransom of a nation underfoot.

The walls were thick, at least the arm's reach of a full-grown man, and the open doorway formed a massive arch that dwarfed all human callers. Carved into the archway's stone were huge figures of grotesques, beings part human and part madness. All were executed in high-relief, with a relentless attention to detail. A cloud-cast shadow passing over one of these almost gave it the illusion of . . .

"It moved!" Don shouted, leaping onto Quintus' back. The saint in turn stumbled into Ambrosius, who was shoved up against Faith. She did not seem to mind.

Gerial's finger flew to his lips for silence. "Of course it moved," he hissed. "A djinni needs to stretch his muscles every fifty years or so."

"A djinni?" Cringing, Don braved a second look at the carving. It rolled its eyes back at him, and stone lips formed the sound *Boo*.

"One of King Solomon's many captives. The walls crawl with them. Look around and you'll see." With a wave of his hand, Gerial gave them carte blanche to the tomb. "Only *don't touch anything*. And keep it quiet. There's a formal procedure for waking our honored guests and I don't want any of you guys jumping the gun."

They all glanced about, timidly at first. Their eyes became accustomed to the shadowy archway, the dim interior, and now they could see that carvings lined all the walls of Solomon's tomb. Sprites and devils of every description were caught in stone, colored like the rosy rock that held them, but still alive. Some of them struggled mightily, a flutter of bat wings, a closely confined lashing of tails. Some had resigned themselves to their eternal fate. Only their eyes moved from time to time, a glitter in the darkness.

Curiosity overcame any hesitation once the visitors saw that the stone-caught demons were securely pent. As the mortals, living and re-living, strolled around the tomb's inner perimeter to study Solomon's captives up close, Atamar spoke to Gerial. "What's all this about don't touch, keep quiet, wait for the ceremonial waking? We don't have time for a lot of formalities."

"You'll have to make time." Gerial straightened his shoulders and made a banker's sound in his throat. "We have our policies in the Valley of Cloud, and we adhere to them."

"I don't recall you being this prissy when we were in the desert together."

"I don't recall smelling you this *purty* then either."

"So I don't reek of dung any more. Strong talk and cheap shots"—the angel's lips curved into a lazy smile—"from someone who used to read *Das Kapital* on the Q.T."

Gerial spluttered. "Shush up, Atamar, for pity's sake! You really want to get me in trouble?"

The angel shrugged, his hands in his jeans' pockets. "You cut the rigmarole about waking Solomon and the only Marx I'll mention will be Groucho."

"Harpo, knowing you. O.K., you win." Gerial raised his voice and called, "Attention, everybody!"

The rest of the party joined the two former demons before Solomon's golden throne. They all looked badly shaken, Don the worst of all.

"The fiends chill my bones, even though I know they are imprisoned," Quintus said, palms pressed together. "Why would David's son surround himself with such horrible sights?"

"He keeps them near against the day that he might need to call upon their services in a good cause," Gerial replied. "Solomon used his knowledge to confine many evil spirits. These are but those in whose capture he felt the greatest satisfaction."

"Rather like lepidoptery, what?" Kent remarked. "Butterflies on pins and all that."

"A FOOL UTTERS ALL HIS MIND." The words resounded from the great dome. "BUTTERFLIES, INDEED!"

"He's awake." Gerial huddled closer to Atamar. "We woke him without any ceremony at all—with an insult! Oh boy, I'm going to catch He—Helicarnassus."

Solomon's voice was a swell of sound engulfing them. "BE NOT AFRAID OF SUDDEN FEAR. NAY, FEAR NOT, FAITHFUL GUARDIAN. I KNOW THEIR PURPOSE. I WELCOME THEIR QUEST."

Hesitantly, Kent took a step nearer the throne. The king's eyes were closed. His hair was the clean gray of good steel, his delicately curled beard falling over his chest like the rush of spring-freed streams. When his voice was heard, his lips never moved, and yet it was a human voice they all heard, not a whisper in the mind.

"I say, Your Majesty, I do apologize most profusely for that comment on lepidoptery. Uncalled for. Frightfully down on myself for it."

A torrent of warm chuckles tumbled from the apex of the dome. "REBUKE A WISE MAN, AND HE WILL LOVE YOU. SO IT IS."

Quintus knelt before the sleeper. "Wise One, you say you know our purpose here. Yet we have not spoken of it. How can that be?"

"THE HEARING EAR AND THE SEEING EYE, THE LORD HAS MADE BOTH OF THEM. HOW MUCH MORE, THEREFORE, SHALL THE SPIRIT SEE, HEAR, AND KNOW, THE SPIRIT WHICH IS THE TRUE PERFECTION OF ALL HIS WORKS? YOUR THOUGHTS TELL ALL. I WILL HELP YOU."

A blue star appeared at eye-level in the sunlit air between Kent and Solomon. It spun there, twinkling, while the visitors gaped at its beauty.

"THE RIGHTEOUS ARE BOLD AS A LION. TAKE IT AND FEAR NOT. IT WILL BE YOUR PROTECTION AS YOU TRAVEL IN UNHOLY REALMS, BUT IN THE END IT WILL SUFFICE TO BRING YOU TO YOUR DESTINATION."

Despite the king's soft words, no one moved to touch the star, though it was small enough for a man's hand to close over.

"TAKE IT, TAKE IT," Solomon urged. "IT WILL NOT HARM YOU, BUT WILL ANSWER YOUR NEED. IF YOU FAINT IN THE DAY OF ADVERSITY, YOUR STRENGTH IS SMALL."

Ambrosius was the only one who dared to step forward and reach for the star. His touch turned light to substance, and when his grasping fingers opened he held a talisman of silver and sapphire in his hand.

"Majesty, our thanks. How must we use this precious gift?"

"THE SLOTHFUL MAN SAYS, THERE IS A LION IN THE WAY. BUT HE WHO IS DILIGENT KNOWS THAT IF ONE WAY BE BARRED, YET ANOTHER WAY SHALL OPEN TO HIM WHO HOLDS THE KEY. BE BOLD, THEREFORE, O SON OF KINGS, AND SEEK OUT YOUR WAYS. WHERE THERE IS NO VISION, THE PEOPLE PERISH."

The voice of Solomon faded. A sense of peace descended on the tomb and all within it. It was a silent dismissal everyone could feel. By unspoken consent, the visitors departed, not speaking until they were in the open air again.

Ambrosius held up the talisman. They all crowded around him to admire it, with the exception of Quintus.

"How does it work?" Don asked. "He didn't say."

"Yes he did," Gerial corrected him. "In his own way. If you think Soloman's big on conundrums, you should visit Socrates' tomb. Drive you right up the wall with questions, questions, questions, and not one hint of an answer."

"Might there be instructions on the thing itself?" Kent suggested. He took a look at its flip side. "Not a sausage."

"Too bad," Gerial opined. "Magical doohickeys like that are sometimes one-shots. You'd better use it right the first time. *Riddles.* What a gyp."

Ambrosius called for their attention. He did not notice the resentful look on his old master's sun-browned face as the younger man held forth: "Solomon spoke of vision, and of a key. I think that if we all concentrate our thoughts on one place, making it a vision we all share, this may be the key to take us there in spite of Raleel's barricades."

"So it might be," Gerial said. "Sounds straightforward enough. Solomon was master of many charms, but I never heard it said that he went in for all that sorcerous mumbo jumbo, burning goo in a brazier, tossing herbs all over the floor, waving his hands around. Things just *happened.*"

"Thought is the greatest magic," Atamar said. "Why shouldn't this talisman be thought-directed?"

"Oh, piffle!" Quintus snatched the talisman from Ambrosius' hand. "How do you expect so many people to keep their thoughts concentrated on one common goal for any appreciable length of time? It can't be done."

"Remind me to tell you about PBS fund-raising week some time, old man," Kent said.

"*I* will handle this." Quintus held the star-shaped talisman by one of its seven points as he thrust it high. Gerial backed off nervously, but the others remained where they were. *"By all that is holy, I command thee to convey us to the realm of the archfiend named Raleel!"*

There was no peal of thunder, no flash of light, not even a puff of smoke for effect. They all simply vanished, leaving Gerial to stare at the newly vacated patch of cloud.

"Gee, I hope they made it," he said aloud.

From Soloman's tomb came the king's sleepy voice: "EV-ERY FOOL WILL BE MEDDLING. PRIDE GOES BE-FORE DESTRUCTION. A MAN'S PRIDE SHALL BRING HIM LOW."

"Uh-oh." Gerial bit his lower lip. "Where did they go, then, Your Majesty?"

A yawn blew from the tomb, and riding it the drowsy words: "YET A LITTLE SLEEP, A LITTLE SLUMBER, A LITTLE FOLDING OF THE HANDS IN SLEEP . . . " It was all Gerial could get out of him.

"*Riddles,*" he snarled again, and returned to his duties.

17

A Cup of Coffee, a Sandwich, and You

"THERE!" QUINTUS SAID with high satisfaction. "You see? I got us here." He turned to reprove Ambrosius. "Don't over-step yourself again, my boy. You seem to forget that I was the first help these good people summoned, and I was your spiritual leader. A little thing like death shouldn't change that. Humility, Ambrosius; you must practice some hu—"

The word died on Quintus' lips. His eyelids fluttered in disbelief. He rubbed one eye at a time, shifting the talisman from hand to hand, then said, "Where's the sun?"

"Or the stars, while you're at it," Atamar said, looking up.

"Never mind that. Who stole the sky?" Don wanted to know.

"I know this place," Faith said, a chill of dread creeping into her voice.

"So do I," Kent said, a little more calmly. "Raleel's realm, all right, by reason of inheritance. You ought to have specified, Quintus." He took out his pipe, filled it with shag, and struck a match under the bleak and lightless desolation that roofed them.

The match's momentary glow drew every eye. Too soon it snuffed out. Though there was no apparent source of light above, they did not stand in darkness. The barren plain of stubble and gravel at their feet was sharply visible down to the last blade of sere grass. The dreary gray of late November evenings touched everything with its own mournful radiance.

"I don't think this is L.A.," Don said. "The smog was never this bad."

"What sin have I committed in the eleventh hour to deserve the Pit?" Quintus wailed.

"What pit?" Don was frantic. "You don't mean, like, *the* Pit-with-a-capital-P, do you?"

Quintus' answer did not comfort him. "Alas, this is fitting punishment for my pride. Ambrosius, my son, I envied you your bravery, to take King Solomon's gift when none of us dared. Rightly he called you son of kings, for your valor."

"Empty words!" Ambrosius responded a little too quickly. "The speech of royal courts, and their illusions."

Quintus continued to bemoan his own failings. "You should have ruled our settlement, not I! I am a jackal, snatching at the scraps of your heroic deeds. You were always the better man."

Ambrosius laid his hands on his old abbot's shoulders. "But you are the saint, Master."

"Saint? What manner of saint am I, to do such things? I am prey to a thousand flaws. Now I have misused Solomon's gift, and transported us all to Hell itself!" He sobbed into his hands, tears falling on the talisman.

"Courage, Master," Ambrosius said with a steadiness his eyes belied. "A little courage can conquer much."

"Even Hell," Faith said. "Only this isn't it."

Ambrosius looked down his nose at her. "And how would you know?"

"Previous experience," Atamar replied twice as coldly as the young monk. "And I don't mean of Hell. She's been here before. So have I, and the memories still sting. This is Murakh's accursed realm: Parvahr."

"*I* never heard of it," Ambrosius sniffed.

"*You* never heard of California," Faith prompted.

In a small voice, Quintus said, "I wish I had never heard of either place. What is this Parvahr?"

"A region neither Heaven nor Hell, Purgatory nor Limbo," the angel said, "where lives incapable of choice must wait, wasting the centuries, until they may overcome their own weaknesses."

"Melisan and Noel don't have centuries," Kent said. "If choice is what it takes to escape this place, by all means, let's choose to do so. Quintus?"

"Yes?"

"Try the talisman."

"I don't know if—"

"Try." They waited while he called upon Solomon's gift again, to no avail. Kent nibbled the mouthpiece of his pipe. "One down. I suppose a miracle's out of the question?" Quintus squeezed his eyes shut in concentration for ten seconds, then relaxed. Nothing changed. Kent clicked his tongue. "Right. That's two. Atamar, you are an angel, are you not?"

"Wait. I'll check my driver's license."

"No need to be facetious. Use your powers."

The angel returned a rueful smile. "This is truly Raleel's realm as well as his blasted sire's. The same effect the isle has on my powers is here as well."

"Three." Don finished the count-off for Kent, his face funereal. "We're doomed."

"We are not!" Faith said staunchly. "We didn't have an angel or a saint with us the last time, and we still got out. But we didn't do it just standing around. Come on!" She unleashed her chipper attitude on her companions. "Let's look for our own answers. Hey! See that flashing red light over there? Just at the crest of that hill, see? Maybe it's our exit!"

"Maybe it's a dragon with the hiccups," Don moped, but he fell into step with the others as they set off.

"Oh, my gosh! Now I *really* know this place!" Faith exclaimed as they gained the hilltop. At the bottom of the slope stood a glittering diner whose flashing neon sign proclaimed:

HONEST ARIEL'S
SHATOW DE QUIZINE
WINE LIST   CAJUN SUSHI   CALZONE
GRAZING PARTIES WELCOME

Faith snapped her fingers. "Shoot, it was a Sandwiche

Shoppe the last time I was here. Best coffee and pie I ever ate, in the tackiest atmosphere this side of Scarsdale.''

Kent went up to the chrome-plated door and pushed it open. An arpeggio of Monteverdi guitar music trilled out as he peeped inside.

"Come in, Faith," he said. "I think your memories are safe.''

Nothing had changed inside the diner, the new sign to the contrary. Faith yelped with joy as she recognized each ratty feature of Honest Ariel's establishment: the tinny bell over the door that announced their entrance; the banquette-flanked booths, their red plastic seats mended with duct tape; the row of skewed stools at the chipped Formica counter; the glass display case filled with pastries. A *Star-Crunchers* video game had been added. It stood in the corner, a big OUT OF ORDER sign taped across its screen.

There were five customers at the counter, not one of whom bothered looking up at the newcomers. A dark-skinned man in sunglasses played an old rosewood guitar. Two slender women danced lightly around and around him, their bodies partially veiled by swirling silks. Their swaying dance never took them far from the counter, where an order of steak and eggs was set before the musician. Though the smell rising from the plate made Faith's mouth water, the man played on.

One stool over sat another woman, hardly more than a girl. She too wore flimsy draperies of saffron and blue, her neck, wrists, and ankles heavy with gem-set gold. Hennaed feet bare, she picked at her portion of lasagna under the cold, vigilant eye of a fat, baldheaded gentleman. There was something about the self-important way he bore himself and the style of his ample gauze robes that made Faith think of Sumerian high priests.

The hem of his robe stirred. A definitely un-Sumerian fishtail swished out, blue and green scales catching the light. It hit the base of the girl's stool and snapped the metal in two. The girl tumbled backwards, taking her plate of lasagna with her.

"Gerha'ar, you *ox!*" she screamed. "I'm sick of you!''

"After this long, Tiamat, the feeling is mutual," the fat man replied dryly. "Why don't you do something about it?''

"Yo! No fighting. This is a class operation now, y'know?'' Behind the counter, unchanged by the years, Honest Ariel swabbed at the Formica with a dishrag the color of a mongrel dog's behind. A lit cigarette bobbed at the corner of his mouth, the smoke wafted up and out the ceiling ventilator by rapid, regular strokes of his filmy wings. He waggled the cloth in warning as the girl picked herself up and clambered onto the next stool over. "You eat up and get out, got it? And *you*"—he flicked the rag at Gerha'ar—"you better order something or I'll slap your butt with a cover charge *and* a minimum!"

"Your offerings are not acceptable." The fat one folded his plump hands across the expanse of his paunch. His lips parted, showing off a double row of fishy teeth.

Honest Ariel was not impressed. "Hey, you wanna play God, do it on your own turf. Whatever you really are, you're not pulling that plague-of-salamanders shit on me."

"In that case, bring me the burnt sacrifice du jour. And a side of fries."

"I say, Atamar, that chap's almost as much a lady's dream as you," Kent said quietly, watching Honest Ariel rustle up Gerha'ar's order, then go back to wiping up spilled tomato sauce and coffee.

"More." The angel pressed his lips together. "I know that one, Kent; know him from the days before the Rebellion and the Fall. When Heaven itself was split by choice, he would not choose. He has been here since before the beginning of time." The angel stepped forward. "Ariel."

The cigarette dropped from his lips. "Atamar?" He stretched out his hands in happy greeting. "Hey, last I heard you were—" He stopped himself, took in Atamar's mortal attire, then sniffed. "What *are* you?"

"Back to what I was in the beginning. Don't let the clothes fool you."

"Me?" Honest Ariel snapped his fingers and a fresh pack of cigarettes appeared in his hand. Another snap and one was in his mouth, lit. "The smokes may kill the ol' taste buds, but it'd take a whole lotta smokes to dull this nose, y'know. I can still tell 'em for what they are. So, if you're back with the winners, howcum you're down here? Slumming?"

Atamar noted the bitterness. "We are all here by chance, not desire, Ariel. We want to get out."

"Preferably by a gateway near public transportation." Faith

recalled the last time she had left Parvahr. She didn't want to wind up in the desert again.

"Directions?" Honest Ariel took umbrage. "Sheesh, I like *that!* Cominta a guy's place of business, don't spend one thin dime, and you want *directions?* Whaddoo I look like, Direct'ry Assistance or what?" The unwholesome dishrag was back in his hand. He slapped it onto the counter and returned to scrubbing, muttering the while, "Next thing ya know, they're gonna wanna use the can, then bitch about how it ain't clean enough for 'em. Scroomall."

He looked up at Atamar. "You want out? You got out. You got outa worse'n this yourself, so howcum you need my help alla sudden? Make like an angel and flap off. Juggle up a miracle, howzaboutit?"

"Miracles are more in this gentleman's department," Atamar said, with a nod to Quintus.

Ariel leaned across the counter and sniffed again. "A saint," he said. His nose twitched over Kent, Ambrosius, Don, and Faith in turn. "Anna buncha Public Works projects. 'Tween you and Mister Beatific over there, what's the beef? You can carry 'em all."

"Sir—" Quintus seated himself at the counter. "Sir, if we could, we would. We can't. Atamar here is not one of the higher ranking Heavenly Host—"

"I'll say he's not!" Honest Ariel enjoyed a chuckle. "Not after what he did. Hey, no hard feelings, Atamar buddy. You got my sympathy. We were in the same wing command before the Archfiend hit the fan. Angel to demon to angel again—shit, that makes you almost as big a waffler as me!"

"Then too," Quintus went on, "—you call me a saint, but I would not say the same of myself."

"You wouldn't?" Honest Ariel was on guard.

"My grasp of miracle is . . . undependable."

Honest Ariel's lofty brow unfurrowed one wrinkle at a time. "*I* get it. Parvahr's got a hold on you, huh?"

"Only on our more helpful powers," Atamar answered. "Which is why we must leave by conventional means, and before the warping of time down here makes for too great a difference on the surface. Now, the directions?"

"Oh, sure, sure, swell, no problem." Honest Ariel rummaged under the counter and dredged up a volume the size of the *Oxford English Dictionary*, unabridged. Dust flew when he flipped it open and yanked out an accordion-folded map. Using his cigarette for a pointer, he casually poked the lit end here and there on the paper.

"Here's where we are, and here's the nearest gateway—it goes up several levels, y'know. See, you take 'er up two flights, cross over through"—he riffled to another page, which he likewise pulled out full-length on the counter—"to this entry here, the other sida the Slough of Moderate Welt-schmerz, take that one up *three,* come out on"—more riffling, and another map was spread-eagled on the Formica—"*this* level here and pass through the low-rent district, then throw a shoe or something at Cerberus, sneak under the brazen gate, take the service elevator, and you'll come up right where you want to be!"

Honest Ariel looked up, beaming, and slammed the atlas shut on his burning cigarette. "Simple?"

No one else was smiling. "Mind repeating that?" Don asked. He had produced a pocket tape-recorder from his jacket. "I only got it turned on around the low-rent district part."

"Sure, lemme just . . ." Honest Ariel sniffed the air, looked down, and saw the telltale wisps of smoke arising from the book. He grabbed the coffeepot from the back burner and dumped the contents on the smoldering volume, but only managed to swamp the guitarist's steak and eggs. The dark man kept on playing; his two attendants never stopped their dance.

Ambrosius threw the book open to the burning pages and whacked the fire out with his toga. It was too late; the core of the book was consumed.

"Shit." Honest Ariel jammed a fist to his hip.

"What are we going to do now?" Quintus asked.

"Why don't you just repeat what you told us?" Faith suggested to Honest Ariel. "Don can get it all on his re-corder. We won't need the maps."

"Yeah, but I do! Sheesh, I'm *rotten* when it comes to giving directions on my own. Oh, I could find my way anywhere, quickest route, no problem, 'thout a map. I mean, I know the turnoffs and transfer points when I see 'em, but I can't *tell* you how many levels up and how far over unless I got the map in front of me."

"Then, like you say, no problem," Faith said. "You guide us out of here."

"Who? *Me?*" Honest Ariel laughed in her face.

Fifteen minutes later, as he was bringing them all their blueberry pie, he said, "No kidding? Murakh's kid? It'd be worth it just to kick that old blister inna teeth, by proxy. Jacked up the rent on this dump again, last time he was here. *And* stiffed me onna tip."

"So you're with us." Faith didn't make the mistake of turning it into a question.

"Yeah. . . No. . . I guess. . ."

"You're doing it again."

"Yeah, but—" Honest Ariel scratched his golden curls and looked miserable. "It's just so hard to decide, O.K.?"

"That's because you've got eternity, my friend," Quintus said. "We mortals don't. We make our choices and take our chances, and the only consolation we get is not having to live with the wrong choice forever."

"And even so"—Atamar gently brushed the exiled angel's starboard wing—"nothing need be forever, except love. Look at me."

"Yeah . . ." This time it was uttered with rising hope. "Yeah, y'know, you're right, Atamar!" Honest Ariel smacked his fist into his palm. "O.K., this is it! I mean it! Eat up and get out, everyone, 'cause Honest Ariel's Slurp 'n' Burp is C-L-O-S-E-D, *finito*, Chapter Eleven, history!"

Faith cheered, then gobbled up her pie while the suddenly decisive proprietor zipped into the mysterious back reaches of the diner.

While they waited for Honest Ariel to reappear, Don turned idly to the dark guitarist. By now the steak and eggs in front of him were icy. "Bad stuff?"

The man's fingers wandered from a French opera score to a Chuck Berry number. "No, man. No better eating in all the world than what ol' Honest Ariel dishes out."

"So why don't you eat it? Take five, you know?" He leaned closer, and spoke confidentially. "Listen, seems like you can get out of this hole just by saying so. C'mon with us. You're *good*. I can get you an in with the musicians' union, a gig in Vegas, talk to some high-powered record people— Whatever you want."

"Whatever I want?" The guitarist tilted his head, a slow

smile lazily parting his lips. "Whatever I want . . . Well, man, what I want's to have me a bite to eat, so whyn't you cut me off a chunk of that beef and help me to it?"

"*Feed* you?" Don was outraged. "Hey, that comes after you ship platinum. You're not crippled. Feed yourself!"

The guitarist shrugged. "If you say so, man." He used his guitar to nudge the plate over in front of Don before he stopped playing.

At once the two dreamy-faced dancers froze. Their eyes went wide, the pupils stretching to vertical slits in blazing yellow centers. Feathers sprouted the length of their sinuous arms, blurred their bodies. Talons sprang from their scaly feet, and with harsh cries, the harpies fell upon the silent guitarist's portion, tearing it to scraps and fouling what they could not devour.

The guitarist leaned back, chuckling, as Don beat the air around his head, trying to ward off the monsters. Quintus and Ambrosius tried to intervene, fruitlessly, until a knowing shake of the head from Atamar called them off.

While the harpies ravaged his original order, and anything that stood between them and it, the guitarist slipped a Danish out of the pastry case and ate it. When he was done, he took up the rosewood guitar again and played.

The music returned the harpies to their first forms. They moved away from Don and went back to their dance without a word or sound.

"Holy crow!" Don scrubbed at his feather- and guano-decked clothes with all the tissue-paper napkins in the counter dispenser. "*That's* your punishment?"

"Only if I stop playing, friend. Or if I go back up there, giving my playing a real try. See, you *say* I'm good, but you gonna stick by me, see me all the way up to the top? Where I grew up, I seen too many men go out, try to make it, come home broke and broken, all the gift sucked outa them and nothing to show for it. So I say, I ain't gonna play that game. I'm good, maybe, but until I know for sure I'm good enough, here I stay."

"You want a guarantee? From life? Hey, join the line! All or nothing, and you won't even *try?*" Don dropped the wadded napkins. "It doesn't work that way."

"Then neither do I, my man." He played a whisper of Brahms. "Neither do I."

Honest Ariel came out of the back room carrying a small Gladstone bag. "Mementos," he explained. He snapped open the clasp and laid his autograph book collection out for admiration.

"Boy, some of these are *old*," Don said, turning the pages.

"Honest Ariel's"—the proprietor winked—"where the world's greatest wafflers wine 'n' dine."

"Machiavelli . . . Henry the Third . . . Ethelred the Unready . . . Merlin . . . Hey, shouldn't this be 'Caesar'?"

Honest Ariel glimpsed over. "Mmmnope, Caesarion, Julie's son by Cleo. Coulda been a contender, only he waffled his way to glory. Time he finally decided to do something definite with his life, Octavius offed him. Poor schmuck."

"You will speak with honor of the dead." A deep crimson flushed Ambrosius' handsome face. "He was royal, of a house devoured by ambition. If he could restrain the worm of worldly greed, let us praise him, not defile his memory! Not all inaction comes from a slothful spirit."

"Ooh, wait right here, I'll getcha medal." Honest Ariel jammed the books back into his bag and started for the door.

"Lord, you forgot this." The girl Tiamat stood at the reformed angel's elbow, holding out what looked like a framed photograph. So gracefully did she move, and so silently, that no one had noticed her tiptoeing into the fabled back room to bring forth this object.

Honest Ariel turned his eyes from it. "Leave it, kid. Some things you can't change."

Tiamat did not move. It fell to Kent to take the picture from her.

"Fascinating creature, Ariel," he said, studying the portrait. "Friend of yours?"

"Summer romance," the rainbow-winged spirit mumbled.

"Indeed?"

"Before the Fall. She picked the winning side, and I didn't pick any, until today. Leave it lay. She probably don't remember me from last week's toothpaste. C'mon, we gonna grow roots here or what?" He shouldered his way out so decisively that the diner door snapped off the entrance bell on the backswing. Kent and the rest hastened to catch up.

"Write when you get work!" Gerha'ar shouted after them. He snapped his fingers and the neon sign above the diner read:

CAP'N GERHA'AR'S
DOCK 'N' DIN-DIN
TRY OUR TURF 'N' WURF: TENDERLOIN 'N' TOFU
FRANK

All the apostrophes burnt out before Ariel and the others reached the first gateway.

18

(I Ain't Gonna Play) Sin City

DON CAST AN astonished backward glance over one shoulder. "He's eating my Guccis, that son of a bitch!"

"Clam it, bub," Honest Ariel advised. "That ain't no way to talk 'bout Cerberus."

"We had nothing else by way of sops to throw him," Kent said. "Our genial guide here only brought one beefsteak."

Honest Ariel looked sheepish. "Forgot 'bout the three-headed bit. 'Sbin a long time. Good thing you got such good taste in shoes, huh? Get it? Good tastin' shoes?"

Don wiggled his toes and contemplated the holes that the rocky upward path had already worn in his silk socks. "I hope the next monster we run into's got a yen for angel wings on toast."

"Awwww." Honest Ariel threw an arm around Don's shoulders. "Tellya what, buddy, when this is all over, I'm gonna fix you up one of my special feeds, y'know? Got someone you really wanna impress, bring 'em around and I'll ambrosia 'em alla way to Anaheim."

"Ariel, you're trying to regain admittance to Heaven, not the Culinary Institute of America," Atamar reminded him.

"So can I help it if what I do best—what I really dig doing—is cooking?" The returning angel's wings rose and fell, their whorls of colors bright even in the sooty shadows of the passageway. "Oughta be a place for that in Paradise."

With a curl of the lip, Ambrosius said, "It would seem that some folk confuse salvation with salivation."

"That does it." Faith rounded on the resurrected monk. "That is the last holier-than-thou crack I want to hear out of you! If not for Honest Ariel, we'd be blundering our way all over creation. He's doing us a favor."

Ambrosius' finely formed mouth merely twisted further. "It strikes me that we are the ones doing him the favor. Our cause lent him the backbone he lacked all these millennia. He would never have made his ultimate choice if not for our lucky intervention."

"You can't lend what you don't have," Faith countered. Atamar noticed the small woman going into her fighting crouch and prudently shepherded everyone else out of range. The rest of the party was well up the path, beyond earshot, when Faith said, "I almost sympathize with your cousin for feeding you those poisoned quail."

"How do you know it was quail? This is witchery. You are an unnatural woman."

"Unnatural, am I? For using my mind? There's no witchery about it. I'm a trained archeologist, and there were plenty of clues about your tastes on that sarcophagus, quail the least among them. You were quite the gourmet, for all your put-downs of Honest Ariel. If Berenice hadn't caught your ascetic palate off guard with your favorite dish, you'd have been a prime candidate for Parvahr yourself."

"I? Are you mad, woman?" Ambrosius drew himself up as tall as the rock-hewn passageway to the surface allowed. "I made my choice long ago. I pledged my life to holy service of my own free will."

"Sure you did." Faith's mouth twitched up at one corner. "Only some people would call it running away, Your Imperial Majesty."

Her laugh was smothered by the hand that fell across her mouth. "What did you say?" Ambrosius demanded roughly, his lips pressed to her ear.

Faith struggled, but he held her fast. The others had vanished around a bend in the tunnel and heard nothing. Her indignant snorts and squeaks stayed muffled until she had the presence of mind to nip him. "I said, how do you expect me to answer you with my mouth covered? And *before* that, I called you Your Imperial Majesty. Or would you prefer one of the old Pharaonic titles instead? You're entitled to both."

"Hush." Ambrosius rolled his eyes in the direction the others had taken, up the passageway. "No one must know."

"Why not? It's safe to come out of the closet now, Ambrosius. No one cares about your imperial ancestry in this day and age. Except you might be good for a week on the cover of *People* magazine, Heaven forfend." Faith took his hand and turned it palm-upward. Almost shyly her fingers traced the route of the veins from wrist to elbow. "It's kind of a shame. You've got the blood of the Ptolemies pulsing here, and the Julian house of the Caesars. All wasted, now."

Ambrosius regarded the unprepossessing Ms. Schleppey with wonder. "How did you know?"

"There's a cartouche on your sarcophagus, among your cousin Berenice's maunderings, that puzzled me for a long time. I was trying to recall where I saw it before. It wasn't a proper name, but a rare royal title. I didn't think much of it while you were still the Unknown Mummy, but when you came back to life, I got curious. Why should a fugitive monk rate an honorific like that? Then Honest Ariel mentioned Caesarion. I remembered then. I'd seen the same title applied to Cleopatra's son by Caesar."

· "You are right. I am of Caesarion's line. My cousin Berenice had illusions of a coup, staged from Alexandria, to seize the imperial crown. She had—let us be charitable— many *friends* in the garrison. I was to be their figurehead first, later her puppet. I was also supposed to marry her and make her Empress." He sighed. "But if my spirit held any ambitions in that direction, it also held a great fear of risk. Other pretenders had tried for the purple, and failed most spectacularly. A live dog is better than a dead lion. I would not cooperate with Berenice, much as I was tempted by dreams of a crown. Fear made me waver. I ran away into the desert to join Quintus' monks."

"It wasn't the first time a religious calling was used as an excuse," Faith said, by way of comfort. "Or the last." She noted with pleasure that Ambrosius did not try to draw his hand out of hers.

"That is so. But when Quintus died, I returned to Alexandria. Perhaps I did long to claim my birthright, but the fear—! Always the fear, to make me take two steps back for every one step forward. You are right, my lady: I did belong in Parvahr, the indecisive shadow of a man. I should have stayed away from Alexandria. Berenice saw my return as an opportunity to renew her pleas. Had she been subtler, she might have wooed me to her side, but all that woman knew to do was nag, nag, nag."

"She wouldn't have lasted a week in Byzantium."

"Would she had been wafted there by demons, then! At last I told her to leave me in peace or I would have words with the authorities about her plot."

"That was a mistake. Never threaten. It's always the ones who say 'I'm going to make you sorry' who end up as the corpses in Perry Mason books."

"Whose books?"

"Never mind. So Berenice silenced you. Tsk. I'm surprised you trusted her enough to eat at her table, after all your diatribes about women's treachery."

Ambrosius' hand tightened around Faith's. "My own flaws came to my mouth and were turned against others. I apologize to you, my lady. You have great insight, to derive so much information about my past from such paltry clues."

"Well, I had my suspicions about you."

"And my defense of my ancestor's honor decided you?"

"No. But your confession right now did. That's another trick I learned from Perry Mason."

Ambrosius stroked his chin. "I must seek out this stoneworker friend of yours. He sounds intelligent. As are you, my lady."

Faith had a winning smile. "Thanks."

Ambrosius sighed. "It was ever thus. By woman's wiles is man deceived, to his own undoing." Then he smiled too. "But this woman's wiles appear to stem from true wisdom, and the scholarly life. It might have been worse. There is no shame in such defeat for me." He smiled back, and clasped both his hands over hers. "If it is defeat."

"It's truce, Ambrosius." Faith was sincere. A little color rose to her face as she felt the pressure of his hands. "Your secret is safe with me. Word of honor."

"Then let it be peace between us." He gave her an equivocal kiss.

"Hey!" Honest Ariel's voice came echoing down the tunnel. "Ya gonna kill each other, do it quick! We don't got all day!"

They caught up with the others at a bend in the passageway. Honest Ariel was leaning against the rock wall, mopping his brow. "Wow. Getting hotter'n I expected down here."

"We are going in the right direction?" Faith asked.

"Sure. I can smell Dis a mile off, but funny thing"—the reformed angel's nostrils twitched—"there's more'n a hint of Eau d'Inferno stinking up this route. It's the real thing, the stench of the Big Boys from Down Under, ya know? They got a smell all their own, only I never snuffed it so close to the surface-world before. It's almost as if someone's been tampering with—"

"The Gate." Atamar looked solemn. "The Gate that bars the worst of Hell from reaching the world of mortals. There is an infernal epic, the *Helliad*, that speaks of how that Gate may be broached, but it seemed mere poetic license, wishful thinking, something impossible. . . ."

"Raleel," said Kent, and suddenly nothing seemed impossible.

"Well, let's put wings on it," Honest Ariel said. "If that brimstone bozo's trying to spring the Big Boys, I wanna hurry up and stop him. And if he manages to break 'em out before I can kick his pointy little ass, I sure's shootin' don't wanna be blocking the road when they come up it, *capeesh?*"

"The road to Hell . . ." Quintus scarcely dared to turn his eyes in the direction from which they had come. "May God have mercy on those poor souls who must travel it the other way!"

The rock beneath their feet shook. A patter of dust and gravel fell from the ceiling, containing some fairly hefty chunks of granite.

"Whoa! Easy with naming names down here, bro," Honest Ariel said, holding onto the walls for support. "You're too close to the competition's turf to mention Thou-Knowest-Who."

Quintus gave him a burning look. "Shall that stay me?"

"Well, hey, yeah. I mean, you're the one jumping at every second shadow. You're scared, right? So don't bring something down on us to *really* be scared of!"

"Yes, I am afraid," Quintus admitted. "But if I fear, it is only for this borrowed skin. My soul will speak."

"Good for it. Bully for you. So while your soul's jawing

its head off, move your feet. I want outa here.'' The once and future angel strode up the rocky path. "We're almost to the surface. Think we can grab a quick bite somewhere up there?''

"Who knows?'' Kent stuffed some shag into his pipe and tamped it down. "One assumes the folk on Raleel's isle are being fed. The Brown Derby was reported missing from the mainland, as well as Pink's. We ought to find some sustenance up there.''

"I shudder to imagine what we shall find,'' Quintus said, doing so. "In a land where demons rule, what sins may not be given full rein? What scenes of depravity and vice, what vile degradations of the human body are not being practiced? Alexandria at its most wicked, Rome at its most decadent, Bubastis at its most depraved can not hope to equal the loathsome panorama of corruption we shall encounter!''

Dixi Dominus sauntered up to the mansion door, whistling a Disney tune. She rang twice, and when the lady of the house answered she said, "Good morning, Mrs. Bradley. I see by my program that you're supposed to be committing adultery with Travis Miller right now. Can I give you a lift over to his place?''

Leonie Bradley stared at the pert young lady on her doorstep and licked her lips. "Uh, honey, I just kinda don't really feel up to it this morning, O.K.? Maybe tomorrow?''

Dixi shook her head and ran her pen down a column of names. "Tomorrow you're supposed to go over to Bella Cavendish's house and steal that dress she got at Giorgio's yesterday. It was the only model, you've been coveting it for days, and you think she looks stupid in it. You don't have time for theft and adultery both tomorrow.''

"Well . . . couldn't I sorta skip it? That dress, it doesn't look half bad on old Bella, and I been tired. . . .''

"My *dear* Mrs. Bradley, what do you think Blessed Last Tabernacle Ministries is doing here? Having a Sunday school picnic? You *heard* the word of 'Sometime' Joseph Lee. We are all in this together, bound and obliged to make our lives a testimony to the special spiritual privileges conferred upon us. If we hold on to outmoded moral directives that no longer apply to us, where is our testimony? Where is our faith in our beloved leader? Where is your husband?''

This last question caught Leonie off guard. "Um, what say?''

"Your husband, Sister." Dixi showed rising impatience. "Mr. Chester Luther Bradley. You and I both know how badly *he's* been slacking off when it comes to testimonial trangressions. I had to put him on a strict schedule of Wrath, Envy, and Lust. Sloth he's taking care of just fine himself. He was supposed to be down at Tom Bergin's Tavern two hours ago, starting a barroom brawl. He did *not* show up." Her lovely brows came together in a fiery scowl.

"Oh, I can explain!" Leonie replied brightly. "He was home with me all day, being just so *sweet,* and building me that bookcase I've been after him to—" She clapped a hand to her mouth, but not in time.

"Bookcase, Mrs. Bradley? As in to hold books? Do you mean to tell me you and your husband have been *reading?*"

"We—we got kinda tired of television, and Chester putters in the garden with me a lot, so's we don't read all *that* much."

"Hm. Well, there goes Sloth, shot to Halifax. I'll have to inspect your library." Dixi elbowed past the mistress of the mansion. She was back almost immediately, and she did not look pleased. "Not one piece of pornography. Not *one*. And all that evidence of industriousness inside. You've even been doing your own laundry! My good woman, *have* you been sinning at all?"

Leonie hung her head and mumbled that her Chester had managed to commit adultery at least once. She thought.

"*Not* according to our printouts, he hasn't!" Dixi flashed a sheet of cream laid writing paper in front of Leonie's downcast eyes. "I also found *this*. It's a love poem. By your husband. To *you!*" She made several slashes across her clipboard. "I'll be back, Mrs. Bradley, and when I return, you'd better have some sins to report!"

As Dixi marched down the crushed-shell pathway, Leonie's whine wafted after her: "But we're so *tired!*"

In the bushes flanking the path, Lura and Lysi crouched unseen. The angel was fascinated with the scene she'd just witnessed. "Making sin an obligation, a duty . . . Tell most humans they've *got* to do something and they'll find a zillion ways to get out of it. Compulsory vice. Why didn't we think of that?" She looked thoughtful. "It's a cinch Raleel didn't."

Lysi was less intent on the ins and outs of mortal frowardness. Her eyes had never left the red Maserati parked curbside the whole time Dixi was conducting her unholy Inquisition. Slumped at the wheel, Noel waited for the clipboard-bearing blonde.

"I'm going to talk to him, Lura," the succubus whispered.

"Wait."

"For what? For *that* bit of bumptiousness to beat me out?" She pointed at Dixi, whose healthily swinging haunches were now almost at the car. Green lights kindled in Lysi's eyes.

"I smell Wrath. Get a grip on yourself, Lysi. We don't dare come out in the open while there's the chance Raleel is watching."

"Unless my darling brother keeps a constant vigil over his spying-crystal, the odds are in our favor against being discovered. I don't like being a rabbit."

"I'm not asking you to be one. I'm just telling you to exercise a little caution until we get some help. Atamar and the others will come after us."

"When? Too much can happen while you're waiting, and that Dominus broad is one thing too much for me. I don't like competition. As long as I'm still a demon, I might as well use what I've got to eliminate it."

"You don't *have* anything. No powers worth sneezing over, remember?"

"I've still got these." Lysi flexed her long-nailed fingers into claws. "And how do we know that Atamar and the rest will have anything more effective if they *do* make it over here?"

At that inopportune moment, Noel called to Dixi, "How's it going?" For answer, Raleel's private secretary laughed, sashayed around to the driver's side, and gave him a joyful kiss.

It was targeted on Noel's forehead, but no way could Lysi know that, or see it, since her darling's head was turned away from her. Innocence be damned, it wasn't passion, but it looked close enough for jazz.

Something nasty snapped out of the earth, the first trickles of hellish power seeping up through the soil of Los Angeles Caídos. Just beneath the turf, the earth was writhing with them, like nests of night crawlers. The Gate had not opened, but minor bolts of evil had already managed to slither out through the cracks, seeking nesting places in human hearts.

The tiny arc of white fire snared Lysi's ankle and sank

through the skin, charging her with its own potency. Wrath and Envy and wounded Pride were there to welcome it and add their sparks to the flame. Lysi felt her lost abilities flood back, tearing a pair of bat wings from her shoulder blades. Talons sprang from her hands and feet, and slashing silver fangs filled her mouth. With a terrifying cry, she launched herself at Dixi.

A scarlet hand with talons of its own snaked up from the bushes on the other side of the path and snared her as she flew over. Lysi was yanked down, back out of sight, just as Noel and Dixi glanced up to wonder what that awful noise had been.

Melisan crouched on Lysi's chest, her goat-legs bunched up uncomfortably, her serpentine hair all a-hiss with agitation. She swatted some of the more aggressive locks back into line and glowered down at the supine succubus.

"You should be ashamed of yourself, Lysi."

Lysi stared up at the horror on her rib cage and was rendered speechless. At last she managed to ask, "How—how do you know my name?"

"Noel introduced us."

"Oh, no, that's impossible. I mean, even when I was working on him to first try sorcery, he never called up anything as—as ugly as you."

"A fine way to talk to your potential mother-in-law!"

Now Lysi's disbelief hit its zenith. *"Melisan?"* She was unaware of just how loudly she shrieked that name.

The bushes behind the crouching horror rustled. One by one, Lura, Dixi, and Noel popped through the shrubbery, all with approximately the same question on their lips:

"Melisan?"

"Mrs. Cardiff?"

"Mom?" Noel's voice ended on a note the Vienna Boys' Choir sopranos would envy. "Is that you?"

"No, it's the Tooth Fairy," his mother grumbled. Under a bush, a yellow kitten chuckled.

"What happened to you?"

Melisan removed herself from Lysi's body. The shock of Melisan's appearance had driven all the auxiliary power out of the young succubus, and with it all changes in her looks. In spite of snaky hair, goat-legs, and pointed tail, Noel's mother retained her dignity.

"Never you mind what's become of me, young man. I am still your mother, and as such I'm entitled to some common courtesy on your part. Stop goggling like a frog; your eyes will freeze that way. And stand up straight! When I saw you do that television show you looked just like a hunchback. And you *mumbled*."

The spate of criticism was a more satisfying positive I.D. than if Noel had asked to see the demon's driving license. He seized his mother's taloned paws. "Mom, who did this to you? Why?"

No one but herself. The yellow kitten detached itself from the shade of the hedges. It cocked its head to one side and winked its single eye at Noel. *And why? For the sake of gaining magical powers strong enough to give her a fighting chance to rescue you.*

"Rescue me?" Noel was confused. "From what?"

"From Raleel," Melisan said.

"My brother, curse him," Lysi said.

"I don't know anyone named Raleel."

"You know him as 'Sometime' Joseph Lee."

Noel's visible disbelief went beyond simple skepticism all the way to you're-out-of-your-mind.

"Would I have done this—transformed myself into this horrible shape—if he were just another human being? Fire to fight fire, Noel, and demons to fight demons!"

"That makes sense," Dixi remarked. They all looked at the golden-haired secretary. She didn't seem to be panicking when confronted by Melisan in her hideous guise. She even reached out to pat down one of the demon's scalier cowlicks. It snapped at her, but a touch of her hand made it subside.

"Dixi, you can say that?" Noel was astounded.

"Well, it does make sense. But if you want to know for a fact, you can handle that yourself."

"How?"

"Magic. You do have that power. You were born to it, so it's still with you here, which is more than some of us can say, isn't it?" She gave Melisan a sympathetic look.

"Who—what are you, to know that?" the demon asked.

Dixi feigned not to hear. "To conjure vision is easy. Ask the seeing that you summon to show you 'Sometime' Joseph Lee, then ask to *truly* see him."

"But that's sorcery, Dixi. It's unclean; forbidden. It ruined my life, other lives, tore the world itself apart—!"

Dixi patted Noel on the cheek, and Lysi saw the harmless fondness behind the gesture. She took an instant liking to her brother's mysterious secretary.

"Don't carry on so, dear. You take things much too seriously, sometimes. You're good, but you never had the power to accomplish a mess this big on your own. You only took the blame. If you don't believe that, call up the vision I suggested. You do have power enough to do that. You'll see."

"I don't know . . . " Noel frowned.

The yellow kitten butted his leg. *Your mother went through Hell to have you born mortal—almost literally—and she tossed aside her own mortal form to save you, and now all you need to do is conjure up one lousy vision to set your own mind at ease and you* don't know? *Yagh! The kid's lazier than I ever—*

"All right. I'll try. How do I do it?"

Look within yourself. There you will find the shaping of your magic.

Noel closed his eyes and concentrated. His fingers snapped, and a perfect circle of silver appeared. He balanced it carefully on one forefinger, then spun it like a plate. The circle whirled, sunlight bright on the surface. Then he breathed on the shining metal, and it fogged over. The mist cleared, and in the center of the spinning disc was the vision:

"Sometime" Joseph Lee at his desk, feet up, a cordless phone to his ear. He didn't look comfortable.

"Truth." Noel breathed the word over the twirling mirror. "Show me the truth."

Again his breath fogged the surface. This time it cleared to a seeing that made the small hairs on Noel's nape stand up and pay attention. A demon sat at the great televangelist's desk, sweating blobs of mercury as he stammered excuses into what had to be the hottest of hot lines:

Damn, I don't know why they're not fornicating any more! Or stealing, or fighting, or anything. Yeah, I know you've had better results from a Little League championship. Shit, I don't know what went wrong. I told those fuckers they could do anything they damn well wanted, and what do they do? 'Side from a couple of real hard-shell cases, they sit home and watch TV and act content! *Fucking contentment never brought*

*down a single soul. . . . Yes, ma'am. Yes, I know the
Underlords expected quick returns. Just warming up the Gate
isn't going to melt it down, no, I know that. . . . Hey, look,
at least I'm snagging you one soul, all right? Melisan's kid,
and he's as good as hellbent right now. He's too busy wallowing
in phony guilt ever to know what real remorse is like when it
does hit him. One good sin to his record, no remorse, no
repentance, and we've got him! And others will follow. All I
need's a little more time. . . . Hey, get outa my face, Mom!
I'm doing the best I can!*

The silver disc shattered, and Noel was shaking in his
mother's arms.

19

Season of the Witch Hunt

THEY EMERGED IN the projection booth of Mann's Chinese
Theatre. Ariel was the first one out, followed by Quintus,
who scurried forward to take a look at the strange machine
whirring away at the other end of the little room. A beam of
smoky light shot from its nose through a small aperture in the
wall. The saint peeped out and saw what was being projected
on the screen up front.

"Good Lord." He had seen the seamier side of the Roman
Empire, but he had never seen *Deep in the Heat of Texas* on a
double bill with *Sorority Rut*.

Gently Ambrosius guided his master away from the window. Atamar stole a peek, and noticed that the theatre was
empty. He made a few shadow-bunnies on the screen.

Outside, the angel held them all up while he tried on Clark
Gable's shoes for size, then insisted they go looking for
Charlton Heston's star on Hollywood Boulevard.

"Never fails," Don said. "Everybody likes to go tourist in
Hollywood."

"I say, old man, got your priorities a bit skewed, haven't you?" Kent inquired. "I thought that our first concern was to find Noel and the ladies."

"And a boat," Ambrosius added.

"What do we need a boat for?" Don asked.

"To get them and us off this accursed isle." To the producer's questioning look, Ambrosius replied, "There would be no other way. Unless your powers are no longer affected by this place's unholy aura, Atamar?"

The angel's wistful expression said it all.

"We still have this." Quintus pulled Solomon's talisman from the bosom of his shirt. The blue star had lost all its shine. It was a dull pendulum at the end of its shabby cord.

"Dead as Darth Vader," Don opined. "And as the Seventh Cavalry sinks slowly into the west, any chance of a miracle?" The rising hope in his question was quickly dashed by Quintus' sorry shake of the head.

"Real miracles demand real saints. I just don't think I have it in me. I never was canonized. For all I know, my earlier accomplishments were just flukes."

"Bringing Ambrosius back from the dead was a freakin' *fluke?*"

"Can you tell me there is no difference between a miracle and an answered prayer, Don?" Quintus spoke softly.

Don thought back to the production of *The Dorm Ran Red, Part One*. Getting that turkey onto the screen had been the answer to his financial prayers. The fact that the Ivy League vengeance slasher flick spawned a whole set of sequels plus a cult—now *that* was a miracle.

"Right," he said. "We'll need a boat." He looked down at his feet. "And shoes." He looked at Ambrosius. "And you are going to have to shuck that bedsheet for some Beltramis." He looked at Honest Ariel. "And *you*—"

"Ah, geddadahere. Whassamarrer with the way I look?"

"You've got wings. Also, you're naked."

"Your mama!" Honest Ariel waggled his soup-stained counterman's apron in Don's direction. "Whaddaya call this? Chop liver?"

From behind, Atamar remarked, "I call it incomplete coverage. Don is right, Ariel. If we lack our normal powers on Raleel's turf, we must remain as inconspicuous as possible.

Come, let's find a hiding place for you and Ambrosius first; then we'll fetch you something appropriate to wear."

"A sterling idea, Atamar," Kent said. "Only, where could we hide a being as Corinthian as Honest Ariel, even temporarily?"

"Hmmm." The angel's smooth brow wrinkled tightly to squeeze up some creative juices.

"Uh-oh," said the Corinthian in question.

Some time later, in the back garden of an unoccupied Bel Air mansion, Honest Ariel flung his apron in Atamar's face and shouted, "I ain't gonna do it!"

"Oh, come on, Ariel, it's only for a little while," Faith wheedled prettily but uselessly.

"You actually 'spect me to stand here like some jerk with a buncha freepin' goldfish chomping on my tootsies?" He gestured indignantly at the marble fountain basin where it had been suggested he strike a pose and wait. "S'pose someone turns on the water, fagoshsakes? You getcher selves another chump!"

"It's not so bad," Ambrosius called from two plinths over. "We won't find a better hideaway, dressed as we are."

Ambrosius was right. The garden they had found held a congregation of the most varied and ill-assorted hunks of statuary on the West Coast, San Simeon included. Many of these were large or larger-than-life ceramics from Mexico, painted and glazed. The cool classic restraint of untinted white marble belonged elsewhere. A summer-winged angel on the mend and a togaed former monk would fit right in.

"We only have to hold our poses if we see anyone approaching. Watch me, it's easy." He raised a stiff right arm. *"Ave atque vale."*

"Blow it out your—"

"Ariel!" Atamar's reproof caused the reformed angel to climb into the fountain, grumbling. "If I get irrigated, I'm gonna sue." The pose he struck was not classic, or graceful, or even polite.

"Reminds me of something I saw in Belgium once," Don remarked as they went off to find their friends some clothes.

In the mansion next door, Dwayne Knox pried himself away from Tivoli's sensuous importunings and dragged himself to the window in time to see the winged statue in his neighbor's garden scratch itself with rude abandon.

The succubus begged and pleaded for another chance, but Dwayne booted her out the door anyhow, lock, stock, and feather duster. His mama had been right after all: You do *that* too much and your mind goes right to Squirrelsville.

"Raleel, *I* am a professional." Tivoli tapped her foot angrily but soundlessly on the thick wall-to-wall carpeting in "Sometime" Joseph Lee's office. "I'm used to being treated like one. Instead of respect, instead of simple gratitude for clearing up his damned complexion, what do I get from the Prince of Puberty? My walking papers! You want to tell me how you expect to get the Gate open like this? Last I saw, little Dwayne was on his knees to *pray!* I call that a rotten waste of knee-time."

Raleel's brow furrowed. "Something is rotten in Los Angeles Caídos," he rumbled.

"Ooh. Original, aren't you?" The succubus stuck her tongue out at him. He turned it into an iguana, almost as an afterthought, and continued to think aloud over her garbled screams.

"Something is wrong. Instead of sinning, my followers sit. They've lost all their get-up-and-go. And yet there wasn't one among them who wouldn't willingly leap into his car and drive for miles, or sprint all the way across town on foot to attend a good book-burning or protest an updating of the school curricula to meet twentieth-century needs. What could be stifling them now?"

Tivoli's hysteria was distracting him, so he rescinded the iguana. The succubus darted her restored tongue over her lips experimentally before speaking again.

"Maybe they need something they could all pitch in on together. Community spirit counts for a lot, down Hexico way."

Raleel wasn't listening to her. "Something is wrong," he repeated, and pressed a button on his desktop. A panel slid back and a crystal sphere the size of a bulldog's skull rose to the surface. It was cradled on a malachite tripod carved with the likenesses of three somber men. Tivoli recognized Savonarola and Torquemada, but not the gentleman in the three-piece suit toting a briefcase.

"Oh, he's the one yet-to-come, baby," Raleel said, reading her curiosity. "And when he does—when good men close their eyes and stick to hoping for the best instead of fighting for it—that's when we'll see the burning to end all burnings!"

"Great. Only what are you going to see now?" Tivoli wiggled her finger, and a chair slid in under her rump. She leaned her elbows on the desk and stared into the empty depths of the crystal.

"What I hope to see," Raleel said, "is the answer. Someone or something's been lousing up my plans for this land, and I want to know what it is."

"Then you'd better look sharp. What if your 'someone or something' has slipped into hiding? A spying-crystal only shows you what's happening now."

"Ah!" Raleel pushed a second button, and the crystal rose even higher. Tivoli saw that the tripod rested on top of a complexly knobbed and toggled black cube, with wires running from one of its faces up under Torquemada's Grand Inquisitor robes. "Clearly you've never seen a spying-crystal with built-in VCR."

The demon tweaked Savonarola's protuberant nose and a series of sweeping scenes washed across the crystal sphere. "I programmed her for all-day, full-isle coverage, and if I see anything interesting, I can just . . . zoom . . . in . . . like . . . *son of a bitch!*"

Raleel smacked the desk hard enough to make Tivoli's head bounce. He hit a toggle on the black cube and the action froze. Another twitch, and a close-up of the big HOLLYWOOD sign up on the hill filled the ball.

Nestled in the single *O* were three figures. Raleel knew every one. His lips trembled as he spoke their names: "Lura . . . Lysi . . . Melisan."

He smacked the desk again, jogging the picture. "*That's* it! That has *got* to be it! Leave it to my sweet bitch of a sister to fuck up my finest hour. And she's got—precious Parvahr, is that really Melisan? Lookin' good, but in baaad company. Looks aren't everything, Mel. I know a disguise when I see one. I'll bet you're just slumming through my playground to make a grab for your brat, aren't you?"

Tivoli ventured closer again. "Who's the third?"

"Her? An angel. Formerly one of our own."

"You mean . . . Lura the Apostate?" Tivoli made the sign against moral contamination and hawked several noisy gobs of spit at the ball, for form's sake. Then she leaned in for a more careful look and said, "She doesn't look half bad. How'd she rate making the changeover?"

Some questions are not all that innocent. This time Raleel gave Tivoli a fiery dismissal all the way back to the low-rent district of Dis.

"Succubi," he said under his breath, still staring at the three females in the crystal. "Unreliable. Disloyal. Flighty and useless as females of any breed must be. Bearing young must unhinge the mind. And yet, I owe these weaker creatures a measure of thanks." His eyes burned as they rested on Lura, Lysi, and Melisan. "Thanks indeed, for they have given me the means I need to reunite my followers and stir them up to a pitch of mindless, remorseless sin that would make Dagon drool."

He passed his hands over the crystal, and flames devoured the vision of the three.

"A demon?" On the couch, Laurabeth Kimball snuggled closer to her husband, skin cold and damp with fear.

Avery's jaw set grimly. "That's what the man's telling us, hon. Hush up some and let me listen."

On the television, "Sometime" Joseph Lee swabbed his brow with a paisley kerchief and spoke in a voice whose pathos might wring a refund from a used-car salesman.

"Yes, friends, it is as I have told you. There is a *demon* in our midst! Oh, I do not speak of those wicked, wicked impulses deep within us all—impulses that wrongfully tell you to disregard the good advice of folks who cherish your souls more'n I do my own; impulses that urge you to disobey and *turn* from the one and only revealed path to righteousness and your proper reward in the life to come! Shoot, I'm talkin' the real thing here, and I don't mean Co'Cola. I mean *her!*"

The screen blared with a full-scale blowup of Melisan at her most diabolical. The snakes' mouths gaped, venom falling in black drops from their fangs. Some of them were cheating toward the camera.

Laurabeth screeched and covered her eyes. Avery's hands went colder than the can of Coors in his clutch. All across the isle of Los Angeles Caídos, people sat up and took notice, except for the few who sat up and fainted dead away.

"Now, why is this spawn of Satan here, friends?" The great televangelist's face was back on-screen. "Shucks, do I need to explain something that obvious to intelligent folks like you-all? It is clear—I say, it is clear as any crystal—that our new way of life as the righteous and the select has obviously been the *right* one all along, in spite of what our accursed *and* condemned detractors on the mainland might be saying. And so there have been dispatched against us certain unholy and *utterly* reprehensible elements by our *un*dying *and* eternal Foe to turn us from the path of our one and only gen-u-wine *and* true deliverance!''

"See, Ave?" Laurabeth whispered fiercely in her husband's ear. "See? I told you this's gonna happen if you and your no-'count men friends didn't cooperate with me and the girls. I *told* you!"

"Aw, now, baby"—Avery fidgeted on the couch—"now, baby, it's not as if me and the boys didn't 'preciate what you girls'd been doing for us, just to help us keep up with all our obligations—"

"We only *organized* just 'bout everything for you lazy lot—who you're s'posed to be sleepin' with every night, on a *strict* rotation basis. When I think back on the everlasting *committee* meetings we held to get you scheduled for proper *and* thorough slippin' around, the unending cups of Irma Josephine Randolph's coffee—near 'bout ruint my digestion for *life!* Why, shoot, I never went through so many danged hen parties since I give up selling that Rosebud Rae line of cosmetics.''

"Sugar, I purely did intend to—"

"You *never!* You never kept *one* 'pointment with any of the girls, and neither more did your men friends! When a man slacks off, what's a girl to do? Can't commit no really good solitaire adultery. *Now* look what's happened!"

She pointed at the television, where Melisan's ruddy face was again being broadcast. In the background, "Sometime" Joseph Lee continued to scourge his parishioners for their lack of team spirit.

"We had a headache," Avery mumbled sadly.

"Hush up! I want to hear this."

"But though this creature walks in our very midst, will we tremble? Will we fear? Will we curl up and just *hope* for everything to turn out all right? *Nossir!* Hope isn't in our vocabulary. For I say unto you, though we walk the road to Hell itself, ain't *nothing* going to stop the Blessed Last Tabernacle Ministries and our loyal followers from going *all the way!* So how about it? We gonna hand off the ball to Satan, or are we gonna go the whole nine yards? I say to you, we can *whup* us this fiend! Armored in our righteousness, we can *capture* her and bring her *down*, that we may all unite and give testimony that ours is the *true* way, ours is the *right* way, ours is the *only* way to spiritual victory!''

"Sometime" Joseph Lee closed his eyes. There was unnatural silence. He raised his hands before him and spoke in an unearthly voice. "I do hereby charge you, as you hope for your souls to come into their proper keeping, to seek out and capture this creature of evil. You will be shielded and armored in your unquestionable rectitude. Be strong, and believe in our cause, and she shall not be able to harm you. But be warned!'' His eyes flew open suddenly and the cameras homed in on his wild, wide stare. "Be warned that such creatures are deception incarnate! With *these very eyes* I have seen her change shape to this—"

A picture of Lysi flashed on the screen.

"—and this!'' It was followed by a picture of Lura. "So go forth, my brave heroes of the right! Go forth unafraid, seek closely, and bring the creatures of darkness and wickedness to their just reward, even as you hope to save yourselves in the time to come!''

"Sometime" Joseph Lee collapsed exhausted into a chair hastily brought him by Brother Beau. The lesser BLT dignitary made a few concluding remarks, mentioning where to bring any and all captured demons. The cameras pulled back to show a room set up with enough hard liquor and soft barmaids to satisfy the most demanding epicurean among the islanders. There was also a big-screen television with a football game being broadcast.

Avery Kimball rose from his chair. "A man's gotta do what a man's gotta do,'' he said.

"Tell that to the adultery committee,'' Laurabeth grumped, but he was out the door.

20

Angel of the Morning

THEY SPLIT UP at Noel's suggestion, though it took some doing to convince Melisan to leave her son again.

"I'm going after that so-called 'Sometime' Joseph Lee," he told her. "I'll make him return you to normal."

"But he's not the one who transformed me to this," Melisan protested. "I did."

"So what? He's still the most likely one to know a way to change you back, and I'll make him tell it."

"Noel, how can you? He's a demon, and you're only—"

"He's no more than half a true demon. So am I, remember?" There was no anger or accusation in his voice when he said that. He smiled fondly at his mother. "We're the same, Raleel and I: half demon, half mortal, even if his mother was a witch and my dad's only with PBS. On the basis of blood alone, we should be alike, but we're not. You and Dad always taught me about choice, even if I didn't always listen. Raleel chose his path freely, I chose mine. The magic isn't evil; it's how we choose to use it. There's one lesson I've finally learned. If nothing else, I'd like to find Raleel and thank him for that. Also, I want to punch him in the nose."

"Please, darling, don't fight with Raleel!" Melisan forgot herself and dug her talons into Noel's hand until he yelped. "Oh! I'm sorry." She bent over his hand to kiss the scrapes and her serpentine hair almost bit him.

With a small oath, Noel performed a sorcerous exodontia on all of the snakes. They gnashed their gums at him in hollow rage and snarled themselves into a mare's-nest of tangles.

"I can recommend a really good creme rinse," Dixi suggested.

"If you can do that to her hair, why can't you change your mother back to the way she was?" Lysi asked.

"Think I haven't tried already?"

"When? I didn't see you do it."

"That's because there was nothing to see; no results. What did you expect, Lysi? Fireworks every time I call on my magic?" He hugged her. "I'm a pretty unspectacular sorcerer, even when my spells do work."

"But they *do* work here," Lura put in. "The spells you have the ability to effect *do* work on this isle. Yet none of us can call up a single *vytkin* of our own powers, right, ladies?"

Lysi and Melisan reconfirmed this. Dixi looked abstracted and remained noncommittal. Melisan's pickup familiar, the yellow kitten, emitted a small mew of despair.

Stuck! That's what we are: stuck! I don't wanna lick hair balls till the day I—

"Noel was born mortal." Dixi spoke up, the ring of authority in her words. "His powers were born with him and will die with him, like any part of his mortality. He never doubted or denied the basis of his own being—his mortal nature—even if he did have trouble accepting his sorcerous heritage."

"How do you know that?" Lysi demanded.

The secretary smiled, and chose not to answer.

"What's doubt or denial got to do with it?" Lura asked.

"Who among us can claim the same?" Dixi countered. "Were you always an angel, Lura?"

Lura shook her long black hair. "Melisan and I were born succubi, if you can call that being born."

"Well, I was born a succubus too!" Lysi protested. "And no one ever turned me into anything else, like those two. So why don't I still have my power?"

"What you were born and what you long to be—are these the same, Lysi?" Dixi's clear, honest gaze would admit no lie. Something beyond her demanded the heart's own truth, and Lysi could not evade it.

The supposed succubus looked at Noel. "I'm like him—a half-and-half; a hybrid. Hey, call me a mongrel, I don't care. I know which path I'll choose: his."

Noel's arms tightened around her. Melisan mused that she had never seen her son looking so happy. *And why not?* a small voice within her asked. *Love enough for all, always, is the abiding miracle. Never doubt it.*

"I won't," she whispered to herself. "I can't."

"You know," Noel said, "from a strictly Mendelian point of view, we could have some pretty weird kids, Lysi."

"First, young man, you're going back to Yale and finishing your education!" Melisan's dictatorial foot-tapping sounded even more impressive when done with a cloven hoof.

"No, Mom. First I'm going to rearrange matters with Raleel, like I said." Before she could renew her protests, he continued: "I owe him this. And it's not as if I'm helpless, magically speaking, or still in the dark about his true nature. Aren't mortal sorcerers famous for calling up and enslaving demons? So Raleel's already called up. Get my hands on a good, tight-stoppered brass bottle and the rest will be a piece of cake."

"Devil's-food, if you're not careful," Dixi said. "If you don't want to wind up with that brass stopper somewhere personal, you should change your plan of attack. You'd have a chance against a lesser demon, but Raleel's on a level with you; you said so yourself. You can't face him down, one-to-one. You'd be better using your wiles to reconnect this isle with the mainland. Once that happens, the old balance of powers will be restored, and you'll have more than a few strong allies to help you give Raleel that fat lip you're dreaming of."

"Punch in the nose," Noel corrected.

"When Raleel is in demonic form, he hasn't much nose to speak of, but he does have a really superb set of lips. This will call for trickery, treachery, and some slick fifth column work." Dixi patted him on the back. "I'll be with you every step of the way."

"You?" Four suspicious glances fell on the lissome secretary—four and a half glances, if one counted the kitten.

"What are you, Dixi?" Noel asked for them all.

Lura crinkled her nose. "I'm not an expert on auras, but there's something about yours . . . "

"A Pleasure," Dixi said, extending her hand.

Lura still looked mistrustful, though she shook it. "Mutual, I think. But you haven't answered the question."

"Yes, I have. I'm a Pleasure: one of the lesser publicized

ranks of the Heavenly Host. The Cherubim, the Seraphim, the Thrones, the Virtues, and even you rookie Guardians get more attention than we do. No one appreciates a simple Pleasure these days.''

"An angel!" Melisan gasped. "Born as one?" Dixi nodded modestly. "Why, then—then you must still have your powers, regardless of what this awful island's done to us!"

The golden-haired angel's face lost some of its brightness. "No. I am not what I was any more than you."

"But if you were born angelic—"

"Parvahr's unwholesome strength holds down those who fear to choose, who make excuses instead of decisions. The same evil spell pervades this land and fetters any being untrue to his real nature. I am as guilty of leading a divided life as you, my sisters.''

Melisan did the best she could to keep her talons from scratching Dixi's skin as she laid them on the angel's shoulders. "Guilty how?"

"Condemned by reason of love for one lost to me." Tears like drops of liquid aquamarine slid from her eyes. Forget-me-nots sprang up where they fell to the ground.

"I'll tell you a sad tale," Dixi said. "The angel Eloe felt compassion for Satan himself and left the realm of Heaven to be with him and grant even the Archfiend some comfort in the midst of Hell. No one condemns her for it. Compassion was her nature, her being, her self, and she was true to its demands! But I remained in Heaven when my heart had left it. For that cowardice, a mortal would have merited Parvahr. For me, my own spirit drove me from Paradise. It drives me to roam the Earth forever. I could not turn my beloved from an evil path because I was afraid to speak and share his fate, and so in penance I set myself to turn mortals from their own destruction.''

"At least it's steady work," Lura said. She stepped in to touch away Dixi's tears.

"Your beloved . . . is he—?"

Dixi took a deep breath and regained self-control. "I'd rather not talk about it further, if you don't mind.'' She shook off her would-be comforters. "If my dear employer has things his way, my work on this world will soon be superfluous. There's nothing more dangerous than establishing the Heavenly Jerusalem on Earth. Look what you've done with the original! Come, Noel. We'll see if we can't trick Raleel into a replay of his own game, linking your power with his. Only this time, I'll make sure that you'll be at the helm."

Noel did not rush off straightaway. First he counseled Lysi, Lura, and his mother to make themselves secure until he did what needed doing. "Hide; and hide separately. You'll be less conspicuous than as a group."

"One of me is plenty conspicuous," Melisan said bitterly. Dixi fetched a beach blanket from the trunk of the red Maserati and threw it over her. "Better." Her voice and the hissing of her hair were muffled. She scooped up the yellow kitten and shuffled away.

"I'll just go look up an old friend and hide out with him," Lysi said, with a pert tilt of her head. "He's dumb, but that's a plus right now." She gave Noel a lingering kiss before she, too, went off. "Be careful, babe."

"What about you, Lura?" Noel asked. "Raleel's got a real ax to grind with you. Will you go underground?"

"Ugh. Nematode City." She shuddered gracefully. "I'll be safe, and I won't have to hide. Lysi was right. Unless Raleel sits up twenty-four hours a day, his eyes glued to his spying-crystal, the odds are he won't spot us. So I'm going to rely on the hide-in-full-view gambit and go the one place he'd never expect to find me."

"Which is where?"

"Rodeo Drive. I'm going to shop till I drop, spend till I end, and buy till I die. Maybe I'll even find something amusing to do when the old gold-card melts. *Ciao!*" Hips swinging, she sashayed right up to the Maserati, slid in, and appropriated the sports car with a glorious sense of panache, flash, and down-home *chutzpah*.

"If he does catch her, she'll go happy," Dixi remarked as the red Maserati roared down the street. She offered Noel her arm. "It will be slower going for us to reach the BLT Ministries HQ on foot, but it'll give us time to lay plans. Are you with me?"

"All the way."

I'm hungry, the yellow kitten said. He nudged Melisan's breast firmly.

"So am I," she replied. "Only what do we do about it?" They were seated under a mammoth azalea bush bordering the patio of Revenge, one of the newer L.A. eateries. The scents of mesquite-grilled meats and freshly baked pastries had been too grave a temptation, luring a famished Melisan and her familiar near despite any danger. They could have picked a worse eatery to case. With its color scheme of scarlet, crimson, and every shade of red imaginable, extending even to the plantings around it, Revenge and its environs provided the demon Melisan with some camouflage.

The one-eyed kitten crept up onto Melisan's beach-blanketed shoulder and peered through the hedge. A second eye of glowing green light appeared for an instant and vanished before Melisan could be aware of it. There were times when depth perception was more vital than artistic integrity.

They're getting ready for the lunch crowd—not that it'll be much, with the population of this cowpat island. Raleel's minions are dressed up like waiters. Sheesh, they may be imps and the also-rans of Avernus, but they'd better look a whole lot nastier if they want to pass for real Beverly Hills table-jockeys.

A couple of customers presented themselves at the little black lich gate leading into the patio. They were greeted by a smiling maitre d' who seated them immediately, handed them open menus, and snapped his fingers for a waiter to bring rolls. Then he hurried back to admit the next party.

The kitten groaned. *Aw, now, that's all wrong. Look at them! He's wearing one of those bill-caps with a beer logo on it and if she's got one shred of natural fiber clothing on her body, I'll eat it! Didn't even check a list of reservations! Didn't even give 'em the cold-and-fishy eye! Didn't even tell 'em that all the tables were taken! Sominex save us, when you can't count on a Doheny Drive maitre d', then this burg really is going to Hell on a dessert trolley!*

He slid down into Melisan's lap. *Shouldn't have said that. Now I'm really hungry. They're putting baskets of rolls on all the tables, and fresh butter, and I can smell what's cooking inside, too!* He opened his mouth to yowl, but Melisan nipped it shut.

"Sshhhh. We'll get fed." She glanced through the flowering hedge with all due caution and dropped her voice even further, until she was addressing her familiar in the merest ghost of a whisper. "You're right about the rolls. Thank goodness they're everywhere, and easy. Just hit the nearest table, and don't worry about the butter. Okay, boy; fetch."

The yellow kitten gave her a ruinous look. *Say what?*

"Jump onto the nearest table and knock the roll basket over in this direction. They call them rolls for a reason, and I'll bet more than two will bounce under this hedge. You can bat a few more to me with your paw."

It took a lot of arguing, but at last the kitten consented to do honest work. *All right, but just this once. I'm no Uncle Benji.* He goal-kicked six rolls into the azaleas and hooked himself three pats of butter with his claws without drawing anyone's attention.

Wolfing down the rolls, Melisan praised him lavishly. Kind words went to his head. He licked some greasy crumbs from his whiskers. *Wait here. If it worked with rolls, it'll work with profiteroles. I see that dessert trolley winking at me, and it doesn't have any more of a guard on it than a sixty-five-year-old virgin. Get ready to catch.*

He bounded through the hedge before Melisan could stop him and jumped for the lowest shelf of the dessert trolley. Unfortunately, it was impossible to see the bowl of *schlag* from the ground. He landed right in the creamy billows and knocked the bowl onto its side in his panic to get out. A whipped cream tide washed him into the apricot torte, and momentum plus improved underfoot lubrication sent him bowling through a setup of chocolate soufflé ramekins. He scored a strike before the maitre d' seized him by the sticky scruff.

"What you got there, Pierre?" one of Revenge's new clients called. He guffawed when the maitre d' held up the draggled kitten. "You bring him over t'here. We got us an empty wine cooler, fulla melted ice. Good a place as any for drowning rat-bait like that."

Cheered on by his pals, the home-grown wit snatched the kitten from the maitre d's hand and dangled it above the large, water-filled wine cooler. "Ding-dong bell!" he shouted, and plunged the kitten in.

The red fury knocked him and the wine cooler and the kitten in three separate directions. Talons ripped open the back of a good Hawaiian print shirt, wasting some mighty fine rayon. The kitten raced for the hedge and sat there, panting and shaking, as he watched Melisan carve a smiley face on the man's back.

She had the vapid grin half drawn when four pairs of meaty hands grabbed her. Her lashing hooves struck air. A tablecloth was yanked into service and thrown over her head and the empty wine cooler brought over.

The man she'd attacked took it, narrowed one eye to judge his target, and slammed it hard against the side of her head. Melisan slumped. He wiped his mouth on the back of his hand and returned the cooler to his chum.

"Much 'bliged."

"Don't mention it, Jim-Bob. Just doing the Lord's work."

Jim-Bob continued wiping his lips as he observed the red stain spreading across the tablecloth. "Amen."

"—and my husband, Ave, he says it's just a matter of time till they catch that demon." Laurabeth uttered a sigh of satisfaction that came all the way up from her newly polished toenails. "Little further down, honey."

"Yes, ma'am," said the masseuse. She paused only long enough to tuck up a lock of her long black hair. "What demon's this?"

"One 'at's lurking round, seeking to lead honest folk astray, distract our mind from the path of righteousness, blunt the edge of 'Sometime' Joseph Lee's holy sword—stuff like that. Oooh, my, you sure do have blessed hands, hon. That feels so *goooood*."

"If it's a real demon," the masseuse said, "what can you do about it, ma'am? The way I understood it, they're pretty vicious, and they've got supernatural powers that would curl your hair."

Laurabeth chuckled into the hard pillow. "Shouldn'ta had me that perm then, huh? Save Ave a whole lotta money, 'cepting everything's free." She arched her back. "Who'da thunk it? Laurabeth Kimball, getting the full Georgette Klinger treatment for nothing. Shoot, I hope they catch that bitch. Sure would hate to have this setup screwed."

"But demons aren't human. You couldn't kill it even if you caught it."

"Aw, honey, where you *been?* 'Sometime' Joseph Lee—

bless his heart—he's been filling up the TV every hour on the
hour, telling us 'bout how folks already been asking that
question. Well, he's got the answer: all of us. One man
against one demon, that wouldn't do no more than make
Satan's servant laugh in your face, but when you got enough
people together, their minds all aimed right at one single
solitary thing, then you got a weapon to *conjure* with! Yes,
ma'am. Catch that demon, tie 'er up real good, and turn the
minds of every man, woman, and child on this isle to directing all the righteous anger, rage, and good, clean, honest
hatred that's in our hearts for any being tries to stand against
us!''

''Still, a demon . . . ''

''Foo. We got the *Lord* on our side! No demon can stand
up to the Heavenly Host.''

''Amen,'' the masseuse said, and gave her client a stinging
smack across the buttocks. ''You're through.''

Swathed in pastel sheets, Laurabeth retired to change into
civvies. Lura had just gotten the massage room tidied up and
was at one of the makeup tables, gleefully trying on every pot
of cosmetic she could reach, when Mrs. Kimball pounced.

''Honey, I just wanna borrow the loan of you for a minute.
Come with me, tell my Ave how good a massage feels, how
it won't turn him into no goddam faggot or pervert if he gets
one for himself, won't you now?''

Laurabeth wasn't one to take no for an answer. She wasn't
even one to wait for an answer. She just dragged Lura out of
her chair and into the waiting room, where Avery sat thumb-
ing through the Donna Rice issue of *People* for the fifteenth
time.

''Ave, there's someone you gotta see here!''

The magazine flapped to the floor. Avery Kimball went on
point, like the best bird dog.

''Shit. I'll say.'' He vaulted over the low table and all its
magazines to seize Lura and hold her fast. Every other husband in the waiting area and the succubus playing receptionist
stared.

''Why, Avery Kimball—!''

''God bless America, Laurabeth, you're a pistol! Know
what you did, babe?'' His grin was incandescent. ''You and
me, we caught us the demon!''

Laurabeth nibbled a gel nail and studied her husband's

sudden captive. At length she sighed. "Never did have me a head for faces. You sure?"

"Sure as death. Heck, you saw the show. You heard Mr. Lee saying as how the fiend changes her looks, and this here's one of 'em. He *showed* it on TV! That's truth enough for me."

"I *did* think she looked familiar, but a demon . . . " Laurabeth sounded doubtful.

"Who'd you think she was, then?"

The lady shrugged. "Cher?"

Lysi rang Dwayne's doorbell. While she cooled her heels on the palmetto mat, she glanced at the odd gaggle of folks walking away from the house next door. One of them wore a long satin cape and was cursing at top volume as his friends helped him along the street. She shrugged. This isle was full of noises, and weirder ones than a passel of profanity. It took all kinds.

The door opened on a security chain. Dwayne Knox's nose thrust through the crack, the end twitching with autonomous life. Lysi pressed her hands together in front of her, which pressed her arms together, which in turn pressed other features of her anatomy together.

"Hi, Dwayne," she cooed. "Remember me?"

She never heard a scream go on that long and loud, uninterrupted. She was still marveling at the boy's lung power when the midnight-blue Lincoln glided up to the curb and four burly men piled out. By the time she turned to go, they were halfway to the house, blocking her retreat.

As they took her away, she caught a last glimpse of Dwayne Knox. He was standing on the doorsill, a cordless phone in his hand. He was still screaming, but he'd managed to dial the Los Angeles Caídos equivalent of 911 while he howled.

The yellow kitten flung himself under Dixi's feet and was almost trampled for his trouble. "Hey! Careful, there, little one!" she exclaimed, picking him up. They were all about a block from the BLT Ministries HQ.

Save your steps, sweetheart. The kitten's small sides heaved as he fought to catch his breath. *You're heading for a real sad and sorry surprise if you're after Raleel.*

Noel stroked the kitten's head. "What are you talking about? Where's my mother?"

The kitten leaned into Noel's caress and purred in spite of the news he had to deliver. Noel's hand dropped, and the little animal came out of his reverie. *Oh, man, that felt better than—Well, maybe not better than* that, *but pretty darn good. Your mother . . . Sit down.*

"In the middle of the street?"

Okay, take everything people tell you at face value and see where it gets you. I meant brace yourself. They've got her.

"They—? Raleel?"

His salvation flunkies. Mouthing off a hundred and one misapplied Biblical justifications a minute for why they can split heads, kick butt, and burn anything or anyone who tells them No. They're still going to Heaven. They'll be the only ones there, but what the hey!

"They have Melisan," Dixi repeated. She sounded almost as stunned as Noel looked.

"No panic," he said, though there was a ragged edge to his voice. "He'd like us to panic. We have to think."

"What do you think he'll do to her, Noel?" Dixi sounded really scared.

"That's one thing *not* to think about. Knowing Raleel, whatever he does decide to try on my mother, he'll do it in public, before the biggest audience he can muster. He's a demon, but he's a showman number one."

"You're right. Listen, I'm going in there." She passed him the kitten and indicated the glittering towers of the BLT building. "If he's got your mother, Raleel might figure he doesn't have to toy with you anymore. He'll use her as a chip to force you all the way into his power. But he can't do that if you're not there. Like I said, I'll go inside, and I'll see what I can find out about."

She squeezed his hand and started for the building, but his fingers tightened and he would not let her go. "Dixi, if Raleel suspects what you really are—"

"He hasn't a clue."

"Are you sure?"

The angel shrugged. "I'll risk it. No single demon can utterly destroy an angel. Unfortunately, it works the other way around too." She forced a smile. "I'll be fine."

Noel let her go, not without a nagging sense of misgiving.

The yellow kitten butted his hand for further petting. *Since you're not doing anything useful, pay attention to me!*

"What can I do? She told me not to go in there."

So you obeyed. You let her go after Raleel alone. What a good little boy are you. A cat—even a kitten—is born master of the scornful sneer.

"She'll be okay," Noel mumbled. "He can't destroy her."

There are some things he can do to her that might make destruction seem mighty tempting, the kitten rumbled. *Or is that another one of the things you won't bother thinking about?*

"Well, then, why—why did you let her go?"

Me? One perfectly round eye blinked at Noel's startled expression. *Things have come to a pretty pass when you think even a common kitten's got more say-so in this world than you.*

"It's the truth, though." Noel's shoulders rose and fell, accepting it. "I'm always the one things happen *to.*"

Yeah; if you let them. There's a powerful lot of magic in you, kid, but you still believe that hiding under the bed with your eyes closed makes the nightmares go away. Growing up's not something that just happens south of your belt buckle. It's opening your eyes and taking on the nightmares yourself, without calling for Mommy or Daddy or even God. It's facing down evil, even when you know it might be the last thing you ever do.

"That's . . . "

Frightening? Isn't it. You think heroes don't care if they die? You think saints go looking for their martyrdoms? You think you're the only one alive who's ever been afraid, for all your big talk about punching Raleel in the snoot? The power of Hell is the power of purest evil—trust me, I know—and there's nothing more frightening than that. You humans make demons in your own image to reduce that power to something you can handle, but you know there's something worse lurking on the other side of all those horns and tails and pitchforks. Stand up to it, Noel. Know evil where you find it, and don't run away, though you see Hell itself through the eye-slits of the demon's mask. When you can do that, you'll be a mage to reckon with. It'd almost be worth staying awake to see.

The kitten dug his claws into Noel's flesh and sprang

lightly to the ground when the boy cried out and released him. He switched his tail restlessly and sifted the many smells of a passing ocean breeze. He sounded amused as he added, *You stare at every kitten that way, kid?*

"What are you?" Noel asked, the breath torn out from under his words. "What are you?"

Very truly yours, a friend. You sound like you could use a few more, though. Follow me. Still sniffing the breeze, the kitten led Noel down the street, away from the horned towers.

21

Living Hell Is the Best Revenge

"DAWN," BRAZLYP GROANED, dragging himself down the backstage hall to his superior's dressing room. "Of all the corny gimmicks, this death-at-dawn *shtick* has got to be the tiredest. The boss is losing his touch."

He found Raleel's door and knocked. In the star-studded history of the Hollywood Bowl, many a prima donna of the entertainment world had commanded decorating changes made inside that room. Only Raleel had thought to invert the shiny gold star on the door into the demon's pentacle.

Raleel opened the door and leered at his subordinate. Just behind him, Brazlyp spied the succulent Ms. Dominus' face and form divine.

"Oops. Sorry if I'm interrupting anything, bo—Brother Lee." *Good thing I kept this stupid "Brother Beau" face on,* he thought. *Wonder how a sweet young nugget like her'd take to the sight of a demon?*

"Not interrupting a thing, Brother Beau, not a thing." Raleel emerged from the dressing room, rubbing his hands together rapidly enough to cause spontaneous combustion. "I was just explaining to Ms. Dominus there 'bout what's been going on down to HQ whilst she's been—Where'd you say you'd been gone, sugar?''

"Looking after the interests of the souls in your charge, sir," Dixi said, with flattering self-effacement. "Just making sure they were all doing what you told them they were supposed to do."

"Now that's devotion, Brother Beau, idn't it?" Raleel threw an arm around Dixi's waist. "You learn anything from what you saw, precious?" he added hopefully.

"Human nature's a wonderful thing, sir."

The chief demon raised an eyebrow at that. Then he relaxed and chuckled. "Any time you want yourself s'more lessons 'bout human nature, I'd take it *most* proud were you to 'low me the honor of being your guide."

"Oh!" Dixi's eyelashes batted like a hummingbird's wings. "*Would* you? Right now?" And she took the fiend aback by an abruptly uncharacteristic gesture: She pressed the wrinkles out of the front of her blouse, using Raleel's chest for an iron.

The attack was as unmanning as it was unexpected. Brazlyp observed a fine dew form on his master's brow. It took real doing for Raleel to place Ms. Dominus at arm's length. "Not for what we're 'bout to handle now, out on stage, I'd take you up on that," he said, recovering a shadow of his former homespun aplomb.

Dixi's voice sounded as if she'd been suckled on single-malt. "Can't that wait?" It dipped another octave as she insinuated herself back to armpit-range. "For me?"

Brazlyp was astonished. Was this the demure and pure typing machine he'd gotten used to bypassing in his master's anteroom? *Maybe the atmosphere on this island's getting to her,* he thought. *Raw, unbridled self-indulgence thick in the air, untamed sensuality on every breath—sure beats the Hell out of smog!*

Raleel swallowed an invisible toad. He withdrew his arm from Dixi's waist, but she put it right back and cinched it a notch tighter. "Pleeeease?" The demon began to waver.

"SOME-time! SOME-time! SOME-time! SOME-time!"

The chant penetrated even the backstage area of the Hollywood Bowl. The place wasn't filled to capacity, but not one of "Sometime" Joseph Lee's followers had slept in late today. Dawn or not, they were out there, waiting. Their spiritual leader had revealed the whole sordid story on television the night before—how not one demon in three guises, but *three actual demons of unbounded wickedness* had been dispatched to tempt, undo, and damn to Hell the select faithful.

Why should they be surprised, their leader asked them. Every time a bunch of simple, honest, well-intentioned folks got too holy to bear, some supernatural spoilsport got sent up here to tempt them. It went with the territory, like when Saint Anthony was in the desert, or when Watergate happened, or when their no-good, blaspheming, unsaved, and *heathen* neighbors kept asking them if they hadn't sent BLT Ministries enough money this month already. It wasn't easy, being one of the select faithful when you were surrounded by mockers and had three demons on your tail.

Except the select faithful had been too vigilant for them, and now came their turn to teach the spawn of Satan a lesson: a painful, slow, final lesson. And they were the folks to do it.

Noel had been righter than he knew in his evaluation of Raleel. He was a showman first, a demon second. They were waiting for him, his public, his audience. Maybe he never gave suckers an even break, but he'd be cursed from Burbank to breakfast before he neglected to give them a damned fine show!

"Later!" he croaked, stiff-arming Dixi aside, and plunged down the corridor with Brazlyp bouncing after him.

"Oh, poo. I guess temptation just isn't my line," Dixi said. "Lord knows, I tried." She paused long enough to wrench the pentacle from the dressing room door and stuff it into her skirt pocket before following her quarry.

"Sometime" Joseph Lee emerged on the stage of the Hollywood Bowl and breathed deeply of the predawn air. There was the scent of the surrounding sea, underscored by the more pungent and slightly bitter tang of the abutting La Brea tar pits. When the big quake caused so many of L.A.'s tourist lures to migrate out to sea on wings of magic, Raleel had tried to include something for everybody. Now, smelling the reek of sullenly bubbling asphalt, he regretted he'd thrown in the tar pits.

It smelled too much like home.

"Thank God for the tar pits," Atamar murmured from the shelter of one of the concession stands. "He'd catch our scents, otherwise, or I don't know Murakh's get."

"Yo! Watcha mouth, creepo! I took me a shower before I changed inta this rag." Honest Ariel was loud in his indignation as he flapped the satin cape at Atamar. Under it he was wearing jogging pants. "Where'dja find this number, huh? Superman's goin'-outa-business sale?"

"We grabbed what we could that would do the job," Faith said. "Being an angel, you're sort of monumental, and mighty hard to shop for."

"You implying I gotta lose weight, sis?"

"Ariel, there's a time to get on Mr. Blackwell's list and a time to shut up," Atamar said.

"Hey! You gotcher n—"

"*Shh!*" Noel held an urgent finger to his lips. The one-eyed kitten on his shoulder likewise hissed a warning.

"Ah, geddadahere, alla yez," the returning angel muttered. "Who died an' made you King Kazootie?" He scowled at all his shushers in turn, then gave them the cold winged shoulder and pretended great interest in the cookery equipment stored inside the stand. Soon the interest was no longer pretended. Honest Ariel was born to cook.

The ribbed band shell behind Raleel caught the first lines of false-dawn brightness and amplified them by virtue of a subtle spell. Raleel and those on stage with him appeared to be bathed in a heavenly white radiance shot with rose and gold. He gazed out over the seats, where his followers sat in row after row, faces lifted, thirsting for his words.

Thirsting for something else, too, he thought, *or I don't know piss-all about human nature.*

He raised his arms and three picked teams of neckless wonders came onto the platform. There were four men to a team, divided two-and-two—two to push, two to pull the heavily draped structures now creaking and groaning across the boards on badly oiled iron wheels. When the shrouded wagons were in place, Raleel let the effect sink in a little before he spoke.

Look at them, he thought, mentally spitting into every one of those upturned faces. *Sitting out there, looking like they're kids and I'm Santa, bringing 'em what they always wanted for Christmas! Acting like they don't have any idea of what's under those curtains, but it's gonna be the best damn surprise they ever had in their lives! Bastards. Worms. I'd like to give them a surprise! Nothing changes. That was just the way the crowd looked when those iron-ass elders came to our cabin, dragged my mother away, strung her up and watched her dance on air. Oh, they all tried looking stern and solemn, like they were just doing a painful duty, ridding New Ramah, Massachusetts, of a witch, but I saw! I saw the smiles. I saw the blood-lust in their eyes. Well, give the public what the public wants, I always say. Soon all Hell's gonna break loose for real, and then it'll be my turn to get what I want.*

He slashed the air sharply and Brazlyp made the draperies drop simultaneously. A cry of near-orgasmic fulfillment went up from the crowd.

People, the demon thought bitterly. *Hardly worth the brimstone to burn 'em.*

He stepped right to the edge of the stage. A couple of imps manned the boom cameras he'd ordered on the off chance that someone had stayed home to watch the proceedings on television. Now those swung in for tight shots of their leader's face.

"Friends! Friends, we come together this day for the *dawning* of a new era! Oh, we have walked the spider's web above the fiery Pit for longer than you know, without being aware of the danger we were in, but now I say unto you, it is time for that slender strand to *snap!* For our days of uncertainty are at an *end!* Yes, we have had one proof already of the special grace that shrouds us, that sets us apart from ordinary folks. Sugar, didn't ever' last one of you know that long ago? Didn't you purely know it in your *heart* that you weren't like the other folks you walked among? And couldn't they just sense it too, and didn't it make 'em madder'n a butt-stung scorpeen, and all a-boil with ripe green *Envy* which their contumelious souls turned against you any way they knew how?"

The mob rumbled with agreement. They remembered. They knew. There wasn't a one of them who hadn't gotten the rough end of the cob more than once—love scorned, promotion lost, recognition denied. Leave it to good old "Sometime" to tell them why! Not because they were lacking, or unworthy, or unattractive, no. The snubs and spurnings had come because they were too special, too good for the lower souls they lived with, and Envy had a hundred ways of trying to bring the world's true masters down.

Raleel's smile spread out to engulf them all. "I knew it. You knew it. And now, here we have, before our eyes and in our very *hands,* the final proof of our unique destiny. Can you feel it, friends? Can you feel the warmth just a-welling up outa the earth itself, telling you that the fires of true zeal in your hearts will be the means to change this sorry old world?''

"Is getting kinda warm," Laurabeth Kimball whispered to her husband. "Losin' all the curl outa my perm."

" 'At's just 'cause we got us stuck in seats near them tar pits, honey,'' Avery whispered back. The pits mentioned sent up a few steaming bubbles that *blorped* when they hit the surface. "Hmmm. Don't rightly recollect 'em being so dang lively last time we went t'see 'em," he mused. The La Brea pits had been one of his favorite hangouts while avoiding Laurabeth's committee-directed adultery round-robin. More than a few six-packs of Schlitz had gone to sleep with the fossils, courtesy of Avery Kimball.

"Must be what 'Sometime' says is so," Laurabeth told him. "World's changing."

"Fact."

On the stage, Raleel fell to his knees and flung his arms back to encompass the whole tableau behind him. Brazlyp too knelt, and the pickup choir in their cumbersome, sweaty robes. Dixi was the last to get down.

"*Behold!* The spawn of our Enemy has been given into our hands! You have lived your lives in accordance with the *di*rectives vouchsafed me by the grace of *true vision*, done just *pre*cisely what I told you to do, and here is the evidence of rightness and reward for all to see! You think you'd be able to wrassle down not one, not two, but *three*—count 'em—*three* demons if'n you hadn'ta listened to me?"

Someone shouted "Amen!"

"And so now, I just know that I can count on your support and *obedience* in this, our finest hour! From the fire they came, and to the fire they shall go, but not without our consent and help! Oh, my friends, I call upon the faith deep within you all to grant us the means to destroy the demons!"

The tar pits grumbled and burped. The Hollywood Bowl shook with the opening chords from *2001*. A spritz of spangled golden light arced from Raleel's hands, and a thick bank of mist overhung the apex of the Bowl's shell. Nine angels, wearing altogether too much eye makeup, descended from some undisclosed point in the conjured clouds. As they floated down, they sang the theme song from *Heading Home* and bore to earth three sturdy oak stakes, each on a bed of tastefully arranged kindling and fagots. As soon as each team made touchdown, they disappeared.

There were more than a few moist eyes in the house after that apparently divine delivery.

"He's going to burn them!" Quintus gasped.

Kent said nothing, but his fingers hooked into the lip of the service window.

"Lura . . . " Atamar started for the door. Noel and Faith both moved at the same time to stop him. "Let me go! Do you expect me to allow this? I'll kill him!"

"He'll kill you," Noel said evenly. "Or whatever's closest to it. You know you're helpless on this isle. Walk out there and 'Sometime' Joseph Lee sics his flock on you. Four demons to burn instead of three!"

"But they're all immortal beings," Faith said. "How can he burn them?"

"My mother may look like a demon, but looks are as far as it goes." Noel struggled to keep his voice level. "As for Lura and—and Lysi, if it were Raleel alone, he couldn't hurt them."

"He's not alone," Ambrosius observed. "He has that hunting pack he calls his followers behind him. He can glean all their power and add it to his own."

"What power?" Atamar demanded. "There's not a wizard among them. What power can such people own?"

"Hate," Ambrosius said. He looked to Faith. "Love. With these vermin, it will be hate, now as ever, and in the end they will be damned for it."

"Oh, my son, don't say that." Quintus placed his sun-browned hands on Ambrosius' shoulders and made him face him. "You will have me believing that you expect the worst of our brothers, contrary to all I tried to teach you in the desert—for they are our brothers, Ambrosius."

"No brothers of mine." The young monk shrugged off Quintus' hands. "Master, you were always in a cloud, in these times as in the past. You never faced reality. You never saw half of life as it was."

"I saw more than you credit me for, Ambrosius. When you took the one called Melisan for your lover, I saw." He did not recriminate, only stated the facts.

Ambrosius looked shocked. "You did? And you knew what she was?" Quintus nodded. "Still, you let me go my way to perdition, and not a word to stop me?"

"I had faith in you, my son. I knew there was that in your heart that would not allow you to throw away your immortal soul for the sake of a momentary weakness of the flesh. A greater One than I can grant forgiveness for that, so shall I be too proud to do less? Those people out there, their weaknesses run deep, but they are no better or worse than you or I: We are all human."

"Yes, human! We are human, and to be human means to be filled with a thousand petty hungers, grudges, and self, self, self! To give in to humanity means to lose your soul!"

Quintus shook his head, his eyes full of sorrow. "That is not so. From my heart and my soul, I know it. I believe it. Those people—perhaps some are inclined to true wickedness, but for the rest . . . ignorance. It would be a pity if they lost their souls for that." His expression hardened. He grew determined. "They shall not."

He bolted from the concession stand before anyone could guess his intentions.

"After him!" Ambrosius cried. "Raleel will—"

"Raleel's gonna be on us like drosophilae on doo-doo if you don't plug it," Honest Ariel said. He cast a quick glance out the service window and saw Quintus well down the aisle. None of the audience paid much attention to him. He was dressed to blend in, wearing the same nondescript sports clothes as most generic Californians, and his Egyptian tan was the capper. They thought he was a latecomer, if they thought about him at all.

Honest Ariel snapped his fingers. "Awright, we gotta make a move, don't we? Quitchabitchin'. Taking off like that, ol' Quintus just gave me the butt-kick we all needed ta get it in gear. Huddle in fast, kiddos: I got plans."

"And where does my master's death fit into your plans?" Ambrosius demanded.

"Death, shmeth. He's done the Big Snooze once already. Ever wonder what it'd take to off that guy a second time?"

"No; nor do I wish to find out."

"So shaddup and listen! Quintus isn't sitting in here on his keister jawing about powers he *don't* got; he's out there getting ready to use what he *does*. And that's what we gotta do, too. Yo!" He threw aside his cloak and herded them all in beneath the shelter of his wings.

Quintus had not an inkling of what was happening behind

him. His eyes were ablaze with renewed zeal. He had a cause to defend, a point to prove, and all the strength of his belief in mankind's true nature firing him up. He reached the end of the aisle just as Raleel's neckless wonders were opening the women's cages.

"DEMON!" The power of his own voice startled him. Here in the open air there were no microphones he could see, though there were two of those infernal red-eyed machines hovering from their black perches. He resolved not to look at them if he could help it. "Fiend! Deceiver! Come down and fight, in the name of God!"

Raleel's teeth grated at the word. He fought down his lurching gut and spread on the biggest oil-slick of a smile in his repertoire. "Why, looky yonder who's here again, brothers and sisters! I betcha you-all remember this poor, wandering soul from one of our last mainland broadcasts of *Heading Home*, now don'tcha? Come right up here on the stage, friend! We're always ready for a healing."

He gestured, and another of Raleel's cream-cheese-complexioned "angels" appeared behind Quintus. She grabbed him by belt and collar and heaved him onto the platform before he knew what was happening. Singing something about the infirm of mind deserving much pity and little attention, she disappeared in a mascara-rimmed poof of talcum-scented smoke.

Quintus leaped to his feet and glared at the demon. "Manhandle me how you will, I will speak! I will be heard but not by ears stopped up with centuries of stubborn hate!" He turned towards the audience. "Oh, my dear ones! My children! Look into your hearts, before it is too late! Find the goodness there, the everlasting flame, the love within you that will save you more certainly than any gilded words and false promises. Have you forgotten the greatest lessons of true faith, of all faiths? As you desire mercy, grant mercy. As you seek love, give love. As you hope for forgiveness, forgive!"

"Sure 'nough," Raleel drawled. "We all heard tell 'bout mercy for demons. Happens every day, don't it?"

"All things are possible, through the power of—"

"—and as you let your enemies live, they ain't *never* gonna come back some dark night an' stab you through the ribs, now will they?" He upstaged Quintus with one neat sideways stride, shunting the saint behind him as he spread his arms out to his congregation. "How many of you gonna be fool 'nough to believe that? Remember this man? *Sure* you do! Remember him just a-cringing and a-moaning on the floor, overcome by the demons trapped inside him? Well, I can see the pity welling up outa your sweet, good, loyal souls. I can see you all asking me, ' "Sometime," can't you heal this man of his demonic affliction, same as you've healed so many others afore him thanks to the sacred and *holy* powers vouchsafed to you and you *alone* as proof of the *rightness* of your message?' " Every tooth in his head caught the tender sunlight. "Friends, shall I heal him?"

The *Amens* and the *Hosannahs* and the *Go it, Joes* battered the stage. Then the chanting started up again: "SOME-time! SOME-time! SOME-time! SOME-time!" Quintus tried to be heard over the waves of sound, and failed. Raleel waved for silence, and got it.

"Then as you have commanded me, my friends, so shall I serve you! For behold, the deaths of the demons shall bring this man the rebirth of his reason, and of that deeply desired death *you* shall be the instrument!"

The whiteness rose up out of the earth itself, a monstrous geyser of snowy light made even more dazzling by the sun's rays. Up and up it flowed, towering, a pillar of ice with wings stolen from a legend of Paradise. The crowd shuddered, too awed to draw breath. Hair the blinding yellow of the sun streamed from the apparition's head, and the halo of glory behind it was a sparkling blood-red.

"Good Lord," Faith breathed as she helped Honest Ariel make the final adjustments on the wheeled cart. "It's got the face of a Cabbage Patch doll!"

She was accurate. Raleel's newest "angel" was designed to inspire fear, but at the same time to keep that fear from erupting into panic. Though it was so huge, though it held a flaming sword in its hands, the creature's bland, reassuring face allowed the audience to keep their seats.

"Sheesh! Godzilla shoulda been a panda, y'know? He woulda wrecked Tokyo anyhow, but everybody'd just stand around saying, 'Awwwww, ain't that cute?' "

"Pandas don't carry flaming swords. More ribs?"

"Yuh."

On the stage, Raleel focused his followers' attention on the giant "angel." "See how we are singled out, my friends! Behold the judgment that is *yours alone* to execute! Oh, look into your hearts, as this poor madman has already said, and as you hope for your own salvation, turn—I say *turn* the power of your wrath against these three minions of *evil*, that the fires of righteousness consume them utterly and they *die!*''

Three of the neckless wonders shoved Lura, Lysi, and Melisan against the oak stakes and bound them there securely with iron chains. The other three shoved Quintus back when he tried to interfere. Melisan's cloven hooves gave her little balance on the kindling underfoot. She kept slipping, bruising herself on the chains. Lysi snarled curses at her brother, who paid her enough attention to signal one of the men to slap her silent. Lura stood tall against her stake, whispering a loved name.

''*Turn* your anger to them! With all your hearts, *turn your* power to their annihilation! *Turn,* and witness a miracle of your own making, that they may *burn* in the cleansing fires of your hate!''

The crowd hummed as if an electric current were running through them. Eyes grew cold, turned to chips of stone, narrowed into small, bright slits of hate. Fists clenched, each man's lips parted to drink chill wrath from his neighbor. Even the dream of mercy died, frozen and shattered. The air thrummed with vengeance, blood-lust, and the shadow of the sword.

The sword. The fiery sword that slowly began its descent, in the ''angel's'' hand. Each passing moment, each closing heart forced it farther and farther down. Lura felt the heat of it on her face. She knew that soon it would touch the kindling wood of her pyre. The three stakes stood close together, and fire lit to one pile would leap to the next and the next, in quick succession. Melisan's stake stood farthest from the ''angel's'' sword. She would see Lura and Lysi die first, before her own death.

For they would die. Not their spirits—never that—but enough of their substance to cut them off forever from life as they had known it; life precious, because familiar. Even for an angel, there was terror on the threshold of the unknown.

The sword came lower still. Quintus' pleas for the crowd to stop, to open their eyes, to see their own souls burning away in that flaming blade, went unheard. Brazlyp uttered a wild huzzah. Dixi didn't look at all unnatural, kneeling with hands clasped and eyes uplifted in fervent prayer.

''OKAY, FINE, GREAT, SUPER, AWESOME! THAT'S A WRAP!''

The sword froze, the fires along its edge shrinking ever so slightly. Bellowing into a bullhorn, his by Noel's courtesy, Donald Swann came swaggering down the aisle. His outfit was also sorcerously crafted—battered sneakers, tattered jeans, a rumpled shirt open at the chest, and a baseball cap tilted back on his head. His breast pocket bulged with pens and sticks of beef jerky, and he carried a packed clipboard under one arm.

They just had to look at him. Noel's magic didn't have to enhance Don's own Hollywood-bred charisma. If you couldn't make 'em look at you, you didn't deserve to survive in this town. Don was a producer and a survivor. He crammed a beef stick in his mouth like a stogie and blasted the people nearest him through the bullhorn.

"YOU! YEAH, YOU IN THIS ROW HERE! YOU GET-TING SCALE OR WHAT?" The people only stared. Don thumbed his baseball cap back an inch and dropped the horn. The excellent acoustics of the Bowl made it unnecessary now. He lofted a woman out of her aisle-side seat by the elbow. "You. Sweetie. Don't be scared. I only bite agents. I just wanna say, you people in this row here, you are all *naturals,* you know what I'm telling you? You were *beautiful.* I mean, I really thought you *believed* all that shit old Joe was shovel-ing onto you from up there. Now *that's* acting!"

"A-a-acting?" the lady stammered.

"You know it, cutie. I mean, when this flick hits the theatres, don't be surprised if your best friends come up to you later and ask you if you really *could* swallow lines like that. Hey, but what can I say? Third writer we brought in on this project and they're *still* giving me televangelist speeches that wouldn't convince a skunk to stink. I'm telling you, if *Crosstown Rapture* makes it big, it'll be thanks to real actors like you, all of you, you're beautiful, I mean it. Gimme your names. I want you off the extras' roll. I want you to have *lines!* I want you to have *billing!* Hey! You guys over there!" He waved the wet end of his jerky at another row of people. "You were good, too! I want you in on it when I kick butt over in Screenplay, okay? I want your *feedback!* Come on, we're going over there *now!* And believe me, I want all you guys who give us good input—I mean really viable dialogue—I want *each and every one of you* to have a speaking part in the final cut, O.K.?"

He picked up the bullhorn and waved it once overhead, like a railroad flagman. "Actors, *hoooooooo!*"

Hasty whispers riffled through the rows Don had picked, and others besides, as they all got to their feet.

"Actors?"

"Yeah, sure, actors! That's us! We're here to make a movie, remember?"

"Oh, yeah. I forgot."

"You mean we been making that movie here all along?"

" 'S why we come out to L.A. in the first place, wasn't it?"

"But the earthquake—"

"Special 'fects, honeypie."

"You mean they've been filming *everything* we've been doing here?"

"Impossible."

"Yeah? Tell that to Allen Funt!"

"Uh-oh. I'm in trouble. Think if I come 'long, ask the director, he'll edit out that scene with the lime Jell-O and the trained—?"

"He wants a PG-13, he will."

"Oooh, Ave, I'm so happy! We're gonna be in a real movie after all. Nothing more thrilling than that."

"But Brother Lee said—"

"Brother Lee sure could use some new lines."

"Fact. That last speech of his, 'bout hating for the sake of righteousness, you set back and *think* 'bout it—really think it through—and it just don't *scan*."

"You think he's acting, too?"

"Hey, out of my way! I got some great ideas for rewrites on some of ol' 'Sometime's' speeches."

"Yeah, me too. That director guy's right. Not really too convincing, lotta what he said."

"And the F/X—kinda poor stuff. I mean, you see that woman in the demon costume? Too corny. Didn't fool me a minute. Prob'ly see the zipper up the back when the prints come out, like the Cyclops in *The 7th Voyage of Sinbad*, less'n they airbrush it."

"Who made you an F/X critic?"

"Saw *Star Wars* sixteen times, is all."

Raleel's jaw dropped like a bad set of Nielsen ratings. "Where'n Hell you-all think you're going?" he screamed.

"Fine, gorgeous, beautiful, golden!" Don shouted from up the aisle. He gave the camera-imps the high sign. "Pan on in on us, fellas! Keep shooting! Don't lose it! Maybe we can splice it in later, work up a documentary—*The Making of 'Crosstown Rapture.'* I love it!"

Nearly a third of Raleel's followers were out of the Bowl before he could stop them, following the Pied Piper of the silver screen. Even the imps swung their cameras around and obeyed the voice of cinematic authority until they realized what they were doing.

"*Crosstown Rapture:* Fact or cinemafictoid? Documentary or *Götterdammerung* of Middle American sensibilities?" The new voice didn't come blasting through a bullhorn. It insinuated itself across the warming morning air with impeccably good breeding and understated sophistication. It was words and music, a symphonic hymn to culture personified, comfortable as well-worn tweeds, polished as a Fred Astaire routine.

It was Kent Cardiff, at his best, in his element, with a discreetly small microphone pinned to his lapel and Ambrosius Minimus taking the role of his attendant cameraman. They were there before Don and his train were entirely gone, playing uppercut to his left jab.

They stood in the very midst of Raleel's followers—those who had not departed after Don's promise of speaking roles in a nonexistent movie. Now the compact black unit perched on Ambrosius' shoulder purred smoothly, bringing the cinematic mountain to a host of fascinated Mohammeds.

"If we were to have asked a groundling of Shakespeare's day whether or not he was witnessing dramatic history in the making, what would the answer have been?" Kent's pipe sent up a misty question mark as he stepped in among the seats. "Here we have a contemporary parallel—a milestone, perhaps, in the centennial history of that undisputed urban matriarch of *les rites du passage du film,* Los Angeles."

Ambrosius kept the camera trained on him, and as was only natural, most eyes in the vicinity stared back at the black box. Kent made a subtle yet visible slashing gesture, and Ambrosius shifted the minicam from his shoulder. "Is that a . . . wrap?" the one-time monk asked.

"Quite so, quite so. Now, my dear sir"—Kent leveled his

leather-and-brandy charm at the man nearest him—"you look as if you are a person of opinions."

"Uh—I guess so."

"Excellent. Opinion is precisely what we at PBS are seeking for the documentary presently in production here. We could use any number of you—that is, provided that you wouldn't mind too awfully being seen on television?"

"Television?"

The word flew from a myriad eager lips at once. One or two dissenters pointed out that PBS was not ordinary TV but rather "all that British intellectual stuff."

"Don't be that way, Jeremy. TV's TV. Tell me when you'd ever get the chance to be on the air otherwise!"

"Well, I've been working on my bowling—"

"Jer', what's going to impress Kathy Sue back home more—you chucking a big round lump of plastic at a lot of little wooden sticks, or you sounding off like you got an actual brain in your head on PBS? Women *dig* brains."

"You sure? I mean Schwarzenegger, Stallone—"

"Woody Allen. Trust me; I read it in *Playboy*."

"Hmmm. Kathy Sue *does* belong to Book-of-the-Month."

It was done in less time than Don's foray had taken, and just as well. Raleel's recovery was swifter this time. He actually was able to hurl an empty cautionary curse at anyone who left his seat before Kent and Ambrosius made off with an additional segment of his audience. The people left anyway.

"I don't believe it," Brazlyp said aloud. "He lured 'em off with something *intelligent* as bait! *This* crowd?"

"Stupidity never should have been confused with ignorance," Quintus answered. He had moved closer to the junior demon, and now regarded him with a volatile mixture of loathing, anger, and menace.

Brazlyp saw for whom the fire was kindled in Quintus' eyes, and he didn't care for the heat. "Uh-oh."

"Servant of Hell, begone from my sight!" Quintus thundered.

And Brazlyp vanished.

Quintus blinked. He had been expecting the fiend to run away, or maybe put up a struggle. He'd been looking forward to smiting him with something—the Lord knew what—but this abrupt disappearance smacked of more than a voluntary leavetaking. There was a sooty ring on the stage where Brazlyp had been standing.

"A miracle," Dixi breathed.

"Who, me?" asked Quintus.

"A MIRACLE!" she repeated at the top of her lungs, for the benefit of the cheap seats.

Someone in the audience liked what he saw and started to applaud. Someone else joined in. Soon a new rumor was rushing from mouth to ear to mouth. Could a madman perform such a feat, the vanishment of Brother Beau? And why would anyone—mad or sane—want to make "Sometime" Joseph Lee's second-in-command wink away like that? There had to be a reason. These L.A. movie-makers—heck, wasn't the place just a-crawling with them?—they didn't waste special effects like that without a reason. Motivation, they called it. So how-in-the-world come . . . ?

"What in Hell's name have you done with Brazlyp, you damned old man?" Raleel bawled.

"Torn your right arm from you, fiend, as I shall tear these innocent women from your grasp!" Quintus pointed at the three captives, still under the watchful eyes of their bill-capped and bull-necked guards. The promise of filmed or televised fame had not moved them. They were the rocks on which Raleel had built his base of power, and there were others like them in the crowd.

"Innocent?" Raleel let fly a down-home roar of laughter and reached out to take his audience back into the bosom of BLT Ministries. He played out to the substantial remainder of his flock, and he played it past the hilt. "Friends, by your kindly leave, do you *hear* that? Hear this sorry remnant of a man call demons such as these *innocent?*"

He didn't get the immediate response he had come to depend upon from his followers. Gone were the automatic *Amens* and the *We're with you, Joes*. The crowd—what was left of it—looked ill at ease. A lot of them kept glancing over their shoulders, or peering at particularly thick stands of shrubbery and trees near the Bowl and the adjacent La Brea tar pits.

It was Raleel's first true revelation, if it could be called such: *Son of a satyr! They think they're still on camera! Those lumps of buzzard snot are too fucking scared to burp without it gets recorded on film for all posterity!*

The truth of the demon's theory was confirmed when a ham-faced man in the front row lifted a questing finger towards his right nostril and had his wife tug it away, whisper something to him, and jerk her head towards one of several good places to hide a camera. The thwarted gent looked sheepish and pretended that all he'd wanted to do was scratch his temple in a photogenically pensive manner.

With the instinct of a showbiz natural, Raleel knew he'd have to win back his viewer-share fast. Eyes still set on the would-be nose prober, the demon shot an invisible bolt of dark magic.

The man leaped from his seat with a bone-grating screech of pain. He grabbed his belly and doubled over, foam bubbling from his mouth.

"See, my friends!" Raleel shouted exultantly. "See how the fiends have power to strike against us, while they live! Why do you hesitate in the holy task I have set before you? Will you wait until *you* are the one they strike down with their cursed sorcery?"

Raleel's victim rolled on the ground, his limbs thrashing. His wife attempted to restrain him, and he bit her savagely. She fell back, her arm torn and bleeding. The foam on his lips turned pink, and a thick green substance oozed from the corners of his eyes.

"*Who* will be next, while we stand idly by, gawping at the hollow shams and carny *tricks* of this crackbrained *charlatan?*" Raleel pointed dramatically at Quintus. Dixi's cry of *Miracle!* he punctured with a loud, "Will you lose precious moments, suffering *fiends incarnate* to live, for the hysterical ravings of an *overwrought woman?* You know how they get, certain times of the month," he added.

The pink foam speckled red. One last scream tore the man's throat open. He convulsed once, then died.

"Will *you* be next?" Raleel asked, without raising his voice at all.

The crowd was galvanized. Fear coupled itself to hate, added its strength to make up for the loss of those who had gone away after Don and Kent. The "angel's" sword flamed up anew, renewed its slow descent toward Lura's stake.

Raleel laughed and urged his people on with blessings.

"No!" was all Quintus could say. He raised his hands as if they alone could freeze the sword in midair. "No!"

"No!" Dixi echoed beside him. "There, Quintus. Your true calling is there." She made him look away from the grotesque "angel," down into the hate-filled mob where one forgotten woman wept over the body of her man.

"*See* how the power of your own hearts shall wipe this evil from our midst!" Raleel cried. "Even so, I vow unto you, brothers and sisters, we shall *expunge* all iniquity from this whole blasted *country!* Cleave—I say *cleave* unto me, and guided by that one true vision which I and *I alone* possess, we shall *redeem* not only this isle, but the *entire all complete* U.S. of *A.* from the snares into which she has stumbled. Who d'you need to help you send your souls the right way? Who d'you gotta get *behind* and *support* any which way it takes if you wanta save your country from the devils visible and *in*visible, Hellspawned and *human*, who are destroying, undermining, sapping, *sub*verting and *per*verting everything we alone know to be *right?* Who's gonna give America one of the hottest wake-up calls of the *millennium?*"

"SOME-time! SOME-time! SOME-time! SOME-time!"

"OH, *NO!*" Raleel threw his head back and slid across the stage on his knees, stopping just at the footlights. A glorious pyrotechnic display of the flag crackled wildly across the entire back of the Bowl. "Not *sometime,* brothers and sisters! Sometime's too late. *Now,* I say! I will lead you in our holiest of holy crusades *now!*"

"BUT BEFORE YOU SET OUT TO REDEEM AMERICA, TAKE THE TIME TO SIT BACK, RELAX, AND ENJOY A TALL, FROSTY GLASS OF HOLYCOLA!"

The fireworks flag was still burning brightly, but across the sizzling Stars and Stripes was the face of Faith Schleppey, smiling as she held up a purple and orange can.

"YES, HOLYCOLA, BOTTLED IN CANS EXCLUSIVELY BY 'SOMETIME' JOSEPH LEE ENTERPRISES, INCORPORATED. EACH CAN, EACH OUNCE, GIVES YOU ONE HUNDRED PER CENT OF THE MINIMUM DAILY ADULT REQUIREMENT OF NINE VITAMINS, IRON, CALCIUM, AND FORGIVENESS FROM ALL INDULGENCES OF THE FLESH. NO CAFFEINE, NO PRESERVATIVES, AND NO GUILT. COMES IN DIET, TOO."

Faith and the flag blacked out. Raleel tore his eyes from his desecrated special effect in time to see that his towering "angel" had traded her flaming sword for a six-pack of

Holycola. A bill-cap with his own "Sometime" Joseph Lee likeness was on her head.

"Noel . . . " He gritted out the name, and banished the "angel." Her vanished sword had plunged into his own innards. He could feel a burning inside like no other, a thick, infernal heat stronger than any human rage could be. Under his feet, he could feel the sweet powers of Hell retreating as he lost one soul after another—too few, too cursed few of these mortals were capable of living for hate's sake alone. The destroying flame burned too small within them, hardly more than a spark that needed careful fanning. Too easily it died. Too readily they were turned from the darkness by the bright lures of life and joy and love. Too many of them still harbored the faithful heart of a child within them.

Sometimes it took enchantment to bring that heart alive. He knew the only one on this isle who had such magic at his command. "Noel . . . "

"Heya, heya, heya! Lunch break! Take five! Getcher munchies right here!" Wings outspread to help him brake and steer, Honest Ariel came sailing down the aisle at the tiller of a huge pedal-driven commissary cart. He jabbed down the kickstand and flung the top lids open. Fat brown paper bags flew through the air, giving off savory smells that were harbingers of their succulent contents.

Faith's Holycola commercial had cut the wind from the crowd's collective sails. Apart from the few hardcore adherents to "Sometime" Joseph Lee's doctrines, most folks were confused, wondering what they ought to do next. Go forth and smite the heathen? Proclaim the rightness of their cause throughout the land? Send "Sometime" Joseph Lee to Washington? Send a postcard home that Los Angeles was a nice place to visit but . . . ? How many pieces of luggage were you allowed to take on a holy crusade anyhow?

Honest Ariel and his incomparable way with food gave them their answer: Have lunch. It wasn't anywhere near noon, but for food like this, they weren't about to quibble. Suddenly the idea of going forth and smiting the heathen didn't seem that attractive. Life was too short and sweet to waste it bludgeoning your brother into accepting your way of seeing Heaven. Though a scant few of their neighbors were still paying rigid attention to "Sometime" Joseph Lee, most of the crowd took one bite of Honest Ariel's spareribs and decided this was close enough to Heaven for them.

They were so enraptured by the delectable brown bag buffet that they hardly listened to Honest Ariel make a pitch for his diet book, *Thinner Thighs by Armageddon,* exercise video extra.

They had to listen when the woman screamed.

"He's alive! Oh, merciful God, he's *alive!*" She gazed from her husband's newly opened eyes to the brown-skinned man who had wrought the miracle. "You did it!" She pressed Quintus' hands to her bosom, tears streaming down her cheeks. "You did it!"

"Not I, my daughter." Quintus gently withdrew his hands from her and helped her husband into her arms. "I am nothing. You yourself have named Him rightly: Merciful." He touched her arm, where her husband's teeth had torn it in the demon-sent madness, and it healed. "As you desire mercy . . ."

"NONE! IN THIS LIFE OR ANY OTHER, NO MERCY!"

The redoubled blast of an exploding furnace blew those nearest the stage several rows back, head over heels. Brows and lashes singed away, and the sun itself darkened in the smoke rising from the stage. The neckless wonders fell to their knees and worshiped what they saw.

The shadow "Sometime" Joseph Lee was dead. Raleel lived, and hate in its full, magnificent power lived in him.

22

The Patience of a Saint

HONEST ARIEL SAT motionless at his commissary cart, blind and deaf to the hordes of screaming people running up the aisle past him, fleeing the demon on the stage. He couldn't take his eyes from the platform, though it wasn't Raleel's transformation that had him so hypnotized. His satin cape slipped unnoticed from his shoulders and was pounded into the dust. His wings unfurled, their beauty undimmed by the murky millennia he had passed in Parvahr.

She saw them. Their swirling colors formed patterns as distinctive and identifiable as a mortal's fingerprint. She rose from her place and walked to the edge of the stage like a somnambulist. Raleel's demonic presence, the rage and hatred pouring from him in fiery waves, was no more than an inconvenience. One sleeve of her synthetic blouse melted away. Her plastic belt dribbled down her charring skirt, her pantyhose steamed off, and her shoes became puddles of molten patent leather when she passed too close to Raleel, but she didn't notice.

Ariel? She called to him with her mind.

His answering thought was not a word or even a name, but a musical sending whose sweetness and immediacy formed an arrow of light that pierced her heart. It bloomed and brimmed and resounded with a joy too great for any but herself and him to understand. It went beyond the bound of any human embrace and held the two of them immobile while spirit flew to long-beloved spirit.

Meantime, the departed "Sometime" Joseph Lee's flock stampeded out of the Hollywood Bowl. They allowed for no stragglers, and their screams were articulate enough to pass the word on what they'd just seen. The groups that Ken and Don had lured off heard them, saw the wild look in every eye, turned their heads for a brief glimpse of the sulfurous flames leaping up from the Bowl, and decided to put their big- and little-screen careers on hold. They bolted too.

It was a sight to see. The mannequins in the windows of the Rodeo Drive boutiques and bazaars regarded the onrushing tide of gibbering mortals as *pas du chic, pas du chien, pas du "cool."* Shoes were squandered on a scale that left Imelda Marcos a mere amateur. No one bothered to snatch one of the many orphaned BMWs or Lincoln Continentals and make a motorized getaway; they were too busy clambering over them. For once in L.A., it was the cars being run over by the people.

The rearrangement of the streets made it impossible for them to know which was the best way to take, but that didn't matter: They were all tourists, themselves, and the only sight they wanted to see now was EXIT. Blind luck made them head for the light, the morning sun. They didn't even want to see their own shadows.

Running in one direction at that speed, they reached the cliffs in record time. The precipice stopped the front-runners for a second—long enough for the next-in-lines to collide with them and send them hurtling into the sea. Rank followed rank, over the brink and into the drink, with all the inevitable symbolism of lemmings out for a morning's plunge.

The lemmings didn't have the Coast Guard waiting for them offshore. The flotilla of patrol boats were soon harvesting the Pacific of its weirdest crop yet. Three or four of Raleel's refugees were such strong swimmers that they hit the water doing the Australian crawl, knifed right past the scattered cutters, and would have sidestroked all the way to Santa Monica if a lesser armada of leftover idealistic surfers hadn't paddled out to retrieve them and shoot the pipe all the way home.

They were all rescued and brought to the beaches where a third argosy—strictly dry-dock stuff—was waiting for them: the press gang.

Spirit-guides and reincarnation gurus would have claimed the credit if they could for what happened next. Without a word or a signal exchanged, without an instant's rehearsal, every last living one of the folk who'd escaped Los Angeles Caídos had the same tale to tell the poised pens and the jabbing microphones:

"Due to certain irreconcilable differences between myself and Blessed Last Tabernacle Ministries, I have decided that my spiritual needs will be better served elsewhere."

One reporter asked, with the genteelly lifted lip of cynicism, "And how did you come to this conclusion? Divine revelation? A personal message from God?"

The interviewee, a thoroughly dampened Dwayne Knox, replied, "Whoever gave me the message, mister, I sure as Sunday hope he don't leave me a call-back number! Can I phone my mama now? Please?"

Their united front could not be broken, or any further details extracted. It wasn't ESP, Harmonic Convergence, or even the Vulcan mind-meld. It was that simple principle of Middle American survival: A closed mouth gathers no one-way tickets to the Observation Ward.

But long before Raleel's fugitive congregation were being asked to do guest shots on *Good Morning America*, the handful of their number who had not run away—fifteen stone-eyed men and women—formed ranks behind the demon on the stage of the Hollywood Bowl and smiled in the face of his fires.

Raleel felt their presence. It charged the marrow of his bones with a great, gloating might. "You do not run," he said to the brawniest man among them. His lips stretched out, showing teeth that nothing mortal could own. "Why?"

"You're our leader," the man answered.

"Just that?" Raleel felt their loyalty, a web of invisible threads binding them to him. It gave him the confidence to toy with words and ask, "Don't you see what I am?"

A woman stepped forward. "You're our leader," she repeated. "The way we see it, you always gave us the right message. You told us we were saved if we obeyed you, clung close to you. Well, aren't we saved?"

"For greater things than this," Raleel murmured.

"Like you said, there's always going to be sinners jealous of us, using every trick of man and Satan to turn us from the one true path. What you look like now—how do we know it's not just more of those three demons' doing, to cheat us of our just reward?" She jerked her head at Lura, Lysi, and Melisan, still bound to their stakes.

"Are you crazy?" Lysi screamed. "You keep listening to my damned brother, you'll get a reward, all right, and it won't be—"

A second man hauled himself to the top of her pyre and punched her in the face. Blood mixed with tears smeared her cheeks and chin.

"Give us the way to shut 'em up forever, Brother Lee!" the hero called from the woodpile. He jumped down to the stage and approached Raleel. "Call up another angel, and let's burn the Earth clean of Satan's own!"

Raleel let his head tilt back as he filled his nostrils with the satisfying reek of small hearts and mouldering souls. Selfish greed for their own salvation pulsed from those fifteen in waves he could almost touch, and damnation take anyone who dared to stand between them and the Heaven for which only they were good enough. Icy tears of happiness ate into Raleel's flesh, but he let them fall.

He could almost say he loved these people.

"Oh, yes! O be it as you say, my brother!" he cried. His claws raked the unseen strands of malice, discord, intolerance, and blind bigotry from the air, and braided them into a torch that blazed in plain sight in his fist. He broke the fire into fifteen smaller flames and gave them to his followers with what sounded like a blessing. He kept a sliver of their garnered hate for himself, a dagger that he hid against his forearm. They cheered his name and started for the stakes.

"You shall not touch them!" Quintus was on the stage, his arms barring a pathetically narrow portion of their path. "For the sake of your souls, I forbid you! In God's name—"

"What do you know of God, you old loon?" The same man who had struck Lysi bulled his way to the front of the mob. The others circled in with him. Raleel chuckled and conjured up a pile of stones. They saw, and grabbed them up without question, surrounding the saint.

"Only maybe you're not crazy," the man spoke on. "Maybe that's the disguise Satan laid on you, to keep us off our guard. Maybe you're one of them, too!"

"Burn him!"

"Stone him!"

"Tear him open, see what color he bleeds!"

Quintus clasped his hands in prayer. He had died before, but that didn't make a second death impossible. The world was full of too many possibilities, sometimes. He felt the breath of fire, and was afraid. Yet through his fear, he closed his eyes and prayed.

He prayed for them, his enemies.

Fifteen silver spears fell from the sky, biting deeply into the stage in a ring around Quintus. When they hit, their shining shafts spread out, widened until a fence of fifteen mirrors ringed the old abbot.

"Leave him alone," Noel said sternly. Raleel wheeled to see his former disciple standing at his back, robed in the bright power of inborn magic.

The demon cursed, then called out to his followers: "My friends, my brothers, see! Here is the true cause of my transformation! Oh, we have nursed a serpent in our bosom! Manifold and *cunning* are the ways of Hell! Yea, but by the power granted me through *righteousness*, together we shall overcome him! Behold!"

A spurt of blue fire roared out of the demon's body and bathed the stage in an eerie, watery glow. "See now, I have by *grace alone* shielded you and all this place against any and *all* unholy illusions that this accursed and *false* sorcerer may bring! Stand firm, my friends. He shall not frighten you with false monsters, imaginary armies, lies!''

''You're right, Raleel,'' Noel said calmly. ''No lies.'' He raised his hand. ''Only the truth.''

Images filled the mirrors.

The woman who had spoken saw herself in a strange uniform, smiling as hollow-eyed children marched past her into a huge gray building with heavy, gas-tight doors. On the horizon, smokestacks filled the air with greasy clouds.

The man who had struck Lysi saw himself on horseback, in an antiquated policeman's blues, clubbing the heads and bodies of pinch-faced workmen who carried signs. One fell, and the horse trampled him, spurred to it by his rider.

Every mirror gave back a similar image. The bodies of men dangled from ropes slung over old sycamore limbs. Schools burned. Women were tied to chairs, force-feeding tubes shoved up their noses. Townsfolk in shabby medieval garb were cut down by gorgeously mounted knights. Infants were cast down from stone ramparts onto waiting lances while cities blazed and churches fell to ash.

A man in animal skins took up a flint-tipped spear and stabbed the stranger who didn't smell the same.

And then, with a swiftness too great even for Raleel to counter, the spell of true seeing in the mirrors leaped out to engulf his followers. Their clothing changed to sober Puritan drabs, relieved only by their white neckbands. The man who had struck Lysi held a coil of rope.

''*Mother!*'' Harsh memory hit Raleel between the eyes, memory too rude and intense to allow reason a moment's intervention. The impact flung him back through time.

He was young, little more than a child, dwelling with his dam and sister in that isolated woodland cabin. He knew from the first that they were different. He learned abruptly that difference meant danger.

They came in the night. They ringed the cabin with fire, broke down the door, held up their black book and their cross while they dragged his mother outside. They reached for him, too, and for Lysi, but he sank his teeth into the bony white hands that groped for him, and leaped through the oiled paper window—too small for a boy's body, large enough for a young wolverine.

Lysi ran beside him, herself transformed. They ducked into the forest undergrowth, lay with their bellies to the dirt, waiting, watching. They saw the noose fall over their mother's head. They saw the light of torches, so bright and unforgiving, shining on the white neckbands, on the hungry eyes of the crowd. They heard the rope scream, the branch groan with the sudden weight on it. They watched their mother die, the life slowly strangling out of her, and heard the hymns, the prayers, and the cheers.

Hypocrites! Fiends worse than my sire! I'll bring you all down, some day. I'll best you at your own game. By the same cant of holy duty and divine will and slaughter in the name of righteousness, I'll give you all to Hell!

Raleel saw, remembered, reacted. He leaped for the nearest human he could reach, talons slashing, seeking to cut away the dark cloak of pretentious piety, thirsting to spatter the stainless neckband with blood.

He slashed air. "They're not yours to kill," said Noel.

"He *is* mine! They are all mine, to taunt, to betray, to kill, if I will it! Where is he? Tell me, or—"

"Don't bore me with threats, Raleel. There." He pointed skyward.

Fifteen mirror-wrapped bodies arced through the air like missiles, launched by Noel's power. All struck the water aft of the departing Coast Guard cutters. They turned back to pick up the glittering shells. On deck, the Coast Guard hatched a clutch of very weird, very shaken chicks, still dressed for a Thanksgiving Day pageant. They babbled everything that had happened to them—Raleel's spell left no room for self-protective fudging of the facts. Truth had its just reward: They were taken to the nearest hospital for "observation."

"Not mine to kill," the demon hissed across the empty stage between them. "But you are."

"Try."

"Noel! No!" Melisan sobbed and strained against her chains.

"Let him alone, damn you, Raleel!" Lysi shouted. "If you don't, I'll destroy you!"

"First you'll have to save yourself, sister dear," Raleel snarled, not even bothering to look at her. He didn't take his eyes off Noel. This prey would not escape him. Soul or no soul, he wanted Noel's skin.

"And I will! You've lost your secret weapon, you bastard. No more bigots to drain hate from and turn against us! You can't kill us by yourself, and the Underlords have snatched back your hellbred cronies.''

The demon glanced up involuntarily, looking to where the imps should have been manning the cameras. They were gone, called home. Hell could scent failure coming in from the farthest distance. Below, a great Gate clanged shut, cracks melting to seal themselves. He heard Lysi laugh.

"You've lost, Raleel!" Lura called. "Cut your losses before it's too late! You have nothing to use against us, and you know it!''

Why are you his friend all of a sudden? A familiar voice reached out to Lura telepathically.

Atamar? she responded

A hand touched her crossed wrists just above the point where the chains bound them. *At least we're left this much of our powers on this accursed isle, or I'd have to whisper. Now let him ignore you, or he'll see us lurking back here.*

Us?

Kent and Don are hiding behind Melisan's woodpile—praise be, these stakes are wide enough to shield a couple of people, if they're careful—and Ambrosius is with Faith, working on Lysi's bonds.

Then Noel—

A diversionary maneuver—or so it was to be, at first. Now look at him. He wants a real fight.

Thoughts flew faster than words, in utter silence. Raleel was unaware of what passed between Lura and Atamar, but he heard his sister's laughter only too well.

A glowing dagger shot into his hand. "No weapon, Lysi?" He stabbed the sky, and would have turned to face her with it, but Noel feinted with a gesture that might have been a prelude to a full sorcerous attack, distracting him. Raleel jerked his head back to the boy, just missing Faith as she ducked behind Lysi's pyre.

"One knife won't help you," Noel said, not knowing what that blade was made of. "And my magic is the equal of yours. I should thank you. You taught me how to use it better, faster than I could've done on my own."

"Brave . . . '' Raleel's feet sprouted hooked claws that rent the stage as he dug in. "Or stupid." A mane of twisting green and yellow filaments grew in a fringe around his face, twined down his body. His whole outline blurred, swelled, enlarged to twice its original size.

Noel countered with an expanding cage whose bars were spiraling flights of bees the size of hummingbirds. The cage swallowed the demon, who laughed at the fragile bars and burst out of his foe's weak illusion.

He had forgotten his own spell, which barred all things but truth from the battleground. The bees were no illusion—they had been transported, not woven of air—and they got very angry when they were pushed around. Raleel burned with a thousand tiny stings and dwindled back down to human size. The pain shrank with him; the provocation did not.

The gall—!

"Well, Teacher?" Noel stuck in the needle. "Do I pass?" He stepped back and snapped his fingers high, kicking out one foot like a Greek dancer. A rain of apples, whisked from their orchards in the north, thudded down on Raleel's head. "Do I get an *A*?"

Now Raleel could not have looked away from Noel if he tried, no more than a coiled cobra would look away from its victim before it struck. The rescuers saw, and hurried to their business while Noel continued to play his dangerous game. They put their hands to the chains and found that Raleel's unlamented helpers had only fastened these with twisted bits of coat-hanger wire. They worked with all haste—sometimes with too much—as one pair of hands got in the way of another.

Above the dance of demon and magician, above scurry of rescuers and captives, two spirits still held each other in a thrall that seemed never likely to break. Their bodies remained where they had left them, like lovers' quickly shed garments.

Don released Melisan, who fell into Kent's arms.

Way to go, the yellow kitten said with a snaggletoothed grin. *Let me see if I can speed up those other klutzes.* He bounded to the next stake over.

Stupid wire! Why they couldn't use a padlock. . . . Atamar complained silently.

Because where would you find the key to it, Atamar? Calmly, calmly and you'll—Ah! The wire was off, the chains down, Lura free.

"Let me." Don climbed the middle woodpile, where Ambrosius and Faith still struggled with Lysi's bonds. A turn

of the wrist, and Raleel's sister was released. She let out an
exuberant war whoop and slid down the mound of kindling.

That made Raleel turn. He saw how he had been duped,
heard fresh laughter from his sister, from Noel. The others
climbed down and ranged themselves against him. For a time
he forgot that on his island realm they were nearly powerless.

Even Quintus was not above lording it, in what he saw as a
victory. "So all your plans come to nothing, demon, like
your promises to those you deceived for so long. What
have you now? No allies, no unlucky souls to play the
fool for you, no captives . . . you are defeated. Begone."

Raleel's eyes began to glow the color of molten steel.
"Save your sermons, they won't save you." He took a
menacing step towards Quintus, but came up short against a
barricade he could not see. "Is this more of your damned
sorcery, you puppy?" he shot at Noel.

Noel yapped at him sarcastically, and howled for effect.
"Damned? Why, *shoot*, boy, if'n I use it to do the Lord's
work, guess that don't make it *damned* no more, now do it?"
He reeled himself in a choirboy's robe from a small church in
Claremont and flicked it away again. "The *Lord's* work,
Raleel! One of those names you wouldn't name, those words
it pained you to hear, all the magic in me, and all the miracles
that go beyond magic, together they're telling me I don't have
to be afraid of using what I've been given."

" 'Thou shalt not suffer a witch to live,' " the demon gritted.

"And guess who can cite Scripture for his purpose! I'm not
scared anymore, Raleel. I'm free of fear, and nothing you can
do will make me your prisoner again. Fear was one of your
biggest allies. It's gone, and you don't have a thing."

"Aren't you forgetting something, Noel?" Raleel's voice
was syrupy, the dagger in his hand squirming with purple
crackles of barely harnessed force. "There is one ally my
kind have had to use against yours since the day of Cain."
His arm swept out, and violet light leaped from the blade.

They didn't see its target, but an instant later they heard a
dull bubbling, smelled a bitter stench, and felt the ground
beneath them heave and shake. Dark shapes lifted themselves
into sight, towers of palpable shadow, and then the clinging
blackness oozed away. Eyeless sockets the size of a man's
head stared vacantly at their awakening. Paw by monstrous paw,
the bones of dead beasts pulled themselves free of the tar.

23

Hell in a Hand-basket

"HOLY HARRYHAUSEN," DON whispered, and ran. The beasts stomped forward, every one ten times as frightening a *memento mori* as the philosopher's tabletop skull. Raleel's tar pit legion at once reminded the producer of how fragile his mortality was, and promised to write the bottom line on it Real Soon Now. Don didn't want to stay around for the big boffola finish. He scooted.

Not everyone could run. Melisan teetered on her cloven hooves and clung to her husband. Lysi wiped her still-bleeding nose on the back of her hand and cursed her brother clear across the firmament. The punch she'd taken had left her seeing double, so she swore at both Raleels. He showed her all his teeth and then sank arrow-straight through the stage boards.

"Blessed Ones, save us!" Quintus shouted at Lura and Atamar.

"We can't," Lura answered, her eyes reflecting the on-coming tusks and talons, the sharp horns and tearing claws of the ancient monsters. "We haven't the power."

"Only Noel," said Atamar. The massed skeletons swayed closer, then split ranks. Their fixed grins appeared to grow wider as each singled out his prey. "Noel!"

"What should I—?" A rotten apple smacked him in the eye.

You ask for help? Don't you want that A *.anymore, boy? Then show me how you fight with death!* Raleel's thoughts crisped through Noel's mind. The demon himself was gone, vanished in a moment soon after the first creature pulled itself free of the La Brea quagmire. Only Lysi had seen him make his exit.

"A-plus, dammit." Noel wiped the juicy fragments from his eye. "And extra credit for your hide."

Noel threw out a blanket spell of shielding, but it fell short of covering all those he loved. Only he and Quintus stood beneath its golden dome. "A miscalculation?" the saint asked meekly.

"I formed the spell for strength, not distance. I can fix it." He moved to strip it away and recast it, but the unseen demon sent a shielding of his own out of nowhere. It covered Noel's spell like a blue shrink-wrap skin. Under the green bubble, Noel discovered that Raleel's spell was meant to keep things in, just as his had been intended to keep them out. What was worse, the demon's sorcery had a toughening effect on Noel's own casting. Calling back the golden shield changed from an afterthought of conjury to a will-straining labor that taxed Noel's magic to the limit.

Noel dashed his powers against the trap's curving walls with all his might. Small patches of blue began to show on the green surface as he removed his own spell's power, then set to the even more arduous work of piercing Raleel's magic. He began to breathe hard. Beside him, Quintus knelt and seemed to pray.

The bones walked, and many of their targets who could, ran.

This is what I get for sleeping through those Paleontology lectures, Faith thought as she sprinted up the aisle. *Now I'm going to get killed by some Miocene mother and I won't even have the scientific satisfaction of knowing the name of the beast that hit me!*

As she scrambled over a pile of crushed metal in the middle of the aisle, she looked over her shoulder. The mountain of bones with her name on it didn't move fast, but it didn't have to. Knobbled antlers lowered, it plodded on her track with the stolid endurance of a tax assessor. Its huge hooves churned up whole shovelfuls of soil with every step, and its mouth was full of thick teeth meant for tearing saplings in two. Failing a sapling, Faith's body would do.

She ran as fast as she could, hoping that if she couldn't evade the monster, she might outdistance it. A wild thought told her to run for the sea, swim for the new California coast, and pray that her friends had the bright idea and good wind to do the same.

God bless aerobics! Pumping her knees faster up the aisle, Faith never imagined the day would come when she'd think that. *I can get away eas—*

An elephantine skeleton was waiting for her at the top of the aisle. Its narrow skull was adorned with tusks that made more cloverleaf turns than the Golden State Freeway, and the first step it took towards her turned the refreshment stand into a tortilla.

She yipped and cut cross-country. Her sharp turn let her catch sight of the others. Lura and Atamar were still on the stage, standing back to back. A ring of tiny skeletons of rodentlike creatures surrounded them—tiny, but furnished with sharp horns on their snouts. The two unarmed angels could only kick them away while Raleel's echoing laughter hung over the platform. If he couldn't destroy them, he could annoy them.

Oligocene, Pliocene, when was it that everything including the vegetables grew horns? Damn it, why should I care what epoch those little horrors came from? Good Lord, woman, turn that brain off for once and put some of that power into your feet! Faith's self-flagellation gave her a new spurt of speed.

Useless. Another huge pile of articulated bones stood ready to intercept her. She pivoted and ran in yet a third direction without bothering to play Name That Fossil. She ran one way across a row of seats and met Don running the other way, pursued by a relic that lumbered after him on two legs, forepaws ending in long, heavy claws like steam shovels.

"Aha! I *know* that one!" Faith shouted. "It's a giant sloth!"

"Hooray for education," Don panted. He tripped over his own flying feet and sprawled.

Ambrosius popped up from under one of the seats. "I don't think hiding's going to help me this time, either," he said. He helped Don up, then grabbed him and Faith by either hand. "Up and over!" he commanded, standing on a bench and hurdling over the back of the one ahead. They aped his maneuver because it was either that or tumble and be caught by the pursuing skeletons. When their own legs tired, he lifted them along with him by a combination of strength, enthusiasm, and plain pigheadedness. He wouldn't quit, nor would he let them.

"Another! Now another! They can't follow us this way!"

"You know—you're kind of—frisky—for a former—monk," Don gasped out at every landing stage. Vaulting the hard-bottomed seats at the Hollywood Bowl tended to knock the wind out of you. The producer made a silent vow that if he lived, he would devote his life to Good Deeds and upholstering every row of bleachers in L.A. County.

"*Mens sana in corpore sano.*" Ambrosius wasn't even out of breath. He leaped on to the next row down, and the next, dragging them onward. "Classic education."

"Fat lot—of good—that'll do us. Just look—back."

Ambrosius paused. Since the time of Mrs. Lot, the temptation to look back was undeniable. This time, the sight he saw was no less petrifying. The skeletons of the La Brea tar pits had re-formed ranks in a wall of bone at the back of the open-air auditorium. Heavy heads swung back and forth slowly, as if their bony sinus cavities could sift the wind for the scent of their quarry. Plant-eaters and meat-eaters stood shoulder to shoulder, at the brink of an unseen watering hole. Their bones shone white—not the yellow of old ivory, not the brown of deep age, but a white that was blinding in its intensity, cold and desolate as the moon.

A signal was passed. Each no longer hunted alone. They took a pace forward in unison and the earth shook. Another step, and the rearmost row of seats was crushed.

Crushed . . . Faith remembered the wreckage blocking the center aisle. In her first seizure of blind panic, she'd dashed straight over it without thinking. She could see it clearly and calmly from where she stood now, and what it was—what it had been—registered. "Honest Ariel!"

A brightly colored scrap of something flimsy flapped from beneath the ruin of the commissary cart.

"They're coming faster," Ambrosius observed of the skeletons. "We must keep moving." He tried to take them with him over the next seat-back, but Don pulled his hand away, and Faith was in tears.

"Moving where?" Don demanded. "To the stage? Right back *to* Raleel? I'd rather get squashed by Dumbo's grand-daddy. At least it'll be over faster."

Kent Cardiff's familiar voice rang out from the nearby stage, his pear-shaped tones and good breathing habits making a microphone unnecessary and just a little vulgar. "I say,

Donald! Mr. Swann, sir! Rally to us, if you can. There's hope!''

"Cardiff? Where are you?" Don shaded his eyes. He couldn't see the gentleman of PBS anywhere, on the platform or off. He jumped over a couple of additional rows, trying for a better view.

"Here we are!" Kent and Melisan emerged from behind one of the woodpiles. She held a length of the very chain that had bound her there; he carried a billet of wood. Lysi popped up at the top of her own pile like a prairie dog, more tangles of chain in her hands.

"Courage, friends!" Kent hailed the three of them as they made the few remaining row-hops to the stage. Melisan gave them a hand up as Lysi passed the chains down. "No coda until the last Wagnerian aria, what?"

"It's not over till the fat lady sings," Lysi translated. "Atamar! Catch!" She tossed the beleaguered angel and his mate a chain with two twists of wire still attached to the ends.

Ambrosius yanked a sturdy log from the pile nearest him and hefted it like a major-league slugger coming up to bat. His eyes narrowed as he watched the oncoming line of Raleel's uncanny army. Then he glanced aside to the fossil rodents still bullyragging the angels.

He bent over, grabbed one of the small skeletons up by its spine, lofted it, and slammed it into right field with one swing of his improvised Louisville Special. The wind whistled through the flying rodent's rib cage. It struck an approaching giant sloth fairly in the eye-socket. The beast stopped in its tracks and pawed madly at the unexpected missile. It staggered about, trying to dislodge it, tripped over one of the benches, and fell with a monumental smash. Sloth-parts scattered. Its osseous companions looked riled by this unseasonable shower of carpals and molars, despite their past experiences with L.A. weather.

"Hallelujah!" Ambrosius shouted, waving a fist. "They *can* be stopped!" He picked up another of the little fossils and whammed it too enthusiastically. It shattered into fragments for a foul tip.

The others saw, and seized hope. Don knotted his chain around a smaller log and used it to scythe away half of the chittering little creatures around Lura and Atamar. Through the break on the ring, Lura ran out to claim two nearly identical pieces of wood.

"Atamar! The chain!" Her mate passed it to her without question. The wire at the ends was hard to twist; still, she managed. It wasn't a pro-quality nunchuk that she made, but there weren't any armaments critics in the house. She jumped from the stage and charged up the aisle. The smilodon that tried to get familiar soon got decapitated with a snap of Lura's weapon. Atamar almost got similar treatment on the nunchuk's backswing.

"Will you *watch it* with that thing!"

"Stop grousing, Atamar, and yank those fangs!" Lura tapped one of the smashed smilodon's awesome canines with her shoe, then waded on to meet the next horror.

Atamar did his part for the history of dentistry. "Faith! Here!" He threw her one of the heavy teeth.

"Oh, Atamar," Faith simpered, cradling the fang, "you always know *just* what to give a lady. Where *do* you shop?"

"Olduvai's of Olvera Street," the harried angel snapped. "Now will you *please* take that fang and go out and kill something?"

"Yes, O Messenger of Peace." Faith winked at the angel. She weighed the tooth, considered it, and ran up the aisle hollering something akin to a Greek battle cry as she brandished it overhead. She ran head-on at the first giant ungulate she saw, swerving aside when it was almost upon her and dealing it a ringing blow just below the shinbone. The skeleton creaked, heeled, and toppled into the seats, going to bits and pieces.

Faith took out two more in the same way before leaning back against the stage for a breather. Ambrosius had been doing his bit from on the platform proper, but he had run out of bone baseballs. Melisan was using her chain like a morningstar, minus the spiked ball on the end. Kent and Atamar were playing it primitive, using their respective wood and bone weapons like clubs to fell the creatures of the tar pits. Lura had her nunchuk to keep her busy, and Lysi was attempting to perfect the rib-bone boomerang, with varying results. Don climbed up to take the controls of one of the abandoned boom-cameras. He raised, lowered, and swung it sideways at top speed, whacking more than one mastodon upside the head and back to eternal sleep. The whole scene looked like Bargain Day at the catacombs.

Ambrosius slipped from the stage to Faith's side. "You were wonderful," he said. With his toga exchanged for contemporary clothes, he looked like any typical Angeleno male, and a good deal handsomer than many—this in a city whose biggest cash crop was hunks and hunkitas.

Faith felt scientific detachment and pure scholarly concern go to blazes whenever she looked at him. "Wonderful? Me?" She sounded like every sugarbrained heroine of stage, screen, or formula romance.

"That battle cry—stirring! And the way you handle your weapon, like a warrior born!" He seized her hands in a grip at once firm and tender, like good steak. "I never thought to find a woman like you: the cunning of a Cleopatra, the boldness of a Caesar." His eyes kindled with something more than historical interest. "If Eve had possessed your courage, your intelligence, and your way with a weapon, they'd have eaten the Snake and we'd all still be in Paradise."

Thoughts of Eden turned Faith's mind to Ambrosius garbed according to the reputed dress code of the Garden. She blushed like a magnum of cranberry juice. She also decided not to tell him that the war shout and fighting style that had so captivated him were both relics of her time served on the girls' field hockey team in high school.

"I will—I *must* show myself worthy of such a woman!" Ambrosius lifted his chin, defying the substantial numbers of skeletons still standing to nay-say him. He bawled something nasty in Latin and attacked.

In that instant, Faith saw all her happiness on the brink of being trampled into fertilizer by some infant gorgon the Ice Age had overlooked. For all his talk of admiring the things of the intellect, Ambrosius was too much a berserker at heart. Carried away by a dream of glory, his headlong rush into the teeth of battle made the Light Brigade look like a bouquet of shrinking violets.

Faith was not about to stand by and see the man she loved become part of the Californian geological structure. She had waited too long for a love like this in her life, and God knew how long Ambrosius had been waiting! She tossed aside her smilodon fang and whistled shrilly for the angels.

Lura was too deep into her own sector of the battle, but
Atamar managed to respond to the call. "What is it, Faith?"

"We're piddling here. Get Don and Kent and—Oh, that
should be enough, with me."

"Enough for what?"

"No time! Come on!"

Ambrosius' imperial ancestors would have been proud,
seeing how his newly beloved laid plans, gave orders, and
whipped them through to execution, brooking no arguments.
As it was, Ambrosius himself was in the midst of unequal
combat with the living bones of a testy prehistoric camel
when he again heard Faith's thrilling battle cry at his back.

"HO, HO, HUCKUM, HUCKUM, GET THAT BALL
AND REALLY F—"

And on the word *fight*, she and her three followers annihi-
lated the camel, two giant ground sloths, and a quartet of
mammoths who had been bringing up the rear.

"Amazing thing, momentum," Kent said, dabbing his brow
with a wadded handkerchief as the four leaned against their
improvised battering ram, catching their breath. Tiny chips of
bone were still falling around them.

"Hit 'em again, hit 'em again, *hard*er, *hard*er!" Don
gleefully bounced in place beside the stake he'd helped Atamar
dislodge from the center of the right-hand pyre. He was
getting into the spirit of things. The heavy oak log looked
frayed to splinters at the end, but good for a few more runs.

Atamar did a fast nose-count of the bone-beasts still intact
and moving. "We'd better." He didn't share Don's work-
should-be-fun attitude at the moment. The producer's direc-
tive that he "lighten up" was met with a chilling look.

No . . . Raleel watched them trot the battering ram back
toward the stage—Ambrosius now helping—and make another devastating rush through his army.

This time when they hit their targets, there was a report
louder than the mere shattering of bone. The dome holding
Noel and Quintus had exploded. The boy stepped clear, a
pearly globe of swirling plasm in one hand. He cast it into the
midst of the skeletons.

Iridescence fountained up where it struck the earth, bathing
the fossils in viscous radiance. Their bones began to shim-
mer. Shins bent like rubber, skulls lolled to the ground on
vertebrae suddenly as elastic as overchewed gum. All turned

the dingy color of liquid asphalt and seeped back into the ground.

"I'm back, Raleel," Noel told the empty stage, "and you're next."

The spell he cast this time formed crinkling claws of supernatural electricity. Like ordinary hands, they groped their way through the air, searching, searching. . . .

Under the platform, under the earth, Raleel saw them penetrate first the boards, then the ground itself. He sensed their power as readily as they sensed and sought his presence. Something was wrong. The boy shouldn't have so much strength left after fighting his way through two shells of containment.

Where did he get it? With what source did he link? How—? The demon sniffed the approaching spell, and his blood became cold clay in his veins. *Quintus . . . Miracle!*

He fled in fear, for refuge through the rocky heart of the earth, but a bar lay across his path below. Seared and battered, Brazlyp stood on the far side of the barricade, looking apologetic.

Brazlyp! Let me pass! There's more than magic on my tail. If I can reach Dis—

Sorry, boss. You know the Underlords' policy: You screwed it up, you play it out.

Raleel turned aside sharply from the barricade, his mouth and mind filling with obscenities. The Underlords never had known pity. Success was all they understood, or wanted to. Noel's searching spell dove deeper to meet him. The demon knew that once it had him, it would be the end.

Then he sensed her. He saw her through the layers of earth above as through shallow water. Her clothing was more than half destroyed by fire no mortal could have endured and survived. How could he not have known her for what she was? He cursed whatever pride and blindness had muted an aura so strong.

In my own house! Taken in by beauty like the most gullible mortal! For how much of his failure was she to blame? No matter; he would take payment now. She was just above him, unaware, distracted by something he didn't bother to analyze. Like a shark gliding beneath an unsuspecting swimmer, he moved up suddenly, fiercely.

"Call it off or I destroy her!" He had the hate-braided

dagger at Dixi's throat, her hands pinned to her sides with one arm. "Call back your spell, Noel, or when it hits, she comes with me! You know I can do it, with this!" His fingers tightened on the hilt.

"You're bluffing! She's an angel! One demon alone can't—"

"He's not alone, Noel," Atamar said into the great silence. "That dagger holds the heart-strength of fifteen cold souls. It can harm. It can do worse. Believe it."

Noel hesitated for a breath's time, reading the truth of Atamar's words in Dixi's eyes. He dropped his hands. The questing spell hissed to nothingness, like a match going out in the rain.

24

Chain Gang

HEY, THIS IS MY HIDE-OUT. The one-eyed kitten raised his paw and made a halfhearted swipe at the soul brash enough to seek shelter beside him at the apex of the Hollywood Bowl shell. *Don't you belong down there, with the others?*

"Yeah, I guess," Honest Ariel replied, peering over the edge to where enchanted chains were shackling all of Raleel's prisoners into a line. Kent couldn't restrain a cry of pain as the iron bit his flesh. Honest Ariel winced and said, "I mean *no;* no, I don't. I mean—Ahhhh, rats, I dunno what I mean no more."

How did you get up here? Fly?

"With this?" The reformed angel held out his left wing to show off a massive tear in the fabric. The gossamer tissue still oozed a faintly blue translucent liquid that smelled of lemon and lavender. " 'Swatcha call aerodynamically unsound, ya know? So I crawlt. Boy, that smarts." He blew a cooling breath on his injured pinion. "Musta been a whole freakin' rhino stomped on it, tore a hunk out. Flattened the ol' chuck wagon, too; scrunched up that dog-ugly satin cape they gimme to wear . . . I was lucky to get away alive.''

Do you always sit around waiting for freaking rhinos to pulverize you? The kitten sounded amused. *You're an odd angel, you are.*

"Odd angel out's more like it." Honest Ariel looked disgusted. "Going gets tough, and I take off for Tarzana, just leave *her* standing there, touching my spirit, so's Raleel can spring on her while she's wrapped up with me. She never changed. After alla those years, she didn't. Still the same sweet kid, stars inner eyes, trusting, believing in me . . . Like I deserve it or sumpin'. Long's she held onta my spirit, she didn't care what was goin' on with our bodies."

Admirable. Dull, but admirable.

"But me, I haul this body outa reach so *fast*—"

With your spirit elsewhere? Ingenious.

Honest Ariel was in no mood for jests. "Just the part that loves her. Just only my whole heart, 'sall. Mortals can do that alla time." The kitten looked skeptical, so he added, "Din'cha never hear about 'My heart's in the highlands, my heart is not here. My heart's in the highlands a-chasing the deer,' huh?"

Pity the poor deer.

The exiled angel rested his chin in his hand and sighed. " 'Sno use. All those years, I din't change any neither. I'm still a coward. Little thing like a demon to fight or a Revolt in Heaven and I'm outa there, fence-sitting like sixty. S'prised I don't got picket-marks all over the old wazoo." Honest Ariel patted the nonexistent pockets of his sweatpants. "Sheesh, I need a smoke."

You need something, friend. The kitten picked his way along the outermost lip of the band shell and looked down at Raleel's triumph. *So do they.*

Down below, by dint of his own magic, Raleel had managed to get his conquests organized. Silent commands caused the discarded chains to respond with the alacrity of Laocoön's serpents, weaving themselves around Dixi, who Raleel had set up at one of the stakes still left in its original place. More chains held the others, Noel first among them. A solitary figure remained unbound: Quintus. Raleel had run out of chain by the time he reached him.

"Now what am I to do with you?" His wide mouth quirked over a secret joke.

"Why don't you call up more chains from Hell itself, if you have that power?" Quintus replied boldly.

Raleel jingled the links binding Dixi. "From Hell? I got these from the hardware department at Zody's. I could order chains from Hell for you—not competitively priced merchandise, but damn the expense. Ah! But I may soon have need of all my strength. It is no easy thing to destroy an angel. Shall I waste my substance on you? You're no threat any more, old man," the demon mocked as he sauntered away from the stake. His nostrils flared and snuffled rudely around the former abbot's person. "Not a whiff of miracle. What happened? Lend a friend a cup of power when you could've used it yourself?"

Quintus faced the demon, unafraid. "When we were trapped within that infernal prison of glass, I prayed that Noel might win through. It was not my place to specify how, or even if my prayers were to be answered. I rejoice that I was worthy to be heard; it is enough."

"Only you were heard too well! The boy is a link, a joiner, a tapper of others' powers. He's greedy, too, like all the young, and he drained you dry of every drop of your disputed sanctity. You're a husk now, Quintus; a hull; more of a fossil than my poor defeated pets." His hand swept towards the tar pits. "After I have disposed of the others, perhaps I will sink you in the mire over there. At one stroke I'll be rid of you and drive future archeologists out of their minds with an anomalous find."

"Then do so," Quintus replied haughtily. "Death at your hands holds no fear for me."

Raleel looked thoughtful. "No, it wouldn't, would it. It's old hat, for you, dying. Then I think I shall let you live. It will be instructive to see how a man of your times copes with these last days of the world."

"Last days?" Quintus looked around, as if scanning the skies for notice of an immediate appointment with Armageddon. "You fabricate, demon."

"Do I? Ask anyone, when you wander among men again. For I do intend to set you down on the mainland, once I've cleared away your friends here. People over there will tell you how the world goes, how doom is waiting in the wings, just licking its flaming lips, how the world is about to end in fire *and* ice both, to satisfy everybody. That is, if we don't all die from some abominable plague before we can push the button. Oh, you mortals have been naughty!''

He wigwagged a taloned finger in Quintus' sun-browned face. ''Your inclination to evil is legendary, among my kind, but lately you've managed to surpass even our worst expectations. It takes real effort for a demon to outdo a mortal, these days, and with some mortals, we don't even try. 'A little lower than the angels,' indeed! Sing *that* Psalm verse around Hitler and Goebbels, Idi Amin and Jim Jones and all the others! It wasn't the last time King David screwed up as a judge of human nature.'' His lips curled back. ''You should be proud.''

''Pride's your line, Raleel!'' Lysi shouted. ''Leave Quintus alone!''

''My exact intentions, sister.'' His whole manner was smoother than a game-show host. He balanced his hate-forged dagger on the palm of one hand as he strolled back and forth in front of his captives. ''Alone completely; alone forever. First however, we have some old business to clear away: our sire's business. Or have you forgotten him? Languishing in exile in the Egyptian desert . . . hungering for the one thing that will set him free. You're not a very dutiful daughter, Lysi. Daddy wants a soul.''

''Daddy can want it till Doomsday,'' she countered.

''Oh, I think he'll get one sooner than that.'' The demon's eyes slued along the line of his prisoners, coming to rest last of all on Noel. ''You're halfway to Hell already, Wizard. Why not shuck out payment for a full trip, all expenses paid? Save us a bundle down in Bookkeeping. I can make you a very attractive offer.''

Noel made a biologically explicit suggestion.

Raleel's scaly brows went up in feigned shock. ''Such language! Well, since I can't tempt you with power, perhaps we can bargain on another table.'' He looked meaningfully at Kent and Melisan. ''I understand the Pacific is rather difficult to swim when you've got chains on. They gave you life. Care to return the favor?''

''No!'' Melisan sobbed the word. Her husband said nothing, at first, but his expression alone forbade Noel to make such a deal.

''No bargains, son. Not with him, not for us. What's to

stop him from taking your soul now and our lives later? Don't
trust—"

A backhanded slap from Raleel cut off Kent's words. Noel
lunged against his chains, uselessly. The demon looked bored.

"And what is to stop your son from seeing you free now,
and reneging on our agreement later? Repentance is a nasty
thing. Both sides take chances in such compacts, Mr. Cardiff,
but since you and your bride seem determined to die no
matter what, I suppose I could threaten to kill my sister,
instead. Noel *is* sweet on her—a stomach-turning phrase for a
very handy bargaining chip." He idly ran a finger up the
dagger's blade. It left no mark.

"That sticker won't hurt me, Noel!" Lysi called. "Look!
It's made from stuff too close to a demon's nature to touch
me!" She stared boldly at her brother. "For once, I'm glad
I'm still a succubus."

"We could prove the truth of that with this blade against
your hide," Raleel said quietly. "But if you are right, what a
waste of all this power. No, Noel. I'll stand with what I know
will work." His gaze shifted over Lura and Atamar, then
finally returned to Dixi.

"An angel. Not just one of the lower ranks like those two
rebuilt jobs, not a humble Guardian, but a Pleasure. She has
known Heaven and all its sweetness since before the beginning of time. I shall teach her to know Hell."

He ambled back across the stage to stand beside the bound
Pleasure, wrapping her long golden hair around his forearm
so that her neck was fully exposed. He held up the shimmer-
ing dagger for Noel to see.

"Do you know what she will feel when this point pierces
her throat? The hatred of over a dozen human souls. Do you
know how cold and killing *one* soul's hate can be for heavenly creatures? The pain has echoes, infinite echoes, I assure
you. She will feel every one. And at the same time this blade
takes her spirit from her, casts it into the cold and the dark
and the solitude, each of the souls this blade contains will fall
with her, as certainly as if they had their hands around the hilt
at the moment I destroy her. Fifteen souls!"

The demon's eyes glowed. He was caught up in the deadly
net his own words wove. "Fifteen . . . and why not more?
Those fifteen will still live, and spread their poison to others,
and on, and outward, like ripples in a pond. A new age of

man, then; an Ice Age greater than any of your nuclear seers ever predicted: A winter of the heart, the mind, the soul!''

He dropped Dixi's hair abruptly. "But you could change all that, Noel. One soul for many. And I'll even hand over this dagger, a pledge for you to hold, if you feel you can't trust me without one. Have we a bargain now?''

Noel's face was gaunt, horrified. He saw too well the possibility of Raleel's words coming true. He had stood on stage with "Sometime" Joseph Lee too many times to brush it all aside as improbable. The winter of ignorance *could* come, the cold stoked by a thousand bonfires. There would always be loveless souls ready to kindle such blazes with their neighbors' books, or dreams, or children. The dagger pulled at his eyes. He could actually see the braided hatred, fear, and folly of the hearts within. It was a force of more deathly power than any sorcery. No price was too great to stop it.

He opened his mouth to speak.

"Don't, Noel!" Dixi cried out to him. "If he gains even one soul, it's too many. I'm less afraid to lose my spirit than to watch you lose yours. Don't give in.''

Noel shut his mouth again, and closed his eyes against the tears. He had seen Raleel's eyes blaze with wrath at the captive angel's words. He had seen the demon's jaw grow taut, how he shifted the dagger rapidly in his hand. It wasn't a toy now. Raleel clutched it, raised it for the killing stroke.

He couldn't bear to see more. Let the others witness Dixi's death. In the darkness behind his sealed lids, Noel heard Quintus murmur, " . . . to save them, to save those poor fearful souls! Not hate, but hunger . . . Oh, let there be love enough . . . freely given to the hungering . . . love enough . . . please. . . .''

In his heart, in the silence of the waiting soul, Noel prayed that Quintus' own prayer might find an answer.

"BANZAI!"

It wasn't the typical celestial reply to mortal petitions, but it was spectacular enough to put any number of traditional angelic greetings on the back burner. With his torn wing streaming out behind him like a rainbow comet, Honest Ariel plummeted shrieking from the top of the Hollywood Bowl's shell and landed smack on top of Raleel. The wood piled around Dixi's feet skittered and rolled everywhere with the double impact. The soul-dagger flew from the flattened demon's grasp and whipped across the stage like a free-flying helicopter blade.

"Ow," Honest Ariel said, sitting up on Raleel's back. A shy grin lit his face. He appeared to address the sky as he added, "Hey, thanks for the, y'know, encourage—"

Raleel recovered in a snake's strike. He pushed up on one arm, throwing the angel off. His talons stabbed deeply into Honest Ariel's chest, tearing skin and flesh, scraping the ribs cruelly. The revenant angel struck back, but all he had was his fists. Blood striped his body. His punches were wild, doing Raleel little harm, only serving to rile the demon when they did happen to connect.

"He'll kill him!" Dixi shrieked.

"He can't," Atamar said, though he watched the unequal combat with a strained expression. "One demon to one angel . . . he can't."

Oh, yes he can, said a small voice at Quintus' feet. The former abbot looked down at the one-eyed kitten that butted at his ankle.

"Little one, if Atamar says Raleel cannot—"

Atamar doesn't know it all; never did. Ariel's no angel— not fully, not yet. He's not even sure of what to call himself, which is why he needed—the kitten extended and retracted his claws nonchalantly—*some encouragement to heroics. What he is, is anybody's guess, but he'll be dead before you can slap a label on him.* A single eye and a single word transfixed Quintus: *Unless . . .*

"Unless . . ."

Quintus flung himself onto the abandoned dagger on the boards and pressed the length of the blade to his bosom. He could feel the souls inside, all the hunger in them, the hurting, the dearth of love that made them so small. His lips moved in words that had no earthly meaning while his spirit reached out to theirs. The withered souls cried out for more. He set the point against his heart and silently offered them his last miracle.

The dagger glowed. Noel opened his eyes to see Quintus' body fading away as the light pulsing into the blade became brighter, warmer. The captive souls drank greedily, and Quintus freely gave them what they craved. The dagger burst into the brilliance of a small sun, then clattered to Noel's feet as Quintus vanished altogether.

Take it, the yellow kitten told him. *Take it up, Noel, and use the greatest gift you'll ever know.*

Noel bent quickly and picked up the dagger. He could feel the change in its substance, and his own talent latched onto all the metamorphosed power in the blade as he focused his will on it.

There's no place like home, the yellow kitten whispered just before the island of Los Angeles Caídos exploded with the sound of a million snapping chains.

25

You Oughta Be in Pictures

THE SUN HUNG at the very center of the sky.

Melisan lay gazing up into its single burning eye, feeling the sand and grit beneath press into her scarlet flesh and goatish fleece. The tops of weathered wooden buildings leaned in over her on either side. Her eyes were doing funny things, making the ramshackle structures look like they were swaying back and forth in a strong gale. Her head ached terribly.

"Here, my dear. Allow me." A clawed hand thrust itself into her blurry field of vision. Raleel clasped her wrist with calm firmness and hauled her off the ground, even letting her hold onto him until she was able to balance on her hooves. "Never let it be said that I can't accept an elegant defeat."

Melisan looked all around. The saloon, the emporium, the feed and grain, the assayer's office all returned her stare with their empty windows. A silvery green tumbleweed bounded leisurely down the street, riding a gently moaning wind. It lodged behind a barrel near the assayer's office. Apart from a brown lizard basking on the rim of a dust-dry watering trough, she and Raleel were the only living things visible for the length of the packed-dirt street.

"Where are they?" she asked, trying to keep her voice from rising too precipitously. "Where are the others?"

Raleel leaned back against a hitching rail and thumbed an imaginary Stetson off his brow. A quid of chewing tobacco suddenly pooched out one cheek and a blue pentacle materialized on his chest where a U.S. Marshal's badge should be. "Why shucks, ma'am, I reckon they jes' saddled up an' rode on outa these parts. Why'd they want to stay? Way I reckon, this hyar's demon country."

"Demon—"

"Yup." Raleel's leer hadn't lost a single degree of its native maliciousness. "Y'got no call to gawp at me thataway, ma'am. You shore are a fine lookin' piece of demon flesh, if'n I do say so myself."

Melisan knew he was right. She had only to run her eyes over those portions of herself she could see, only to listen to the low susurrus of serpents' breath in her ears, only to feel her transformed hair curling and uncurling itself around her neck.

Why did I even hope that would change? she thought.

"You still look a mite corn-fused, ma'am." Raleel spat a brown gob clear across the street. It ricocheted off the horseshoe hung above the livery stable doorway. "Way I see it, that boy o' your'n is tidy-minded. Ever'thang's all back where it belongs—the land, the people, all them purty houses, the tourist sights. A place for everything, and everything in its place." The leer pulled itself wider and meaner. "What's a demon's place but Hell?" He proffered his arm. "Shall we?"

Melisan bowed her head. Raleel was right again—he had to be. For what she had done, there could be no other payment but this. She'd been given the gift of mortal life and she'd thrown it away.

But Noel is all right. She consoled herself with that thought. *Wherever he is now, whatever he thinks of me, he's fine; I feel it. Let him be happy. As long as my child is well, I can bear Hell. Goodness knows, I've done it before.* She felt her skin crawl, instinct defying her every attempt at self-comfort and rationalization. Just because she had spent the greater part of her existence as a demon didn't make it any easier to return to that life. Precisely because she did know what awaited her below, it was that much harder to face again.

But what choice did she have? She took Raleel's arm.

"Honored, ma'am," he said. "If'n my kinfolk could see me now, squirin' round a purty li'l filly like you . . . " He taunted her with every sagebrush-sprouting word. "Shucks, why not? I'd be 'bliged if'n you'd 'company me t'visit my daddy 'bout now, Miz Melisan; *powerful* 'bliged.''

She blinked away the hot tears and said a silent farewell to all she'd loved in mortal life. She would go where he would lead her. He waved his hand, and a doorway into a sun-washed sea of sand opened before them. A demon perched alone on a spur of dead black rock. Murakh's head turned owl-slow towards them. Melisan thought she saw gloating recognition in those icy eyes. Raleel escorted her forward, to the threshold of the gate.

"She isn't going anywhere, Raleel." A clear voice resounded from the roof of the Excelsior Hotel. The unmistakable sound of a revolver being cocked snapped through the hot, still air. The gun spoke, and a silver streak tore through the air, piercing the desert doorway, smashing it and all it contained like a mirror. Star-shaped shards of shattered magic tinkled down.

On top of the Excelsior Hotel, a tall, lanky figure blew smoke from the barrel of his six-shooter. He was dressed all in white from the crown of his Stetson to the dyed leather fringes of his boot tops. The only exception was the black mask he wore across his eyes.

"Step away from that gateway real careful-like, Raleel," he directed.

"You've got no right!" the demon shouted. "She's mine, one of Hell's own, by her own decision!"

"Hell's own?" The sharpshooter tilted his hat back with the nose of his gun. Then he raised his weapon and fired off four shots in succession. Smoke rings rose and linked into an overhead canopy of vision. Inside the misty borders, a mortal Melisan bent over the book she'd stolen from Don's house and the paraphernalia for her spell of transformation. Again she reached the part of the spell demanding blood. The yellow kitten with her was scrawny, worthless, nothing to anyone, but still she let it go. Her own blood fell, and the little creature went unharmed.

The vision blew away on a puff of noontime air. "Looks ain't ever'thang, pardner," the man on the rooftop drawled. "Not even in Hollywood."

"Who the fuck is that masked man?" Raleel demanded.

Melisan made a "search-me" gesture. Her shrugging shoulders had scarcely fallen back into place before the white knight of the cinematic West was down off the hotel and right behind them.

He looked a lot less healthy, up close. Anyone with skin that yellow should have been in the last stages of jaundice, or recovering from an encounter with an instant-tan product. He aimed his six-shooter right at Raleel's heart.

"Got the last one with your name on 'er, son. Best to let the little lady go."

The demon bristled. "Whoever you are, you're dead." An overlay of hellish magic shivered across Raleel's skin. He brought his clenched claws up to direct a deadly bolt. The blue pentacle on his chest pulsed with power.

"Hiiiii-*yah!*" A second star came flying out of nowhere. It whisked past the man in white, skimmed just under Melisan's startled nose, and slapped itself right side up on top of Raleel's pentacle, forming a blue and gold ten-pointed star. It was like opening a hole in the bottom of a water barrel. Every drop of the demon's power drained into the linked stars and was quenched. Raleel felt it perish, and howled like a spine-crushed jackal.

At the far end of the long street, Honest Ariel jumped up and down gleefully, raising clouds of dust until Noel bounded out of the Sheriff's office to trade high-fives.

"Whaddye tellya? Huh, whaddye say? Liketa hear some-one rag on me forwatchin' alla them *ninja* flicks now! Can I chuck shurikens or what?"

"I just hope Louis L'Amour doesn't mind," Noel said.

Melisan moved well back from Raleel, who sank to his knees, both hands folded over the joined stars. The demon looked up at the masked figure. "Atamar?"

"Here I am." Noel's male guardian angel hailed their mutual foe from the balcony of the saloon. He wore the full splendor of his angelic robes. Lura stepped onto the roof of a building across the way, likewise in her heavenly guise.

Raleel's head felt heavy as a draft-horse's. A brilliance at the opposite end of the street from Noel and Ariel called his glance. More stunning in her glory than Lura and Atamar combined, Dixi held out her hands to him.

Wearily the demon looked back at the masked figure. "Who are you?"

A hand went up to peel aside the mask. A single eye, perfectly round, winked at Raleel. "An old acquaintance of your sire's. Back to normal, now, with all my old powers restored like everyone else's. Brother, if I'd had to swallow one more mouse—Oh. Where's my manners? The name's

Horgist.'' He stripped off his white gloves to shake Raleel's paw with a taloned extremity of his own.

"Horgist . . . " Raleel knew the name and the demon that went with it from his sire's endless grievance recitations. He was stunned. "But you're—you're an incubus!"

"Now there you go again, son, judging by appearances. Heck, maybe we'll make a full mortal outa you some day, with that kinda attitude. But for right now, you got a choice to make."

Raleel was instantly on his guard. "What choice?"

"Slip ol' Melisan there a shot of change-back magic, and we'll let you go." The yellow demon grinned.

Raleel didn't see the humor. "Why should I? Have her son do it. Have your pet angels work the spell!"

"Well, we *could* do that. I just thought—seeing as how your sister turned out okay, and your sire and I *do* go way back, even if he is a monkey turd—that you might want the chance to work a little changing magic on yourself. It's never too late, you know."

Raleel spat on Horgist's white boots, splattering them with brown. "Do what you will. I am outnumbered. Bonded together—Noel, the angels, even a turncoat demon like you—you can destroy me. Do it, then! But I will never help you."

Horgist pursed his lips. "Suits me." He shot the demon right between the eyes. Raleel disappeared in a lick of silver flame. The twin stars fell to the ground and split apart.

"Bravo! Bravo! Oh, I *do* say, bravo." Kent Cardiff strolled out of the saloon, applauding briskly.

Don Swann emerged after him, looking dubious and framing imaginary camera angles with his hands. "I don't know. That last scene could maybe use some doctoring. Horgist, baby, when you're offing a demon, you think you could say something a little more—well—*deep* than 'Suits me'? You know, like about good destroying evil, right conquering all, justice triumphing, maybe some New Age metaphysical crap?"

"Justice, shmustice. What is this—*Masters of the Universe* cartoons? I'm an incubus—a male sex-demon! Or I was." He stroked his chin. "Whatever I am now, the dreams are still pret-ty good. So don't make me into a hero. All I wanted was some sleep." The yellow demon yawned, to back up his own statement.

The angels fluttered in closer. Dixi retrieved the fallen gold star. "I'd better return this to that dressing room door at the Bowl," she said. She blew on it and it vanished.

Atamar picked up the blue pentacle. "Return to sender." It was gone in a puff of sulfurous smoke.

"Tight shot when the stars split," Don muttered, finger-framing like crazy.

Noel touched Honest Ariel's ravaged wing and healed it, allowing him to fly to his beloved. "Rhonda, baby!"

"Rhonda?" Lysi peeped out of the general store and rushed to Noel's arms. "*Rhonda?*" she repeated.

"Sure," he said. "What kind of a name's Dixi for an angel?"

Faith and Ambrosius appeared at one of the upper windows of the Excelsior Hotel.

"I think we missed something," the former monk said apologetically, patting down his rumpled hair.

Faith groped on the floor for her glasses, then rested her arms on the windowsill with a contented sigh. "I don't," she replied.

Noel and Lysi made their way through the crowd to his mother's side. Kent had reached her first. The four of them formed an embrace that no fear or sorrow could penetrate.

"It's over," Melisan said, hugging her son. "Thank God, you're safe and it's over."

Noel pulled back a little. "Not quite," he said.

"What?"

"Makeup." He kissed her. The demon's skin melted away, snakes, hooves, and all.

Across the street, Don picked up the tumbleweed and checked the label. " 'Made in Taiwan.' " He sounded peeved.

Horgist tried to soothe him. "Like I said, looks aren't everything."

"Yeah, but props are! Told 'em once, I told 'em a hundred times, buy *Korean* tumbleweeds!" He stamped through the assayer's office door and slammed it so hard that the entire flat keeled over.

"Hollywood." Horgist shook his head. He gauged the hour by the sun and called, "Hey! Anybody know where I can catch the next out-of-town sunset?"

Epilogue

THE DOME OF Solomon's tomb in the Valley of Cloud rang with the sleeping king's voice. "EVERY FOOL WILL BE MEDDLING. LEAVE OFF YOUR RUSH AND BUSTLE, GERIAL. ALL LOOKS WELL."

"Easy for you to say," Gerial retorted grumpily. He ran a scrap of woven light over the carvings one last time. One of the more ticklish captive djinn wriggled and squirmed under the dust cloth's attentions. "Is it every day we have such a visitor?"

"A SAINT LIKE MANY OTHERS. WE HAVE KNOWN THEM, IN OUR TIME."

"A saint," Gerial repeated. "But like few others."

"Thank you." Drenched in a soft radiance, Quintus Pilaster stood in the entryway. "I'm just getting used to the idea myself. It's kind of you to say so—other people's opinions are always so legitimizing. As for me being like few others . . . " He dipped his head modestly. "I do think the underlying principle was the same for all of us."

"THE MERCIFUL MAN DOES GOOD TO HIS OWN SOUL," Solomon agreed. "WHAT YOU HAVE GIVEN FROM THE HEART WITH NO THOUGHT OF REWARD HAS BROUGHT REWARD OF ITS OWN."

"Quintus, old friend!" Gerial hastened forward and swept the saint inside. He clapped his hands and two imps, generously tethered to their usual places in the wall by ropes of flexible rock, flew to fetch tabourets, a low bronze table, and the wine of Paradise.

"Sit! Drink!" Gerial shooed Quintus onto the fragrant leather cushion overhanging the sides of the stool. He filled one of the opalescent glass goblets and urged it on his guest. "It's an Eden Premier Cru; a *very* good aeon."

"Won't he be joining us?" Quintus' eyes indicated the enthroned King of Israel.

"WINE IS A MOCKER, STRONG DRINK IS RAGING."

"Oh. I suppose not, then."

The conversation was light and pleasant, excepting only those moments when Solomon chose to drop a lead-weight Proverb into the midst of the chat's natural ebb and flow.

"A restaurant!" Gerial exclaimed. "Think of that."

"Ah, and what else would you expect to occupy Honest Ariel while he sets his soul fully in order? It already bids fair to become one of the more fashionable Los Angeles eateries. With Rhonda at his side, how can he fail? Atamar does keep niggling at him to change the name of the place."

Quintus caused a newspaper clipping, advertising the new bistro, to materialize in midair. Gerial wet his lips and read aloud:

"For Real Olde Tyme Authentic California Cuisine
You Can't Pass Up Try
DONNER'S!
Family Cooking!   He-Man Meals!   People Served Right!
Bring The Kids.
Always A Pleasure To See You There.
(Honest Ariel Smith, Prop.)"

Gerial looked at the saint. "I don't see the problem."

"Nor do I," Quintus affirmed. "Our recovered friend won't qualify as a full-fledged angel until he gets certain spiritual details tucked up, but he appears to be in no hurry for reinstatement. In the meantime, he's not unhappy managing Donner's. If Rhonda wouldn't object, I think he'd turn fully mortal on a second's notice."

"Mortality . . . " Gerial let his eyes rove over the enchanted beauties of the Valley of Cloud, his voice growing dreamy. "It has its attractions. There are times I think I wouldn't mind a second go at it myself."

"Hmph. Ambrosius would side with you there."

"Still with Faith, is he?" Gerial poured more wine.

"Still." Quintus clinked glasses. "She's gotten a post at Yale—sees Noel and Lysi all the time—told me something about how New Haven seems to attract certain weird ele-

ments, so she and Ambrosius fit right in. He's signed up at
the Divinity School.''

"Happy?"

"So I pray. She says she's always liked older men. But
that Donald Swann person . . . Forever on the phone, after
poor Ambrosius to sell him his autobiography, going clear
back to Caesar and Cleopatra.'' He sipped his wine. "*Mummy
Dearest,* Swann wants to call it, don't ask me why. Says he
wants a 'treatment' from Ambrosius. I thought you had to be
sick to want a treatment.''

"You do.''

A loud snore rent the tranquil atmosphere of the tomb.
Quintus jumped.

"Good Lord, what was that?''

"Horgist.'' Gerial remained unruffled. "Back there.'' He
thumbed towards the rear of Solomon's throne.

The saint crept around and found the yellow demon deep in
blameless slumber. He was curled on one side, his single eye
closed, and a smile of transcendent sweetness on his lips.

"What is *he* doing here?''

"It was the least we could do for him,'' Gerial whispered.
"A token of thanks, fully approved by all agencies divine,
diabolical, human, and bureaucratic. All he wanted was some
peace and quiet.''

"Can't he go back to the desert for that? With Raleel gone,
and all, it should be peaceful enough now.''

"Gone?'' The guardian of the Valley of Cloud looked
puzzled.

"Horgist did shoot him.''

"One to one. You know that couldn't do permanent harm
even if Horgist had been an angel. Which, as you know, he's
not.''

"But what he *is* . . . '' It was Quintus' turn to look
bewildered. "It was simpler in my time. You could catego-
rize with impunity. There were demons and angels and people, not all these 'twixts-and-'tweens. Saint Vuox'th of Proxima
Centauri was making precisely the same complaint to me the
other day, until old buttinski Bill came along eavesdropping
and bored everyone in sight with that weary 'More things in
Heaven and Earth, Horatio,' nugget he's so proud of. If
Raleel wasn't destroyed, then where—?''

Gerial laid a finger to his lips. He passed his hands over the sleeping demon's head, and by the powers allowed him, drew out a dream for all to see:

Horgist snorted and twitched with glee. In his dream, he was back in the Egyptian desert, at the site of his centuries' long exile. He hovered above the wasteland on wings of gold. The black rock pierced the sands, a little smaller now, a little more worn by the wind.

The demon Murakh crouched on the black rock's peak, cracking the shinbone of a camel between his jaws. His own exile from Hell had barely begun, yet already looked likely not to end until doom itself cracked like that precious shin bone. A second yellowed tidbit lay beside him on the rock, a bone to pick for later.

Talons crept out of the rock's shadow, reaching cautiously for the other bone. The demon pretended not to see them, though his eyes shifted covertly, following every grope of the questing paw.

The claws touched the bone, retracted with joy, then closed around it. That was what Murakh had been waiting for. He sprang, seizing bone and paw together, yanking Raleel out of the stone, into visibility, and thrashing him all around the rock. Murakh never had forgiven his whelp for that "Sometime" Joseph Lee Whups Satan photo. Raleel squawked and ran, but the unseen boundaries holding his sire in exile held him too. The Underlords had so decreed. Hell was famous for hating failures, but when you got blasted across the galaxy by a creature neither demon, angel, nor earthbound worm, that gave failure a whole new dimension.

Oh, yes, the Underlords weren't pleased with Murakh's little boy.

In his sleep of true dreams, Horgist laughed.

"THE DESIRE ACCOMPLISHED IS SWEET TO THE SOUL," Solomon intoned.

"Say Hallelujah," murmured Gerial.

"Say Amen," said Quintus.